ONE COLD SUMMER

Robert J. Cowles

NEWMAN SPRINGS PUBLISHING
320 Broad Street
Red Bank, NJ 07701

First originally published by Newman Springs Publishing 2020

ISBN 978-1-63692-152-5 (Paperback)
ISBN 978-1-63692-153-2 (Digital)

Printed in the United States of America

1

Eighty-Eight Days from the Night

Richard Morgan sat alone in the front pew of the church. He held his hands in his lap and stared at the coffin in front of him. It lay open, but his eyes were fixated on the framed picture displayed next to it.

It was an old photo, at least a decade old. Richie, as his friends called him, could tell because there was a face partially cropped out next to his dad's. There was no mistaking that the hair was his mother's, dating the photo to before her accident, at least nine years ago. Based on how young his father looked in it, Richie would estimate it was even older.

The tan, virile face in the photo was a stark contrast to the pale, vacant corpse that lay in the coffin before Richie. It was possible to think they were two different people altogether.

Richie's wife, Lana, walked toward him down the aisle of empty pews. Even on the church's thick red carpet, her heels echoed in the tiny, empty house of worship. She wrapped her hand around the back of his neck.

"Hey. You okay?"

Richie put his hand over hers and looked up into her blue eyes. Her long blond hair that usually cascaded down her shoulders was tied up into a bun, although a few strands were already coming loose. He took in her face—her wide eyes, straight nose, and rounded chin—it made him smile for the first time that day.

"Yeah, I'm fine," he said. He turned back to the framed photo and pointed at it. "Did you pick this photo?"

He knew the answer, but he asked anyway. He hadn't been involved in the planning of the wake or funeral. Lana had taken care of it. She had known from their wedding he despised the minutiae of planning events. Always the helper, the one to bear the burden. He was grateful for that. She moved her hand to the top of his head and her hands through his hair, scratching his scalp like she knew he liked.

"Yeah. I showed it to you the other day and asked if it was okay," she said. He had no memory of that interaction.

"Do you remember where the picture was from? Who else was in the photo? What were they doing?" he asked.

She tilted her head. "It was in an old family album, in your mom's stuff, I think." That made sense to Richie. "It was your dad and mom, and you were in front of them. I think it was a birthday or something."

"Huh," he grunted. "I was just thinking. I can't remember him ever smiling like that."

His dad's smile was remarkable. His teeth glowed, and his eyes beamed. Happiness—it looked unusual to Richie on his father's face.

"It was the only one I could find of him smiling."

"Happiest I've ever seen him, and I don't remember it at all," he grumbled. "He must've been drunk."

Lana rubbed his head. "Oh, come on, nice thoughts today."

"I wonder who took it. The picture."

"Well, your brother's not in it. Maybe him?"

"I doubt it."

She remained silent while he continued to stare at the photo. He leaned his head back and closed his eyes to enjoy her massage. She stopped and put her hand out.

"Come on. People will be arriving soon," she said.

Richie let out a deep sigh and grabbed Lana's hand. She pulled, but he remained planted on the pew. She groaned and leaned back, putting all of her weight behind her, and finally managed to get her hefty husband to his feet.

When Richie was upright, Lana straightened his tie. Even though she was tall, only two inches short of six feet, she had to stand on her tiptoes to reach around his neck to fix his collar.

"I can't remember the last time I saw you in a suit," she said. She ran her palms over his broad shoulders and stout chest, smoothing out any wrinkles on his jacket. She reached up and tried to tame a cowlick on the back of his short brown hair.

"I think I wore one for our wedding."

"Was that you? I've been wondering who that handsome guy in a suit was that I kissed at that church."

Richie put his arm around his wife's shoulders. They walked up the aisle to the front doors of the small church to head outside.

"It's going to be a long day," he muttered.

"I know. But I'm here."

"We knew there wouldn't be much family," Richie mumbled.

The husband and wife stood outside the church, waiting for mourners. It was a cool, sunny spring day on the Wisconsin peninsula—the air sharp and clear and the sun warm. The black suit and dress they wore heated them as the sun reached its highest peak of the day.

"At least Luke's here," Lana said.

"Yeah. A brother and that's it. I knew it was a long shot that anyone from Mom's side would show, but I don't know. I still thought maybe—" He left the rest unsaid. Lana wrapped her arms around his.

"A good turnout of friends though," she said.

"It should be. He lived here his entire life."

"It's a good turnout," she repeated. He turned and looked over his shoulder. The church was near capacity.

She looked around and cleared her throat, doing her best to make her voice sound casual.

"What about your brother? Hear anything from him?"

Richie scoffed and gave her a sideways glance. "No."

"You did tell him, right?"

"I left him a message. A voice mail."

Lana sighed, disappointed.

5

"What? I can't help it if he doesn't answer!" he snapped, then turned red at his sharp tone. "Sorry."

Lana squeezed his arm.

"I don't even know where he is. He could be in fucking Canada or Mexico for all I know."

She didn't prod any further. "I'm going to make sure everything is all right inside. You okay out here?"

He nodded, and she left his side. He stood alone. The breeze cooled the sweat percolating on the back of his neck. A portly, older gentleman waddled up the sidewalk and the steps to Richie.

"How are ya, son? My deepest condolences," the man said as he shook Richie's hand.

"I'm all right. Thanks, Sam. Thank you for coming." Sam stood in front of Richie with his hands in his black leather jacket, seemingly resting on his protruding gut. Richie wondered if it was the same jacket he had worn to his mother's funeral.

"Yeah, never easy to lose a parent, no matter how old you get," Sam said, looking off in the distance. "Not that you're even old. You're not even thirty, right?"

"Turned twenty-nine two months ago."

"Least he got to see you married. My parents are still kicking, somehow, and won't let it go that I never got hitched."

Richie had no idea how to respond, so he simply bobbed his head.

"Sorry, I'm blabbing at you. I'll see ya inside."

Richie checked his watch. Unlikely there would be anyone else, he figured. He looked around and saw a figure approach the church from the sidewalk. He had a bag slung over his shoulder. Richie did not recognize him.

The guy was young—at least younger than Richie's twenty-nine years. His dirty blond hair was long, tucked and curling behind his ears. His eyes were covered by black aviator sunglasses. The rest of his face had a scraggly blond beard covering it. He was skinny, which made him look taller, thanks to his long legs, but he still came up a couple of inches short of Richie.

He wasn't dressed for a funeral. He wore a denim jacket and a black Nine Inch Nails T-shirt underneath. He looked like a hippie, a roving freeloader, a loser. Richie assumed he was just a passerby until he looked Richie. The man grinned and gave a quick wave, speeding his strut to a light jog.

Richie stood there, befuddled, as the man hopped up the small steps until they were face-to-face.

"Dicky!" he shouted.

Richie squinted at his face. There was something familiar about it, but he couldn't pinpoint it.

"H-hi," Richie stammered. He reached his hand out. "Thanks for coming."

The guy looked at Richie's hand, his face twisted in confusion. He looked back at Richie and let out a hardy laugh.

"What's a matter, Dicky? You don't recognize your only brother anymore?" he said as he took off his sunglasses.

It was his brother—his kid brother, Nick. Somehow. His hair was long now, and he had a beard. But it was unmistakably him. Even after nine years, Richie knew those green eyes anywhere. He felt his stomach flip inside him, and he blinked several times.

"Come on, man, gimme a hug!" Nick wrapped his arms around his brother. Richie kept himself from shoving his brother away.

When he released the hug, Richie gathered his jaw and cleared his throat until he could form words. "Nick? Jesus, I—I can't believe it."

"In the flesh. You look good! A little softer around the belt, but we all get like that, right?" He winked and patted his brother on the stomach.

Richie took a deep breath and clenched his jaw. "What are you doing here?"

Nick frowned. He thumbed at the church. "Wanted to see the old man off. Thought I'd do the good-son thing and pay my respects or whatever. At first, I wasn't going to come. You know me and the drunk bastard never really saw eye to eye, but I thought I'd try to be the bigger man for the first time and see how it fits. Looks like I just made it in time."

Richie stared at his brother. He looked terrible, which didn't surprise him. His eyes were bloodshot, and the bags in his sockets were dark and heavy. He looked as if he hadn't slept in days.

The organ began to play from inside the church.

"Well, guess I'll see you inside, Dick." Nick patted his brother on the stomach and walked inside, his bag slung over his shoulder.

Richie turned, his hands on his hips, and cursed the sidewalk. Lana passed Nick as she walked toward Richie. "Hey, we're about to start. Richie?"

Richie wheeled and looked past Lana, into the church.

"What? What's wrong?" she said. She followed his eyes to the long-haired guy walking into the church with a bag. "Who's that?"

Richie started toward the church with Lana following. They stopped between the old wooden doors on the threshold. Richie cleared his throat.

"That's Nick."

He rubbed his eyes with his thumb and middle finger. Lana turned to look at Nick, then back at Richie, then back at Nick again, and then Richie.

"Your *brother*, Nick?"

Richie confirmed it was *that* Nick.

"Shit," she said under her breath. A couple in the last pew heard her vulgarity and turned with disapproving looks. "Sorry," she whispered.

"I don't like this," Richie said. He strained to keep himself from shouting, his voice rising in anger. A few more heads turned.

"All right, all right, relax," she said. "This is a good thing, right? He's finally here! He came back home."

"You don't know him," Richie said, shaking his head.

"So introduce me."

Richie bit his lip. She grabbed his arm and nudged him forward down the aisle toward the front pew. Richie could see Nick already sitting in front, his arm slung over and stretched over the wooden pew.

"Nick," Richie said, standing over him. "This is my wife, Lana. Lana, this is my little brother, Nick." Nick grinned ear to ear at the sight of Richie and Lana. He stood up.

"Nice to finally meet you," Lana said, extending her hand.

"Pleasure's all mine, Lana. I'm sorry it's taken so long for us to finally meet. It's long overdue, but welcome to the family, sister." Nick wrapped his arms around Lana before she could say anything.

"Oh," Lana uttered. She patted Nick on the back and laughed a little at his enthusiasm. Richie, standing next to the two, was not tickled by his brother's affection for his wife.

Nick turned and slid his bag down the pew to the other side and sat toward the middle.

"Here, sit down," Nick said, patting the seat next to him. Richie sat by his brother, and Lana joined him on the end.

While they sat, the pastor began the service. Their three demeanors could not have been more different. Nick had a permanent smirk on his face, his left foot resting on his right knee and his arms stretched out behind him. He might as well have been at a baseball game. Richie, meanwhile, stewed. He shot sideways glances at Nick as his mind raced. Lana was somewhere between the two, interested at the surprise of her husband's brother's return but nervous at his intentions.

Eventually, whispers sprang up behind them from the other mourners. Hushed conversations were happening everywhere in the church at the sight of Nick, the mysterious son that hadn't been seen in years. Multiple people seated behind the family leaned over to tap Uncle Luke's shoulder to confirm Nick's identity.

An hour passed in the service. There were readings and songs from Pastor Mark before Richie gave a short eulogy. It wasn't much to remember. Richie was nervous and eager to get through it, but it carried enough genuine sincerity to be labeled appropriate for a son. After Richie spoke, Pastor Mark returned to the podium.

"I believe that will conclude our services for today. Those who would like to join the funeral procession to St. Vincent Memorial Cemetery may do so. A few words will be said before Craig is then laid to rest. The family thanks you all for coming today and God bless."

Pastor Mark gave a warm goodbye to the crowd. The organ in the corner began to play, and the crowd slowly made its way to their feet. Richie rose and buttoned his suit. He put his hands in his pockets. Nick leaped up from the pew.

"Well, that was pretty good, don't you think?" Nick said with a cheeriness that was out of place at a funeral. Richie and Lana both agreed but more solemnly. "Nice speech, Dick," Nick said with a punch on the shoulder.

"I'm going by Richie now."

"What? Since when?"

"A few years now. Just didn't like going by Dick anymore."

"Well, whatever you say, man. Can I get a ride with you guys to the cemetery? I took a bus here."

"Of course," Lana offered.

"Great!" Nick slung his bag over his shoulder. "I'll see you out there."

Richie and Lana watched as Nick stomped through the church in combat army boots. They turned to each other.

"I still don't like this," Richie said.

"I think this is a good thing."

"Not with Nick. It never is."

"Maybe he's changed. Most people do."

Richie still shook his head. Lana grabbed his hand and walked with him up the aisle toward the door. "Just give him a chance. He's still your brother. Your only brother."

Richie heard his wife, but he didn't listen.

*****

Craig Morgan's two sons stood shoulder to shoulder above his mahogany coffin, waiting to be lowered into the ground of St. Vincent Memorial Cemetery. Pastor Mark stood at the head of the coffin, his hands clasped in front of him, his head bowed in prayer.

The other heads surrounding the coffin, consisting of about half of the crowd at the church, were also bowed with eyes closed as Pastor Mark prayed for Craig.

Nick's head stayed level, and his eyes shifted from face to face. He looked over them with scorn. His eyes rolled as he waited for Pastor Mark to finish the prayer.

"Amen," the crowd echoed when the pastor finished. Nick fit his voice with the others.

The pastor began to signal to lower the coffin before Nick spoke up.

"Excuse me, Father!" Nick said, stepping toward Pastor Mark. He approached his side and whispered in his ear. The amiable pastor nodded his head at Nick.

"Of course, son," he said. He stepped aside, and Nick thanked him. He stood at the head of the burial plot. Richie's stomach turned as Nick smirked at the crowd of mourners. Lana could feel her husband tense up. Nick tucked his hair behind his ears and cleared his throat. He stood before them in his sunglasses and denim jacket.

"Good morning, everyone. My name is Nick Morgan, and I am the youngest son of Craig Morgan. I know it's already been a long morning, so I'll make this quick."

Lana glanced up at Richie, his eyes boring into Nick.

"I just have a few words I want to say before my father is laid to rest."

Richie breathed through his nose. Nick took off his sunglasses. He reached into his jacket and pulled out a piece of paper. He unfolded it and looked at the coffin.

"Dad, I'm glad you're dead."

Gasps from the crowd of mourners. Richie dropped his head and covered his eyes with his hands, unable to watch.

"You were an awful father and a worse husband. The worst years of my life were spent growing up with you, and I see the world as a happier, better place with you six feet under it."

Nick folded the paper and put it back in his jacket. He put his sunglasses back on and straightened his jacket. He turned around and gave one last nod to Pastor Mark.

"Thank you, Pastor."

He strutted away.

No one knew what to do or say. Richie reacted first. He huffed after his brother. Lana hesitated before following him.

"Richie—Richie!" she said, her voice rising with each utterance of his name. He either didn't hear her or acted like he didn't. He continued to move toward Nick, his pace a determined stride.

As they got closer, Nick heard Lana's pleas. He turned to see his brother stomping toward him with vengeful eyes and tight fists. Nick watched him approach without a word.

Richie came upon his brother and grabbed him. He nearly lifted him, his powerful hands wrenching Nick closer to his face, bursting with fury.

"Richie!" Lana yelled. Nick said nothing, looking neither surprised nor worried. The mourners watched, still gathered around Craig Morgan's grave.

"Don't!" Lana yelled, trying to pry Nick from Richie's hands.

Richie held Nick inches from his face, his nostrils flaring and brown eyes burning. Nick didn't struggle. When they were younger, Nick teased Richie that he looked like a gorilla. It bothered Richie because with his stout chest, long arms, flat face, close-set eyes, and long nose, it was partly true. Now, with his brother holding him just inches from his face, Nick thought age and his current rage only reinforced that notion. Lana attempted to separate them, but Richie's hands didn't budge.

After more commands from Lana, Richie finally let go, but not before shoving Nick as he did. Nick's thin frame lurched backward easily from the force of Richie's thick arms. He fell onto his back, his sunglasses flying off his face.

"Fuck you!" Richie hissed through his teeth.

Lana stepped between them and pushed her hands into Richie's wide chest. "That's enough," she said simply.

Nick calmly sat up. He grabbed his sunglasses and put them back on. "I'd say sorry, Richie. But I don't mean it. So I won't."

Richie made another move like he was about to jump on Nick right then and there, but Lana stayed between him. Nick didn't flinch.

"Richie, walk away. Now. Walk away." She pushed her husband away toward the road and his truck. Richie stormed off.

Nick gathered himself to his feet. He dusted himself off. Lana took one last look at him, her eyes hovering over him. Her stare unnerved Nick. He averted his eyes, embarrassed, which he wasn't used to. She turned and followed Richie away.

In the commotion, Nick didn't notice Uncle Luke's approach.

"Well, kid," Luke said in his trademark baritone voice. "That was quite something. I'm not sure what."

Nick looked warmly at his uncle. "You know us Morgans, always like to give the town something to talk about."

Uncle Luke chuckled. "You okay?"

"Yeah, fine."

Uncle Luke looked around. The crowd of mourners remained around Craig's coffin as it began to lower. Many still had their eyes on Nick or Richie.

"I don't know about you, but I could use a drink," Luke said. "You want to get a beer with your old uncle, or are you waiting for me to die too?"

Nick grinned. "Yeah. Let's get a beer."

*****

"I can't believe this shithole is still open," Nick mused, looking around the mediocre surroundings of the Walleye Bar & Grill. It'd been a decade since Nick had last stepped foot in the dive, but the only noticeable difference was a slightly larger and working TV.

Uncle Luke drank from his glass. "I always liked this spot. Not many places like this around anymore."

"There's a reason for that."

"I'd rather go here than some bullshit chain like Applebee's or some hoity-toity sushi place. You ever been to those places? Christ, what a scam. Drop a hundred bucks for them to *not* cook your food. The fuck is that?"

"I would've loved to see you try to eat sushi."

Nick acknowledged the easiness in the Walleye that was hard to find in the tourist bliss of Door County. The large U-shaped bar, the dirty billiards table with warped cues, the one-dollar burgers that tasted overpriced. And, of course, the gruff owner Shelley, who manned the bar and watched over it like a dour hawk.

Nick had been coming to the Walleye since he could remember, but he had never seen it busy. Even in the summer. Its capacity always hovered around a few townies at the bar and some miserable married couples eating dinner at the tables without looking at one another.

"Remember when you bought me my first beer here?" Nick asked.

"I think so. How old were you?"

"Seventeen. You were drinking with Craig, totally wasted, and my mom sent me to pick you guys up. You wouldn't leave without buying me a beer and making me drink it first."

Uncle Luke let out his hearty laugh that filled and echoed through every room it appeared in. "That's right. That was fun."

Nick sipped from his can and leaned his back against the wall in the corner booth where they sat, his plastic basket with a half-eaten cheeseburger and fries in front of him. He reached into his jacket and pulled out his pack of cigarettes and lighter.

"You're still doing that?" Uncle Luke asked, disappointed.

"I ain't no quitter."

Uncle Luke shook his head and drank his beer. Nick lit up and inhaled.

"So. You mad at me?" Nick said, exhaling the smoke as he did.

Uncle Luke took a deep breath. "I'm not happy about what you did." He stared at his beer. "He was my brother, and I loved him. But I know he wasn't no saint. I know you two had problems, and he wasn't perfect, especially toward you."

"One way to put it."

"And all that stuff with your mom…"

Nick took another drag of his cigarette. "Either way, it's good to see you, Luke." He raised his can. Luke picked his beer up too and toasted him.

"You too, kid."

Uncle Luke's cell phone rang; its chirping echoed through the Walleye. He wrestled it out of his windbreaker and answered it, getting up and stepping away from the table. Nick thought about how silly it looked, the little plastic electronic phone in Uncle Luke's fat, swollen fingers.

Shelley, the queen of this castle, returned to the table. Nick recognized her. She either didn't or acted like she didn't recognize him. She grabbed the plates off the table without asking if either was done.

"Shelley, how have you been, my love?" Nick said.

She eyed him and grunted in response.

"Don't tell me you don't remember me."

"Should I?" she said without looking up.

"I've been coming here before I could even see over the bar!"

Shelley stood straight, the plates in her hand, and looked at Nick with a complete lack of interest.

"You know, it's that gorgeous smile of yours I missed the most over all these years."

Shelley's face didn't so much as twitch. She looked at Nick's and Uncle Luke's nearly empty beers. "You want another round or the check?"

Uncle Luke appeared from behind her. "Another round, darling. Thank you."

Shelley left the table. Uncle Luke reclaimed his spot. The cushions hadn't even reinflated to their default position before he sat back down.

"I'll get her to laugh one of these days," Nick said. Uncle Luke said nothing until Shelley returned with the two beers. He thanked her. Nick only studied her face. Nick checked his watch, then at Uncle Luke, gulping his fresh beer.

"You're pounding those in the middle of the day."

"It helps with my back pain. Helps me sleep."

"Self-medication. I've been there."

Uncle Luke said nothing.

"Who was on the phone?"

"Oh, no one, just someone from work. Dumb monkeys can't run the place for more than a day without everything going to shit, you know?" His eyes moved to the corner TV on the other end of the bar. He pretended to watch it, even though Nick knew his eyesight was too poor to see what was happening.

"Uncle Luke. You don't have to lie to me."

He rubbed his eyes.

"Look, Lana just told me to keep you here a little longer."

"Keep me here? She gonna come back with a shotgun?"

"No. She's trying to work on Richie—to get him to calm down and come here."

Nick took one more drag and put out his cigarette on the ashtray at the table.

"I hope she's not expecting me to apologize."

"Well, she doesn't know you like I do."

Nick drank his beer. "What do you think of her? Lana?"

"Good kid. Nice girl."

"Too pretty for him, that's for sure."

"I like her. If anyone can get Richie to come down here and make peace, it's her."

"Got him by the balls, does she?"

"I wouldn't say that. She's not like that. He listens to her, is all. You know Richie, stubborn as an ass. Suppose all us Morgans are. But she can get through to him, from what I can tell."

Nick looked away, and the two fell into silence.

*****

An hour had passed since Lana had called Luke.

"I'm telling you, if they just get some starting pitching help, they could make a run," Uncle Luke said. Nick laughed.

"What?"

"Nothing. I just got a very intense déjà vu sitting here, drinking a beer at the Walleye while you tell me this is finally the year the Brewers make it to the playoffs."

"Well, I'm serious—they got some good young players."

"Uh-huh. What's it been, twenty years?"

"It'll be twenty-six this year."

Nick was the first to see Lana walk into the Walleye. He nudged Uncle Luke and pointed her out. They watched her scan the bar before her eyes settled on Uncle Luke with his hand up. She approached with a determined walk.

"Here we go," Nick mumbled.

When she arrived at the booth, Uncle Luke got up and greeted her warmly, hugging her and calling her sweetie. Nick didn't move; he remained with his feet up on the booth and his back leaned against the wall.

"Well? Is he ready for round two?" Nick said.

"He's outside," Lana said. "He's not here to fight. Just to talk. Be nice." Her last words were a demand. Nick began to understand how she could get Richie to do what she says. He stood up from the booth, grabbing his jacket.

"Yes, ma'am."

He began to walk toward the door when he noticed Lana following him. "Sorry, sweetheart, this is a Morgan family conversation. No audience needed."

"Don't call me sweetheart. I just wanted to make sure—"

"If he beats the shit out of me, you can rest easy knowing I deserved it."

He turned and walked out the door, leaving her standing in the middle of the Walleye.

When Nick stepped out into the meager parking lot, he saw the back of his brother, his hands on his hips, looking out into the surrounding trees. He'd taken off his black suit jacket but still wore the white button-down shirt and tie. His sleeves were rolled up to his elbow, and his pits were stained with sweat.

Nick took out his cigarettes and sunglasses. Nick lit up as his brother turned and stared at him. Nick blew smoke and spread out his arms.

"If you're here to kick my ass, let's just get it over with. I won't fight back."

Richie shook his head. "You haven't changed one fucking bit," he snarled. "You're still a fucking asshole."

"I like to think I've changed a *little*. I've tried to get into cooking more. Stuff that's a little healthier, you know, more fish, less red meat. Although, if I'm honest, I still sometimes get a burger from McDonald's for dinner if it's been a long day—"

"Shut up!"

Nick quieted. Richie's eyes burned at him. He took a drag of his cigarette and flicked its ash on the concrete.

"Why did you even come here? Honestly? It wasn't enough that he was dead? You had to piss on his grave to get one last dig? One last middle finger?"

"I don't know about pissing on his grave. I thought maybe I could dance a little bit on it."

Richie stepped to Nick. He was nearly nose to nose with his brother. Nick thought he might punch him then and there. Richie reached out and grabbed Nick's sunglasses off his face. He spiked them on the concrete, shattering them into a dozen pieces.

Nick sighed. Richie turned back around with his hands on his hips.

"Come on, Richie. Are you that pissed? You can play the good son all you want, but deep down, even you knew he was a fucking prick. Even if he wasn't to you."

"That's not true."

Nick rolled his eyes. Richie pointed at his brother. "You crossed the fucking line today. Humiliating him, our whole family, in front of everyone. For the whole fucking town to see. At his funeral!"

Nick took another drag. He thought for a moment. "I didn't mean to humiliate you. I'm sorry about that."

Richie shook his head and leered. "You know, I pictured this for a long time—what it'd be like when you came back. *If* you ever did come back."

"How's it holding up so far?"

Richie turned to his brother. "Why are you here? Did you just come back for that?"

"No."

"Why then?"

Nick took a deep breath. He looked around, avoiding his brother's eyes. "I wanted to see how you were doing. Meet your wife and all that."

Richie scoffed. "Bullshit."

"It's true."

"You could have met Lana at our *wedding*, when I invited you. Or you could have talked to me any of the dozens of times I've called you and you either don't answer or say two words to me."

"I knew if I ever came back here to see you, I'd have to see Craig too."

Richie bit his lip and shook his head.

"But you're right," Nick said. He took another drag from his cigarette. "I've been an asshole, and it's not your fault. But I like to think I'm different now."

Richie gave a mocking laugh.

"It's true! I feel bad about us. We're brothers. We shouldn't be strangers, living on opposite sides of the country, never talking. I want to fix that."

"You're off to a fantastic fucking start."

"Look, Richie," Nick said, trying to keep his voice even. "You were there. You knew what it was like between us. Me and Dad. I'm sorry you were caught in an awkward position today, but I won't apologize for it. You just need to accept that and move on."

"You're telling me to move on? Nick, you were gone for almost a decade because you hated Dad so much! I've never met anyone who holds a grudge like you!"

Nick looked around at the trees and ashed his cigarette.

"Lana says you can stay at our house until you—" Richie exhaled. "I don't know, decide to go back to wherever you came from or whatever you're planning."

"What the old lady says goes, eh?"

Richie gave Nick a look, one that said, *Don't push it.* "Are you planning on staying in town?"

Nick shrugged. "Yeah, I was thinking about it. You know, see some of the old haunts, see how the place is holding up, at least for a few days."

"Fine. I'll grab Lana," Richie said, walking toward the door. He stopped next to Nick, shoulder to shoulder with him. He stared straight ahead as he spoke.

"He asked about you," Richie said. "Toward the end, when he could still talk, but his memory was going." Richie gathered his breath. "He'd ask me almost every day where you were. Every day I had to tell him. You were gone." Nick looked away. "You say you've changed. Well, you never gave Dad a chance to show you that he changed too."

Richie left him and went inside. Nick was left in the parking lot, his cigarette burning down to the filter in the corner of his mouth. He took it out and exhaled. He dropped it on the concrete and stomped it out. He put his hands on his hips and looked out at the forest surrounding the Walleye and the county road leading to it.

He looked at his sunglasses on the concrete. He walked over and picked up the empty lenses, looking them over in his hand. He turned toward the trees, reared back, and fired them into the forest.

2

Eighty-Eight Days from the Night

Inside Richie's gray and rusted single-cab truck, the brothers and Lana sat wedged in the front seat. Richie glowered at the road ahead of him as he drove, and Nick leaned his head against the window, watching the trees pass by.

Lana cleared her throat. "So, Nick, have you—"

"Did he ever tell you the story of how he got this crack in the windshield?" Nick cut her off. He tapped on the asterisk-like crack in the windshield on the right side of the frame.

Lana frowned. "I don't think so."

"Dick, remember when you got this?"

Lana watched as Richie looked out of the side of his eye at the small splinter in the windshield glass Nick pointed at.

"Yeah, of course, I do."

Nick turned to Lana. "I'll bet you'll never guess what caused this little crack."

"I don't know, a rock?"

Richie and Nick both chuckled. "That's what you told Craig, wasn't it?" Nick said. Richie confirmed it was.

"It was 1995, the same year that Dick—sorry, Richie—got this beauty as a birthday present," Nick said, slapping the door of the truck.

"It was only a month after I got it," Richie added. "I'd barely had my license for a couple of weeks."

"Right. And we had a blizzard, a foot of snow, so we got the day off from school," Nick continued. "Everything's closed, there's nothing to do, we're bored as hell. I'm fourteen, Richie's sixteen, so like a bunch of dumb kids, we decide to take the new toy out for a spin. So we pick up a few friends—"

"A few of *my* friends," Richie cut in. "I let you tag along because Mom made me. She felt bad that you would've been home alone all day."

"Whatever. Who was with us again?"

"It was you, me, Cooper, Maddie, and Erica."

"Right, right. Erica M., not Erica F. I forgot about her."

"She and Cooper had a thing."

"That's right. God, I wonder what Cooper is doing these days. Miss that big bastard."

"He works in town. We're still friends. I see him all the time."

"Shit, I gotta see him before I leave."

"I'm sure you will."

"Anyway, so Cooper and Erica were like a thing, right? And Maddie was there because you were with her, right?" Nick asked him.

Richie blushed and avoided his wife's curious gaze next to him. "It was casual, nothing serious."

"Richie, I'm not going to be jealous of you and *Maddie*. We've been married for six years."

"I'm just being honest."

"Bummer," Nick said. "She was fucking hot."

Lana said, "Wait, you were all in this truck? How'd you all fit? We can barely squeeze in here, and we don't even have Cooper."

"Well, the girls were sitting on our laps."

"Ah, of course."

"Yeah, so Erica's on Cooper's lap, and Maddie is on my lap. And, Lana, I'm telling you, Maddie was a legit ten out of ten. Probably the hottest girl in school. And I'm just a freshman, so this is, like, the greatest day of my life."

Lana laughed lightly.

"So we're driving around, and Dick is doing a little drifting, you know, showing off his new truck. I'm holding onto Maddie tight, and she's squeezing into me, and I'm doing my best not to, you know, get too excited."

"Okay, I don't need to know—"

"Come on, Nick," Richie groaned.

"What? I'm just telling the story!"

"Get to the point."

"Okay, okay, okay. So we're drifting, doing donuts and all that shit, having a good time. Then, out of nowhere, Richie starts driving like a maniac and speeds up before this corner."

"You were egging me on!" Richie interjected. "You wouldn't shut up about how you were a better driver and shit! You always did that."

"I did not always egg you on."

"Yes, you did! Like when you got me suspended!"

Nick lowered his voice toward Lana. "I convinced him to cut out of school an hour early one time when he was in eighth grade. They called our parents when they couldn't find us."

Lana laughed.

"I got a day of in-school suspension and couldn't play my next baseball game," Richie said.

"Oh, boo-hoo," Nick said. "You had to miss a middle school baseball game. What a Greek tragedy."

"I'm just saying," Richie said. "You were always trying to get me in trouble."

"I was trying to get you to be cool," Nick said. "Anyway, back to my story. So Maddie is getting comfortable on my lap, and we're hitting it off before Speed Racer over there went crazy."

Richie chortled. "You're so full of shit. She barely noticed you were there."

Nick again leaned toward Lana. "He was getting jealous at how much fun she was having on my lap."

"Would you stop lying?"

"Guys!" Lana cut through the bickering. "Can you just finish the story?"

"Right, anyway, Richie accelerates around this corner and yanks the hell outta the handbrake." Nick mimed pulling on the handbrake and lurching forward. "I honestly thought we were going to flip over for a second. I grabbed the door to brace and let go of Maddie, and the poor girl goes flying headfirst out of my lap and smacks into the frame here." Nick punched the plastic edge frame of the windshield next to him. "I shit you not, that crack came from that poor girl's skull nailing this."

"Jesus!" Lana said. "Was she okay?"

"Yeah, yeah, she was fine, I think," Nick said. "I mean, I don't think she had a concussion or anything, but she seemed okay. She did ask to be taken home after that. Richie barely cared. He was so worried about Dad finding out about the windshield."

"I cared! But if Dad found out about it, he was going to kick my ass and sell the truck."

Nick nudged Lana again. "This girl is crying, can barely see straight, and your husband won't shut up about this little crack in the windshield."

"She was not crying!"

"How would you know? You barely asked her if she was okay!"

"Oh, fuck you! She was on your lap. You were supposed to be holding onto her!"

"Believe me, I was holding on tight. But I thought you were going to flip the damn truck."

"You're such a drama queen."

"Will you two just cool it?" Lana cut in again. "We're home."

They pulled down the long gravel driveway toward the house hidden among the trees. The surrounding forest was so thick, the driveway so long and twisting, that the modest home couldn't even be seen from the road.

Nick surveyed the house as he stepped inside, bag in hand. "Nice place. Looks homey."

"Uh-huh, thanks," Richie said. He could still tell when his brother was being insincere.

Lana gestured at Nick to follow her down a narrow hallway to the right of the entrance. "You can take the guest bedroom. Not much in here, just a bed."

Nick stepped into the small square bedroom. She was right; besides a queen-sized mattress, the room was bare. Its gray walls had zero decorations. There was a small double-door closet, but only a few hangers hung from it. A window let in some sunlight.

"I don't know how long you're planning on staying, but make yourself at home."

"Not long," Richie grumbled.

"Be nice," Lana ordered Richie. "You're welcome here as long as you want."

"Thank you, Lana," Nick said. Nick cleared his throat. "If you don't mind, I'm gonna try to catch some sleep. I was up all night on that fucking Greyhound bus on the way here."

"Oh, of course," Lana said. "I'll just knock on the door when dinner's ready in a couple of hours."

"Thanks, Mom," Nick said as the two left. Richie shot a glare at Nick. They closed the door. Nick let out a deep sigh and dropped on his back on the bed. Only a minute or two passed before sleep took him.

The early morning was chilly, as they always are on the Door peninsula. The cooling Lake Michigan winds make the mornings crisp even in the middle of summer and especially during the spring.

It was barely forty degrees when Nick woke up in a strange bed, his clothes and shoes still on. He panicked, not remembering where he was. Then, it came back to him. His brother's home. His new sister-in-law's home. He rubbed his eyes and propped himself up. He checked his watch. He'd slept for almost fifteen hours.

He could hear a commotion outside his door: a whirring stove vent, crackling bacon, and the patter of slippers on the tile. He stood up. His body felt groggy and his vision blurry. He opened the door and stepped out into the hallway.

Richie and Lana's house wasn't big, being one-story and maybe a thousand square feet. It had a long, curved shape to it. The driveway and garage were on the west side, the living and dining room in the center by the front door, and the bedrooms and bathroom were on the east side, where Nick had slept.

As he walked past the living room toward the kitchen, he noted the decor. Some might describe it as classic, but most would refer to it as outdated. There was wood paneling on the walls in the living room, and the carpet was noticeably old. The only modern touches

Nick could see came in the way of family photos and some sports memorabilia courtesy of Richie.

Nick stepped onto the red-and-white tiled floor of the kitchen. Even with his socks on, the icy tiles made Nick shiver. Lana stood at the stove, her back to him. She wore a purple robe and flannel pajama bottoms. Her long blond hair was tied up in a messy bun. She didn't seem to hear him enter.

"Christ, keep these floors cold enough?" Nick said.

Lana looked over her shoulder with a radiant smile. "Hey! Good morning!"

Ugh, Nick thought. *A morning person.*

"Yeah, I know, I hate these tiles," she said. "There's some coffee ready, and I'm making some eggs and bacon. I'm sure you're starving after missing dinner last night."

Nick helped himself to the pot of Mr. Coffee, grabbing a nearby mug. "Sorry about that. I don't know what happened. I lay down for a nap and was out like a light."

"Don't worry about it! You looked like you needed it. You look better today."

"Thanks, I think."

"Sit down. I'll bring the food over to the table." She motioned to a small plastic table against the wall in the kitchen with three chairs. Nick sat down with his coffee. His stomach rumbled at the smell of fried eggs and bacon.

Nick watched Lana cook as he sipped his coffee. Her hands were busy, poking the eggs and sizzling bacon, grabbing plates from the cabinet, buttering toast, taking the orange juice out of the fridge. She seemed delighted to be cooking breakfast for someone besides herself or Richie.

"You're pretty tall," Nick observed. She was maybe two inches shorter than Nick, who was a hair over six feet.

"I still don't know what to say when someone points that out to me," Lana said without turning around. "Do I say, 'Thank you'? I don't even know if it's a compliment."

"You must have played basketball."

"They all say that too," Lana said, turning with the pan of eggs toward the table. "I did." She put the eggs on a plate in the middle of the table and retrieved more plates and silverware for the table.

"Well, this looks amazing. You always up this early?" Nick asked as Lana put the bacon on the table.

"I'm a nurse. I work a lot of early shifts. Sometimes I work the night shift and get off right around this time, so I guess I'm used to being awake around now. Sometimes I get up early for a run."

This made sense to Nick, observing her lean body. She put the orange juice and toast on the table. The tiny table was filled with breakfast fixings.

"Couldn't be me," Nick said. "If I'm awake before noon it's a special occasion. I can't remember the last time I had a home-cooked breakfast like this."

"It's nothing. Eat up."

Nick didn't need to be told twice. He slid the eggs off the plate onto his and grabbed some toast and bacon, chowing down immediately. "Dick still sleeping?" he said in between bites. Lana sat across from him, drinking her coffee and biting into a strip of bacon.

"*Richie* is asleep, yes. He doesn't usually get to sleep in, so I let him," Lana said. "Plus, it didn't seem like he slept well last night."

Nick looked up from his feasting. "Another side effect of my stay?"

Lana shook her head. "No, he has trouble sleeping most nights."

He raised an eyebrow. "What's the matter? You cut him off or something?"

"What? No! It's just, you know, life stuff."

"Ah, I wouldn't know anything about that." Nick went back to eating. Lana watched and sipped her coffee. Nick looked around the house.

"Do you have a cat?" he asked with a mouthful of eggs.

"No. Why?"

"Dog?"

"No."

"You should get one."

"Why?"

"This just seems like a house that would have a cat or dog in it."

"I don't know what that means."

"I don't either, but it seems right."

Lana rolled her eyes. Nick finished devouring his breakfast. When he was done, he leaned back and patted his swollen stomach.

"Wow," Lana said. "I can make more."

"No, no, please, don't. That was delicious, thank you. I'm sure when you have kids, they'll be adorably fat." Nick leaned back in his chair and took out his cigarettes. Lana raised her eyebrows.

"Do you mind?" Nick asked.

Lana sighed and cracked open the kitchen window as Nick lit up.

"You know, I'm surprised you don't already have a few rug rats running around. I always pictured my brother with a gorgeous wife in a big house with a couple of bratty kids."

Lana reached across the table and grabbed Nick's pack of cigarettes. "Maybe someday," she said. She lit one and took a drag, closing her eyes as she exhaled, savoring it.

Nick noticed how long her neck was as she leaned her head back, blowing smoke. Her lake blue eyes opened, and Nick averted his eyes to his own cigarette.

"Why not now?" he asked, pushing his hair back.

Lana shrugged. "I don't know, just not the right time. Can't afford it."

"Are those the life problems keeping Richie up at night?"

Lana smirked as she smoked. "Yeah, I guess so. He worries too much."

Nick exhaled out of the corner of his mouth. "He's not shooting blanks, is he? If the Morgan family swimmers are having problems, I'd like to know."

"Oh yeah? You thinking of having kids soon?"

Nick ashed his cigarette on his empty plate. "Maybe someday."

Lana smiled and sipped her coffee. The two sat and smoked in silence for a bit, listening to the chirping birds outside the open window.

"Wouldn't peg you as a smoker." Nick broke the silence.

"I'm not. I quit five years ago." Lana reached over and ashed her cigarette outside the window.

"Let me guess—Richie made you quit."

"No, I did myself. Disgusting habit. I only smoked in college."

Nick chuckled as Lana fanned the smoke out of the kitchen window. "I have a feeling he'll blame me if you get caught."

"That's the plan," Lana said with a smile.

Nick put out his cigarette and flicked it out the window. Lana frowned. Nick took his mug to the counter and poured himself another cup. "So how'd you end up settling for Richie anyway? You don't seem like his type."

"What's his type?"

"I don't know. I always imagined him with like a dumb blond who married him because he was tall with big arms."

"Well, I am blond. And Richie is tall and does have big arms."

"Yeah, but you don't strike me as the domesticated housewife I always figured he'd end up with."

"What do I strike you as?"

"I don't know. Cool, I guess."

Lana tapped her chest. "That's real flattering."

"So come on. How'd your options get so bad you settled for him?"

"I didn't!" Lana composed herself. "We met in college. I was in nursing school. A friend introduced us," Lana said, blowing more smoke out the window.

"Was it a Florence Nightingale thing? He got sick and you nursed him back to health?" Nick asked. "Or did he pull a muscle and you gave him a full-body rubdown?"

"Oh my god! Stop!" Lana scoffed. She tried to act offended without laughing but failed. "Richie was nice and sweet. He cared."

"About what?"

"Everything. Me and everything I did. He always cared and didn't change. He wasn't pretending to be a nice guy—he genuinely was. That's rare."

"Makes sense. He doesn't seem to have changed since I last saw him."

"Plus, he's cute. And I have a thing for baseball players."

Nick took another drag. "Looks like a gorilla if you ask me."

"What about you?" Lana asked. "You got a girl back wherever the hell you came from?"

Nick nodded his head back and forth. "I got plenty of girls back where I came from."

"You know what I mean."

Nick shook his head. Lana squinted at Nick from across the table, studying his face. It made Nick squirm, her invasive stare.

"You're lying."

"Excuse me?"

"There's someone."

"There are many *someones*."

"No. Just one."

"I don't know where you're getting this."

"It's not hard to see. It's all over your face."

"What is?"

"Love."

Nick scoffed. Lana didn't budge. He became annoyed.

"Maybe you can hide it from Richie, but I can see it."

"I'm not *hiding* anything. You're just wrong. And annoying about it."

"Mhmm," Lana said. She was enjoying breaking down Nick's facade. It had only taken a few conversations to get under his skin, something Richie never could do.

"You got a job?" she asked.

"What is this, twenty fucking questions?"

Lana laughed. "Touchy."

Nick sighed. "I don't have a conventional job. Per se," Nick mumbled.

"Per se?"

"What's the matter? You don't know any French?"

"It's Latin. And I know what it means."

"You sure?"

"I took four years of French in high school, and it was my minor in college, so, yes, I am sure."

Nick rolled his eyes. "Oh god. Are you one of those people who knows another language and flaunts it at every opportunity?"

"*Tu es un connard.*"

Nick stared, blankly.

"It means, 'You're an asshole.'" Lana smiled, satisfied.

"You really speak it? You're, like, fluent?"

"Yeah, pretty much."

"Huh," Nick said. He scoffed in disbelief.

"What?"

"Nothing. Strange coincidence."

"Seriously though, what do you do for money?"

"I make my way."

"That's a vague and annoying answer."

"Ask me annoying questions and you'll get annoying answers."

Lana was tickled by Nick's growing animosity. Her smile dropped when she heard a door open. She tossed her cigarette out the kitchen window and tried to fan away any smoke left in the kitchen. Nick turned to see his brother emerging from the hallway, walking toward them in a white T-shirt and basketball shorts.

The white shirt was a little tight on him, accentuating his inflated belly but also emphasizing his strong shoulders and arms. He itched the brown stubble growing around his jaw. Nick could hear the scratch of his nails against the short whiskers.

"Thank God," Nick said when he saw him. "I thought I was going to have to answer Lana's questions all morning."

"Good morning to you too," Richie said.

"Morning," Lana said in her sweetest, most innocent voice. Richie smiled at her and leaned down to peck her on the lips.

"Good morning, gorgeous," he said.

Lana frowned after the kiss. "You need to shave today," she said. "It scratches my face when you kiss me."

"Yes, dear," Richie said as he poured himself a cup of coffee. When he returned to the table, he snuck up behind her and quickly rubbed his cheek against hers.

"Ow!" she yelled, pushing him away.

Richie laughed and sat down with his coffee. Lana shook her head and rubbed her cheek. Richie grabbed some eggs and bacon for his plate. He looked from Nick to Lana.

"You two getting along?" Richie asked as he put a forkful of eggs in his mouth.

"Swimmingly," Lana said cheerily. "I always wanted a brother."

Nick sipped his coffee. "I liked Maddie better."

Lana laughed. Richie ignored him and began eating. Before taking another bite of his eggs, he stopped. He sniffed the air.

"Did you smoke in here?" Richie asked his brother.

Nick shrugged.

"Come on, man. At least take it outside. Lana quit years ago. She doesn't need you blowing smoke in her face."

"Sorry, *Lana*," Nick said dryly. She smiled.

Richie went back to eating. Nick stood up and grabbed another cup. He filled it with water and drank. "You don't have to work today?" Nick asked his brother. "Shit, I don't even know what you do."

Richie bit into his toast. "Yeah, you do. I run the bait shop."

"Really? That place is still open?" Nick asked.

The bait shop was the Tackle Box. Opened thirty years ago by their father when he moved to Door County with his wife and a baby in tow. The Tackle Box was never successful. It barely paid the bills. Both Nick and Richie spent time working there during the summer. Nick hated it because he hated fishing, but Richie seemed to enjoy it.

"Yeah. I took over when Dad retired," Richie said.

"Huh," Nick said. He checked his watch. "Shouldn't you be there now?"

Nick thought about all the times his dad dragged him out of bed at six in the morning during the summer so he could man the register, hungover.

"I closed it for a couple of days," Richie mumbled.

Nick raised his eyebrows. "Isn't that bad for business?"

Richie shrugged. Nick began to feel a tension in the room between Lana and Richie, who kept sharing thoughtful glances.

"This'll probably be the last summer of the Box," Richie said.

"Really?"

"It's not making any money. Hard with the recession and all. Worth more to just sell it and get out from under it."

Nick sat back down at the table. "Huh. So the summer of 2008 will be the Box's last summer. I can't say I'll miss that place. What'll you do?"

"I don't know, probably bank the money, live off it while I look for work."

Nick shrugged. "Well, at least you won't be alone. Just turn on the news. Everyone's losing their jobs and houses these days."

Richie said nothing and continued eating. Nick sipped his water, feeling uncomfortable. Lana mercifully broke the silence.

"Oh, honey, before I forget, there's that storage space full of stuff from your dad's old place. Since you're not working today, I figured you could go out there and sort through it: toss whatever's garbage and see if there's anything worth keeping or selling. Nick, why don't you go with him?"

Richie glanced at Nick before standing up with his empty plate. "I'm sure Nick wouldn't want to spend all day going through dusty old shit."

"Come on, Nick, don't you want to go?" Lana said, looking at Nick.

Nick's initial reaction was a flat-out no. Then he thought of the delicious breakfast in his stomach and the comfy bed he slept in last night. He thought of the way Lana had acted as a peacekeeper between him and Richie yesterday. He realized he wasn't in a position to refuse her at the moment.

"Yeah, sure, I'll go. Not like I have anything else to do."

Richie did his best to keep his face blank.

"Perfect," Lana said. "You don't have a job, so you're in no rush to get back, right?"

Nick shook his head. "Not at all."

"Oh, why don't you work at the bait shop while you stay here?"

"Lana—" Richie started.

"I don't think Richie wants me getting in his way at work."

"Oh, come on! It's the last summer of the family business. You got anything better to do?"

Nick scratched his head. "I guess, while I'm staying here, I could lend a hand if you need it."

Richie turned off the sink and dried his hands off. "Okay, sure. But I'm pretty short on cash and can't afford to feed another mouth."

"Don't worry about it," Nick said.

Richie glanced at Lana. He finished drying his hands and looked at Nick. "You sure?"

"Yeah, it's no problem. I'll pay you for the room and the food as long as I'm here."

"That's not necessary," Lana began to say.

"No, I insist," Nick said. He reached into his pocket and pulled out his wallet. He pulled out a wad of cash and began flipping through bills. Richie and Lana exchanged looks as he counted. He slapped $500 on the counter. "There's the first month in advance. I'm not going to be the deadbeat brother."

Richie looked at Lana again. "Yeah, okay," he said.

"Welcome," Lana said.

Richie went to shower, leaving Nick and Lana alone again.

"He sure sounds like he's excited to spend some quality time with his brother," Nick said with a coating of sarcasm.

"He's got a lot of things on his mind," Lana said, standing up and bringing more dishes to the sink. "Plus, he did bury his father yesterday."

"Hey, so did I," Nick said.

"Yeah, you seemed real devastated."

Nick conceded the point and took out his pack of cigarettes. He lit one and emphatically inhaled next to Lana, taunting her at the sink.

"We're not taking your money for rent, just to be clear," Lana said, motioning to the wad of bills still on the counter."

"Try and stop me. I'm not just going to be another mouth to feed."

"Over my dead body."

"If I have to shove cash down your fucking throat, I will."

Lana glanced up from her dishes at Nick. They both laughed. Nick took another drag as Lana began drying the dishes off.

"You know, a lot of wives bail on their husbands when they find out he ran his business into the ground," Nick said.

"He didn't," Lana began to say. "It wasn't his fault. He did his best."

"Still, losing all the family money and divorce tend to go hand in hand."

"Is this your way of asking me to leave Richie and run away with you?"

"You're a little chatty for my taste," Nick said. "But this is Door County. There are old rich guys with Viagra prescriptions everywhere around here looking for a third wife or a mistress. Shit, a young, tall, pretty blond like you could get some married guy to leave his wife in a second. You could be one of those desperate housewives that gets a Cadillac for Christmas and fake tits for her birthday."

"Lovely," Lana grumbled. "As tempting as it is to be a sad, empty woman who doesn't own anything in her life, not even her tits, I think I prefer my life with Richie."

"I don't know. Those girls seem pretty happy with their big houses and diamonds around their neck."

Lana put the last dish away on the drying rack. She turned to Nick.

"*L'argent ne fait pas le bonheur,*" she said, the words dripping out of her mouth like syrup. She plucked the cigarette out of Nick's mouth and put it between her lips. "Money doesn't buy happiness," she translated, blowing smoke in his face.

"Plus," Lana added as she put the cigarette out in the sink. "I don't need fake tits, and Richie doesn't need any Viagra." She clicked her tongue and winked as she passed by Nick, tapping him on the ass as she did.

Nick turned and watched as she walked down the hallway to the bathroom at the end of the hall. She undid her bun and let her blond hair drop as she opened the door to the bathroom. Nick could hear the shower water running.

"Hey, baby," Nick could hear Lana say. She closed the door behind her.

Nick was left alone in the kitchen. He chuckled to himself. "Not bad, Richie," he mumbled.

*****

DETECTIVE VOGEL. This is Detective Harry Vogel recording an interview with Richard and Lana Morgan in their home. Sergeant Kucharski and Deputy Peterson of the Door County Sheriff's department are also present. The date is July 6, 2008, and it is 10:52 a.m. Mr. and Mrs. Morgan, I want to start by thanking you for allowing us into your home on your own accord. We're glad that you've decided to speak with us directly without any lawyers present so that we can hopefully get to the bottom of this.

RICHIE. Richie.

DETECTIVE VOGEL. I'm sorry?

RICHIE. It's Richie, not Mr. Morgan. My father was Mr. Morgan. He's dead.

DETECTIVE VOGEL. Of course. I'd like to start by asking you about your brother, Nick.

RICHIE. Okay. How long is this going to take?

DETECTIVE VOGEL. What's that?

RICHIE. Searching our house, asking us questions—how long will this take?

DETECTIVE VOGEL. Not long at all. I don't want to waste either of your time, so I'll get right to it.

RICHIE. Fine.

DETECTIVE VOGEL. You and your brother, Nick, were estranged for a long time, is that right?

RICHIE. Nine years.

DETECTIVE VOGEL. Did you two maintain any contact at all during that time?

RICHIE. Never face-to-face. Occasionally, I'd try to call him. Usually around the holidays. Mostly to check he was still alive. But we'd go years without talking at all. When we did, it was for a few minutes at most.

DETECTIVE VOGEL. Do you know what your brother did in those nine years he was away? A job or anything like that?

RICHIE. He said he traveled around. Was in California, Colorado, St. Louis. Said he mostly bartended and did other shit like that. Odd jobs.

DETECTIVE VOGEL. Did he mention his time in prison?

RICHIE. No. He was in prison?

DETECTIVE VOGEL. Twenty-five months in a federal facility in California.

RICHIE. For what?

DETECTIVE VOGEL. Assaulting a police officer, among other things.

RICHIE. No. He never mentioned that.

DETECTIVE VOGEL. When did you two reunite?

RICHIE. At my father's funeral, I guess. That was the first time we saw each other since he left.

DETECTIVE VOGEL. When was that?

RICHIE. I don't remember the exact date, early April.

LANA. April seventh.

DETECTIVE VOGEL. Thank you, Mrs. Morgan.

LANA. Lana.

DETECTIVE VOGEL. Right, Lana.

3

Eighty-Seven Days from the Night

Nick rolled down the window of Richie's truck to let the cool morning breeze wake him up some more. Even after two cups of coffee, he still felt groggy from his marathon sleep.

Before leaving, he'd splashed cold water on his face and that combined with the chilly spring air was jolting his system. The rushing wind grabbed hold and uprooted his long hair he had combed. Richie, driving, wore his usual uniform of jeans and a gray hoodie with the Tackle Box's logo on the front.

They arrived at the storage center, where rows of white garage stalls were arranged in neatly aligned rows. They parked in front of stall A9. Richie got out and opened a side door and then the stall door.

Inside was what Nick would describe as a cache of crap: old and broken chairs, tables, Christmas decorations, beer signs, knick-knacks, old toys, decrepit books, and moth-ridden clothes. A musty stench emanated from the stall.

"Jesus, look at this shit," Nick muttered, bringing his shirt up to his face to cover his nose. "Why do you even have this?"

"When Dad moved into the nursing home, we had to clean out his old house. He wouldn't let us throw anything away," Richie said, turning on the light, illuminating even more debris. He went into the stall slowly, navigating the heaps of stuff. He moved a chair out of the way and began sorting through a stack of books against the wall.

"So what are we looking for in this shit heap?" Nick asked, gingerly stepping into the storage space, as if at any moment a snake may leap out and strike.

"Anything that might fetch a buck."

"Who would pay for this shit?"

"You'd be surprised. Come on, start going through this. Anything not worth keeping, throw in a pile, and we'll toss it out."

At that green light, Nick began to roughly handle the dubious antiques that his father had kept for so long. An old wicker chair with a busted seat was thrown backward, splintering on the cement. Richie had a gentler approach but was having a hard time finding anything that was worth hauling back and hocking for even two dollars.

He picked up an old snow globe and blew some of the dust off it. He cast an eye toward Richie, hunched over a cardboard box. Nick cleared his throat.

"It's pretty bad, isn't it?" he said.

"What is?" Richie said without breaking his concentration.

"You're—" Nick searched for the right, delicate words. "Money situation."

Richie halted. He slowly raised and turned to his brother. "What are you talking about?"

"Come on, Richie," Nick said, looking around. "You're selling the Box, and you're looking through Dad's old crap for anything that'll get you a few dollars. I can put two and two together."

Richie turned back to the boxes. "It's nothing. We'll be fine."

"Look, I know you didn't want to say this in front of Lana, and I know we're not close, and I've only been back for a little bit, so maybe I don't have the right—"

"No, you don't."

Nick backed off a little. "But I am still your brother. You can tell me if you're in trouble."

Richie rose again. He turned with what looked like an ornate fountain pen in his hands. He looked down and fiddled with it.

"We're gonna lose the house too."

Nick paused. "Shit, I'm sorry," he murmured.

"Don't."

"Don't what?"

"Look or talk to me like that. With pity. Makes me sick."

"How long do you got?"

"A couple of months, maybe." Richie tapped the pen against his hand. He tossed it aside.

"Even if you sell the Box?" Nick asked.

"Won't matter. Hasn't turned a profit in years. Even if we got twice its value, we'd still be buried in debt."

"I see."

"Forget it. We'll be fine. Lana's still got her job. We'll just move to a smaller place, and I'll get a job somewhere else. We'll be fine."

He turned and went back to his search through the boxes. Nick did the same.

Nick came across three green plastic totes stacked upon one another. He opened the first one. Christmas decorations: plastic reefs, fake snow for hanging on a mantle, and even a nutcracker. He put it aside to bring back. *Christmas shit usually sells*, he thought.

He opened the second box and froze. He found tattered clothes and jeans that looked more like a handful of loose threads than pants. On top of them, though, sat a lunchbox.

Nick's old lunchbox, the one with his favorite cartoon characters: Tom and Jerry. He took it to school every day until the first day of the sixth grade. When he went to lunch that day, he realized all his friends had gotten rid of their colorful lunch boxes over the summer. They brought their food in plain brown bags. He felt like a child. Nick came home that day and threw it away and said he never wanted to see it again. He hadn't, until that moment.

He opened another tote next to it. Again, he recognized its contents: cassette tapes and some more clothes. On top was his old Beastie Boys T-shirt he wore approximately five hundred times throughout high school. Its black cotton faded to a charcoal gray after hundreds of washes.

He opened a cardboard box next to it. They were books. The ones from his childhood like Dr. Seuss and the ones he read in high school from Hunter S. Thompson, Truman Capote, and Stephen King.

Below them were more books, his books. His spiral notebooks and journals. There were almost a dozen of them, their edges frayed and pages filled with ugly scribbles and barely legible notes, outlines, and even sketches. He fanned through them. The first one was a gift from his mom from when he had been in fourth grade. She encouraged him to write his own stories. So he did.

For years, these pages were the most important thing in Nick's life. Even so, he left in such a rush he forgot them at home. He figured he'd never see them again. He gulped as he read over the thoughts and scribbles of his youth.

Richie noticed that he didn't hear any commotion from his brother and turned to see him holding a notebook, standing over a box. He was flipping through its pages, reading pages thick with pencil and pen.

"Surprised me too when I found that at Dad's," Richie said, coming up behind Nick.

His brother's voice startled Nick. He almost dropped the notebook. He closed it and dropped it back in the box. "Mom must've kept them," Nick said. He began to open a nearby tote.

"We found it inside Dad's desk, in one of the drawers," Richie said.

Nick hesitated. "He shouldn't have done that. They weren't for him."

"Well, you left. And you wouldn't talk to him. I guess that was the only thing he had left of you."

"They weren't for him!" Nick slammed the lid back on the tote. Richie jumped at the outburst. "You shouldn't have let him do that."

"It's not my fault. I didn't even know he had them until we cleaned out the house when we put him in the nursing home."

Nick began to open and go through other boxes and totes, roughly handling their contents and tossing them over his shoulder. "Those were personal. That's like going through someone's diary."

"They were just little stories, man. I'd thought you'd be happy to see them. You always had them with you back in the day."

Nick said nothing, moving more boxes and miscellaneous junk. Richie looked at the open boxes next to him with Nick's old things. "What do you wanna do with that stuff?"

"I don't care. Toss them."

"I mean, Dad did keep it all after all these years. I think he would've wanted you—"

"I don't give a fuck what he wanted," Nick said without looking at his brother.

Richie sighed. He began to pick up the books and notebooks, but Nick turned. "Just leave them there. I'll take care of them," he said curtly.

Richie walked away, going back to searching through the compilation. Nick continued as well.

They rummaged through the storage garage without so much as a word between them for nearly a half hour, tossing junk into various piles meant for return or the dump.

After rummaging through mostly crap, Richie came across a different box that wasn't stuffed with old junk. He opened it to find his jerseys. They were his old youth jerseys, all the way from his Pop Warner football and Little League baseball days. He pulled them out and looked through them. The green, red, and blue jerseys were in remarkably good condition for some being twenty years old.

He remembered those times. Saturday morning football and Sunday afternoon baseball games when he was eight years old. The big shoulder pads, sweat-stained helmets, and fraying gloves. The ripped and grass-stained pants. The post-game meals of hot dogs, popcorn, and Mountain Dew. Mostly, though, he remembered his dad the coach.

The best times Richie had with his dad were when he wasn't his father, just Coach Morgan. Pacing the sideline or dugout, Craig Morgan looked born for the title with his tall figure, lean build, thick glasses, strong jaw, and thinning blond hair that was usually poking out of his trademark blue visor.

When he was Coach Morgan, Richie could talk to him. He could ask him questions, and Craig would give answers, not just two-word commands or retorts but thoughtful and meaningful insights into the game and life and being a man. Coach Morgan was different from Craig. Craig was bitter—he drank too much and ruminated on the poor business of his bait shop and the deterioration of his marriage. He blamed the world for his lack of money, the wife he didn't understand, and his youngest son he didn't like very much. At home, Craig barely talked to his family unless it was to argue with Jackie or curse at Nick.

Coach Morgan, though, was a comforting presence. He earned respect and worship from his players with his fair but firm style. He cracked jokes and goofed around as much as he scolded and chided. He smiled much more. Richie, even at a young age, noticed this stark contrast and didn't understand why his dad was so different, depending on where he was. As he grew older, he understood more. On the field he was Coach Morgan: a man to be feared and respected by peers and players. At home, he was only Craig: a husband with barely any money with a wife who only tolerated him and a son that grew more unruly toward him by the day.

Coach Morgan was happiest when it came to Richie, his star athlete. Richie was almost always the biggest and strongest player on the field, and he combined that with surprisingly agile coordination. He sacked quarterbacks, he pinned opponents to the mat, and he hammered fastballs deep over the fence.

Into high school, Craig could only coach Richie in one sport, and he chose baseball. So baseball became the sport Richie was most committed to. He was good—best in the area. But when it came time to choose a college, Richie had no athletic scholarships offered to him, despite promises from Coach Morgan that scouts and college coaches would offer him soon. With few options, Richie chose to go to UW Whitewater and play on their Division-III team without a scholarship.

Craig didn't approve. He thought his son's talents exceeded some rinky-dink D-III school like Whitewater. He wanted Richie to at least walk-on at UW Milwaukee, the only NCAA D-I program in the state, or even a Big Ten Conference school like the University of Illinois or Michigan. He was sure his son, the best player in the town all his life, would prove his mettle against the best of the best.

But Richie didn't want to pay tuition at a big expensive school just to satisfy his father's aspirations of having a D-I athlete for a son. Richie went to Whitewater and enjoyed playing on the team, although it was strange to walk back to the dugout and not see his dad waiting for him. Craig attended a few of Richie's early games but didn't seem to enjoy watching his son compete anymore, so Richie stopped letting him know when he had a game nearby. Every time Richie came back home on break, Craig looked more bitter and drunker than the last time. He decided not to come home anymore, until his mother's death in the spring of his sophomore year.

The setting in which Richie and his dad bonded the most had come and gone. Coach Morgan retired when Richie went off to college. All that was left was Craig.

"Richie!"

The shout startled him. He dropped the jerseys back in the box and realized Nick was right next to him.

"What?"

"I called your name three times," Nick said. "What are you looking at?"

Richie closed the box and slid it away. "Nothing, just old stuff. You need something?"

"There's a dresser back here I think you'll want, or at least want to sell. But I need a hand moving it."

"Yeah, okay."

Nick and Richie made their way to the back of the space where the dresser waited. The two brothers grabbed each end of the antique dresser, a relic that stood in their parents' bedroom for as long as they could remember. They hauled it next to the truck and set it down. Nick returned to the back of the stall and noticed a white cover over a long object hidden behind some plastic totes. He lifted the corner of the cover to see the tip of red plastic.

"Oh, shit, you still got the kayaks?" he shouted over his shoulder to his brother.

Richie glanced over to see Nick taking the cover off the first kayak, the one his family had had since he was ten years old. "Yeah," Richie shouted before returning to a box of tools. "I don't know if we can sell them though. I think there's a crack in one of them. Things haven't been on the water in years. They'd probably sink."

Nick moved some more boxes to take the cover completely off. The old red kayak looked just as it had when he was a kid, albeit with more dust. He noticed another cover behind it and navigated toward it. He took the cover off, and there was the green kayak. He stepped back and studied them both.

"I don't know, I think they look pretty good to me," Nick said, running his hands over the plastic hulls. He recognized the scrapes and scratches on them like he'd taken them out yesterday. "Why don't we do a little test drive? See if they're still seaworthy."

Richie shook his head. "I don't think so, man. We gotta sort through all this crap, figure out what's worth keeping, bring it back to the house, bring the rest to the dump, then I gotta stop at the bait shop for a few things. No, we're not taking a little kayak trip. Besides, it's too cold. Water's freezing."

Same old Dick, Nick thought. "Come on, man! It'll just be like old times! I haven't been kayaking since I left. Have you?"

Richie shook his head.

"It'll be real quick, just drop 'em in the water and see if they float."

"I'm telling you, those things will sink in five minutes on the water."

"You don't know that."

"Look at them! They look older than us."

"You worry too much. It's a beautiful, sunny spring morning. There's no wind; the water will be calm. It's perfect!"

It'd been years since Richie had kayaked, and a part of him did miss the hours he would spend with his brother and friends on the water in the small, plastic rafts during the summer. The few times they could both get away from the Box. They'd paddle for hours, bobbing over the waves of the lake as the sun turned their skin pink and the breeze cooled their sweat.

Richie looked at the sky. It was an undeniably gorgeous day. Without a cloud in sight, the sky was pristinely blue.

"All right," Richie relented. "We're just going to make sure that they still float. Five minutes, that's it."

Nick clapped his hands. "Of course!"

They each grabbed an end of the red kayak and began the human Tetris game to get it out of the space without breaking anything. They loaded the red and green kayaks and paddles into the back of Richie's truck.

"Why don't we go to Cave Point? We always went there," Nick suggested as they finished loading.

Richie looked at him out of the corner of his eye. "We can go to the boat launch by Cave Point, but we're not paddling to the caves. That'll take too long."

"The caves are a Door County landmark!"

"You've seen them a dozen times and never gave a shit before. Why do you want to now? Don't tell me you're nostalgic all of a sudden."

Richie climbed into the driver's seat of his truck. Nick followed in on the other side.

"Maybe a little."

"The answer is still no."

*****

The rhythm of kayaking naturally came back to Nick's muscles. He wondered if that was why kayaking was the only physical activity he enjoyed as a kid. There was no ball, no score, no teams, no coaches, and no fields. It was only him and a kayak on the water. The opponents are the waves and the water and the sun.

Nick could set his body on autopilot, gently stroking from one side to the next while his mind wandered, scanning the horizon and limestone cliffs of nearby Cave Point. He could be alone, out on the water, with nothing between him and the lake but an unremarkable plastic raft and be completely at peace.

Nick glanced at his brother, who was also falling into the cadence of kayaking. He barely fit in the kayak anymore, his knees sticking out. But Nick was impressed at his flexibility in not tipping over.

They nonchalantly drifted out into the lake from the boat launch. Nick turned his south, toward the cliffs and caves of Cave Point.

"Nick! Don't drift too far away!" Richie shouted.

"Come on, Richie! When was the last time you ventured into the caves?"

Richie groaned, knowing he'd lost the battle. Nick was free on his kayak. He couldn't stop him. But he could badger him to finish his trip faster.

"It's too nice of a day! It'd be a shame to waste it on land! I'm going!" Nick pivoted the tip of his kayak back south and toward the shore.

"Goddammit!" Richie grumbled under his breath. He turned his kayak south and followed in Nick's trail. Richie's annoyance faded as he fell into the rhythm of kayaking and felt the warmth of the sun and the cool splash of the lake on his arms and legs.

Nick, a few paddles ahead, studied the shore and its contents. It was, as it was a decade ago, stuffed with the domains of the wealthy: houses and mansions with docks and piers housing expensive speedboats, jet skis, and the occasional yacht.

After about fifteen minutes, Nick saw it. Hanging over a protruding cliff sat a log cabin-style mansion. He recognized its giant windows and its balcony with more square feet than most of the apartments Nick had ever lived in. A stone wall divided the house from the cliff it overlooked, with a zigzagging iron staircase leading down to its rocky beach. On the shoreline, in the shadow of the cliff next to a white dock was a boathouse, like a miniature version of the mansion with the same wood and log cabin look.

Nick stopped paddling and allowed his brother to catch up. When he got within ten feet from his brother, Nick gestured toward the mansion with his paddle. "That's a nice place. I don't remember it. New?"

"Yeah, I guess so," Richie said with a shrug.

"You know the guy? The owner?" Nick asked.

Richie frowned. "How the hell would I know?"

"Maybe he came by the Box or something."

"I don't ask people to see pictures of their houses when they come in." Nick stared at the mansion more. "Why? You know who he is?" Richie asked as they began to float toward each other, side by side.

"No," Nick said in his most casual manner. "Just curious. It's a nice house."

Richie eyed his brother but went on paddling, dropping the subject from his mind.

The sun was beginning to heat up, and the wind was picking up when they finally made it to Cave Point. The waves started to pound on the craggy limestone cliffs, sending splashes and ripples back at the kayaks when they got close.

The caves were as Nick had left them. It was as if he were thirteen again, daring Richie to climb up the cliff and jump into the water. Although Richie complained of the time they were losing on the day, even he warmed up to being outside on the water on such a beautiful day.

When they paddled back in silence and returned to land, Richie didn't complain about wasted time.

4

Seventy-Seven Days from the Night

The dinner table, as usual, was quiet and fraught with silence. The clink of silverware on plates, the chewing of food, and the slurping of beer and wine were the only sounds present. Lana looked around the table. Both Morgan brothers kept their eyes down, afraid eye contact would require conversation.

"Enchiladas okay?" Lana asked, breaking the still tension.

"Not bad," Nick mumbled. He straightened his posture. "Sorry, yes, they're really good actually."

"Glad you like it," Lana said.

She took a sip of her wine. Richie sipped his wine too. Lana's attempt to generate conversation failed miserably, and they returned to an awkward quiet. Nick kept his eyes down and focused on his food.

"So, Nick. Are you itching to leave here again?" Lana said with a forced laugh. "Do you need to get back to, sorry, where did you say you were again?"

"St. Louis," Nick blurted out. He drank his can of beer.

"Right," Lana said. "You need to get back there soon?"

Nick chomped a mouthful of an enchilada. "Not really, no."

"Lived there long?"

"Almost three years."

"I see. What'd you do while you were there?"

"Pour drinks, mostly. Bartended at this shitty little dive called Monty's."

Lana nodded and looked at Richie, who was disengaged from the conversation at the table, staring at his food. Another minute passed before Lana attempted another question.

"Richie was telling me you used to write when you were younger?" she said to Nick. "Said you found your old stuff and writings in the garage."

Nick was in the middle of chewing a large mouthful of chicken enchilada and struggled to gulp it down to answer. "Did he now?"

"That's so cool. Did you want to be a writer when you were a kid?"

"I guess you could say that. It was just a dumb hobby."

"Richie said you used to write short stories and stuff," Lana said, sipping her wine. She sat directly across the table from Nick, with Richie between them at the head of the table. Nick wiped his mouth with his napkin.

"Yeah, some of them were stories."

"What were they about?"

"All kinds of stuff, I guess. I don't remember, to be honest with you."

"Well, I'd love to read some of them, if that'd be okay. Do you still have them?"

"Yeah, but—I don't think you'd like them. They're weird and don't make much sense."

"I'm sure that's not true."

Nick sipped his beer.

"Have you written anything since?" Lana asked.

Nick shook his head. "To be honest, I never felt the need to since I left."

Lana bit her lip, unsure what to say next. "Is home how you remember it? I grew up in Iowa, but my family moved when I went to college, so I didn't go back there for like five years. When I did, it seemed so different. Have you noticed that?"

"The opposite. Nothing's seemed to change."

"What's that mean?" Richie said. Nick was caught off guard by his brother. He had forgotten he was at the dinner table.

"I mean, come on. You know what I mean. This place doesn't change. The food doesn't change. The stores don't change. The music doesn't change. The people don't change."

"The people?" Lana asked.

"It's not hard to notice there's only one *type* of people around here." Richie rolled his eyes. "I'm just pointing it out. Door County likes things a certain way and likes to keep it that way."

"Are you saying that Door County is racist?" Richie asked. "That it's only letting white people live here?"

"I'm just saying I've been here a couple of days and I can probably count on one hand the non-Caucasians I've seen."

"That doesn't mean—," Richie began to say but stopped. "You can't make that blanket statement about everyone."

"I'm not making any statements, just observations," Nick said with a mouthful of enchiladas.

"There's nothing wrong with some things staying the way they are," Richie said.

"It's a little sad. Pathetic, even."

"Pathetic?"

"It's like these people want to live in this alternate fantasy where the fifties never ended," Nick said.

"Doesn't seem like you've changed either."

Nick smirked. "Yeah, how's that?"

"You still think you know everything. You still think you're smarter than everyone."

"Sounds like something's bothering you, Richie," Nick said. "You seem more surly than usual."

"I've been wondering what you do all day," Richie said. "When you take my truck and are gone for hours and never say where you go."

"You wanna ask me something?"

"I just did."

"No." Nick waved his fork. "You shared an observation. If you want me to answer a question, you'll have to ask one first. That's how it works."

Nick went back to eating. Richie did not. Lana took a sip of her wine, feeling trapped between the two brothers. Richie stared coldly at Nick from across the table.

"I just hope you're not doing the same shit you were doing in high school," Richie said.

"What's that?"

"You know what."

Nick chuckled to himself. "What? Selling weed?" Richie put down his fork. "What? It's okay to say it, Richie. It's not like the cops are listening in on our dinner conversations." Nick sipped his beer and looked at Lana. "I sold weed to dumbass kids in high school. Most of them were freshmen or sophomores who didn't know shit. Half the time it was grass clippings from the lawn. It wasn't exactly Miami Vice."

"You're lucky you never got busted. The one time you did, it was Dad who bailed you out, got you off as a favor," Richie said.

"Oh, that was bullshit and you know it," Nick said, aggravated. "It was four guys smoking a blunt in a parking lot. Not like we were moving bricks."

"That wasn't the only time you got off because of Dad. You're lucky he was friends with that cop."

"Sheriff."

"Whatever."

The dinner table returned to the tense hush from earlier. Both brothers looked aggravated.

"You never answered my question," Richie blurted.

"What?"

"You never answered my question."

"I don't remember you asking me one."

"Jesus Christ, do you have to make everything so goddamn difficult? You gotta be clever with everything you say? You can't just give a straight answer?"

"Is it all right with you if my business stayed personal?" Nick said.

"What personal business could you have?"

"You're starting to remind me of Dad."

The statement hung in the air. Richie bit his lip, staring at his brother, who continued eating.

"I just want to be sure you're—"

"What?"

"Staying out of trouble."

"Trouble's not so bad," Nick mused.

"Excuse me?"

"Sometimes you need to get into a little trouble to do what you gotta do."

"What the hell are you talking about?"

Nick ate the last bite of his enchilada. Richie and Lana watched him chew, wipe his mouth with his napkin, and sip from his beer.

"Let me show you something."

*****

"It's a car," Richie said matter-of-factly. He looked up from the photograph Nick had just handed him.

"No shit," Nick said. "But *really* look at it."

Richie shrugged. "I don't know. It's an old car?"

Nick grabbed the photograph from his brother. He held it up for him.

"*This* is not just any car. This is a 1948 Talbot-Lago T26 Grand Sport Coupe. They only made twenty of these French beauties sixty years ago. Today? Including that one, there's four left."

"Okay...," Richie said. "Why are you showing me this? Are you buying it or something?"

Nick scoffed. "Richie, a model in this condition is worth at least three million dollars. At an auction, it'd probably fetch around four million dollars."

Richie's eyes bulged. Lana took the photograph from Nick to study it herself. They both sat on the couch in the living room while Nick paced back and forth in front of them.

"Are you serious? That much for a car?" Richie asked. Nick nodded. "I still don't know why you're showing this to us."

Nick pulled out a piece of paper from behind his back and placed it on the table and slid it toward Richie and Lana.

"This is why," Nick said. "It's a news article from *The Times-Picayune*, New Orleans's newspaper. It's from 2001."

Lana took the paper off the table and read it. "It was stolen," she muttered.

"That's right. For two decades, our French queen was on display in a New Orleans automotive museum. Then, one morning, the manager walks in to find two dead security guards and the Talbot-Lago gone. No sign of forced entry, no alarms set off, security cameras disabled, no fingerprints, no tire tracks, and no evidence that anything happened besides the two dead security guards, still sitting at their post."

Richie took the paper from Lana and read it himself. "Jesus."

"The hunt for the thieves and murderers was one of the largest ever, but they had no idea. They had no leads, nothing to go on. After a few years, they gave up. Technically, it's still an open case, but it's cold as ice."

Richie put down the article. He looked up at Nick. "Okay, I'm waiting for the punch line."

Nick grinned. "I found her."

"*You* found the car?" Lana asked.

"That's right."

"Where?" Richie said.

Nick leaned forward, his voice an intense whisper. He pointed to the floor beneath him.

"Right here. It's right here—in Door County! I'm telling you, I've seen it with my own eyes. It's practically right down the road. Can you believe that?"

"Bullshit. How do you know?" Richie said.

"I got a tip from a guy I used to work with. This was his kind of thing, tracking down priceless cars and things like that. This was his white whale. I knew him for two years, and he never shut up about it. Finally, he found it. I don't know how he found it, he didn't tell me, but he found it here, sitting in a garage right in my neck of woods."

Lana said, "Has he seen it? Have you?"

Nick reached behind him into his bag. He pulled out a glossy black-and-white photograph and handed it to them. It showed the car in front of a garage and a man polishing its hood.

Richie studied it. "This is here?"

"Big house by Cave Point. The one I was asking about while we were kayaking."

"You're sure this is the one? The one that was stolen?" Lana asked. "Couldn't it be one of the other ones you mentioned before?"

"Definitely. Every other known one is accounted for."

"Maybe it's not a known one," Lana said. "Maybe it's just that no one else knows he has it."

Nick scoffed. "Lana, this thing is worth millions. It's one of the rarest models in the world. If you have one, you don't keep it to yourself! There's no point to that unless you don't want people to know you have it."

"Who's the guy?" Richie asked.

"Some rich guy, George Collins," Nick said, grabbing a notebook from his bag and leafing through it. "I asked everyone who might know anything about him, whether he had some connections or something. I got nothing. I think he's just a rich guy with a penchant for old cars."

"So he didn't steal it?" Lana asked.

"I don't think so. My guess is he just bought it from whoever did. Maybe he paid to have it stolen, but I doubt it. I haven't sniffed any connections to criminal business."

"So this is what you've been doing?" Richie said, flapping the photograph in his hand. "Spying on this guy because you think he has a stolen car?"

"It's *the* car."

"What about the other guy?" Lana said.

"Who?"

"The guy who told you about this. Where is he?"

Nick clicked his tongue. "He's not around anymore."

Richie raised his eyebrows. "What's that?"

Nick coughed and cleared his throat. "He passed away about six months ago."

Lana and Richie stared at Nick.

"I didn't kill him!"

Richie rubbed his eyes.

"But if you heard about it, other people would too, right?" Lana asked. "How do you know you're the only one with this info?"

"Trust me, I'm the only one who knows this. He only told me because he knew I was from here and wanted me along because of my experience in the area."

Richie took his hands away from his eyes. "Okay, so where is this going?" Richie said. "Why are you telling us this?"

"Well," Nick said, scratching his head. "We're going to steal it. Now, before you say anything—"

"Are you out of your fucking mind?" Richie yelled.

"Richie—"

"No! Stop, enough!" Richie said. "Not a fucking chance in hell."

"It's *already* a stolen car!" Nick yelled. He picked up the article. "You can't steal stolen property!"

Richie said nothing. He stared, bewildered at his brother before him. Lana stood up from the couch and stood next to Richie.

"You know, I'm not surprised," Richie paused, grasping for words. "That you became whatever you are. A thief, a criminal."

"Richie, if you just take a second and listen to me, you'll see I'm trying to help you! We're talking millions of dollars here, and it's not behind some gigantic safe in a bank. It's sitting in a garage! I'm trying to help you keep your house—"

"*Don't!*"

The sudden shout startled Lana and Nick.

"I knew I shouldn't have told you that." Richie shook his head. "Don't try to make this like an offer to help me when we both know you don't do anything unless it's for yourself."

"Okay," Lana said, stepping away from Richie and between the two brothers. "Let's take a breath for a second. It's a lot to think about."

"A lot to think about?" Richie repeated.

"See! Lana gets it! She gets the opportunity!"

"I didn't say that!" Lana said. "I'm just saying, let's take a break and catch our breath."

Richie stomped away to the kitchen, leaving Nick and Lana alone in the living room. Nick kept quiet. Richie reappeared in the living room, a beer in his hand.

"This is why you came back, wasn't it?" he said, twisting off the cap to the beer bottle and tossing it in the trash. "Wasn't for me, sure as shit wasn't for Dad. You heard about some easy money, right?"

Nick rubbed his forehead. "It wasn't the *only* reason."

"Get out." Richie took a drink and began to walk across the living room toward the hallway and bedroom.

"You're serious?" Nick said.

Richie stopped inches away from Nick's face. "If you're still in my living room in five minutes, I'll throw you out myself." He swigged his beer and walked away.

"Richie!" Lana shouted after him.

"No, that's all right, Lana," Nick said. He collected his papers and photos from the table and stuffed them back into his bag. "I knew it was a long shot. I'll admit, I didn't expect to get thrown out, but if that's what Richie wants…"

Nick went into the guest room and quickly stuffed his belongings into the bag. Lana stood in the living room, exasperated. When Nick reappeared, heading for the front door, Lana cut him off.

"Listen, let me work on him. I'm not going help you with… whatever the fuck that was," she said. "Don't leave. He wants you here, even if he won't admit it."

Nick checked his watch. "I'll be at the Walleye. If he doesn't change his mind though, I'm on the first bus out tomorrow morning." He opened the door and walked out into the night.

Lana closed it behind him. She stood alone in front of the door and rubbed her face. When she opened her eyes, Richie stood in front of her in the living room, drinking his beer. She took a deep breath.

*****

Lana spotted Nick in seconds after entering the Walleye. He sat at the bar, alone, with his duffle bag on the ground next to him. He drank from a can and was chatting with Shelley. Well, he talked at her while she wiped down the counter.

Lana walked up and hovered behind him.

"This seat taken?" she asked. Nick turned and gave her a friendly nod before motioning for her to sit.

"Didn't think you were coming," Nick said, his eyes wandering toward the TV in the corner showing the Brewers game.

"Well, I tried to get Richie to come here," she said.

"Did he send his woman to apologize for him instead?"

"No. Don't call me his woman," Lana said. The directness made Nick glance at her and bowed his head apologetically.

"So why are you here, then?"

Shelley approached. Lana ordered a gin and tonic.

"I wanted to make sure you didn't disappear from town again," she said.

"Nothing keeping me here."

"What about your only brother? The only family you have left?" Nick drank his beer. Lana rubbed her eyes. She felt so tired of this. "What about the car? You won't stay for that?"

Shelley approached with the gin and tonic. Lana quickly shut up. She dropped a few bills on the counter and told Shelley to keep the change to get rid of her.

Nick drank his beer and watched the TV. "It's not a one-man job," he said without looking away from the game.

"Well, that's good, at least," Lana said.

"Yeah, throwing away four million dollars. Out-*fucking*-standing."

Lana sipped her drink. She looked at the screen Nick stared at. "Richie told me you hated sports. Especially baseball."

"I do." Lana waited. "I'm seeing if maybe being back in Wisconsin, drinking at a bar helps make it less boring." He sipped his beer. "It doesn't."

Nick swiveled in his seat and looked at Lana. "Why do you care? I mean, if I leave or not. We barely know each other. I don't even think you like me. My brother—your husband—thinks I'm just trouble and wants me gone. But you want me to stay. Why?"

Lana took a sip from her drink. "Richie's too proud to say it, but he could use you right now."

Nick raised his eyebrows, amused. "Richie's never needed me a day in his life, and he's done all right. Well, it sounds like lately he's had some problems, but in the general sense, he's done fine."

"You two are the only family you guys have. Doesn't that mean anything?"

"Do I come off as a guy who's close with his family?"

"And how's that going for you? Are you happy with your life so far?"

Nick looked at her sideways and sipped his beer. "I think I'm doing all right."

"Yes, clearly. You steal cars and have no friends or family."

Nick grinned a little. "Ouch."

Lana took a deep breath. "I'm not asking you guys to start acting like twins, but your dad is gone, your mom is gone, and your one uncle lives in Indiana. Richie's having a really hard time lately, and I know it would hurt him—it would kill him—for you to leave now. He wouldn't ever say so or even show it, but I know it would."

Nick rubbed his chin as he took in her words. He took another drink. He curled his hair behind his ears. He glanced at Lana and saw she was staring at him, waiting. He took a deep breath.

"I guess I can stick around for a while."

Lana smiled. "Thank you."

"I'll get a hotel or something. Give Richie some time away from me."

Lana was about to disagree but gathered herself. "That's probably a good idea. Do you need some money for a hotel?"

"No, I'm fine." Nick turned his attention to the Brewers game again. Lana did too. They watched in silence over the next few minutes until shortstop J. J. Hardy grounded out to end the inning.

"Can I ask you something?" Lana said when the game went to commercial. Nick kept quiet. Lana took a pause, debating how to phrase the question. "What was your mom like?"

Nick blinked at her. "What do you mean?"

"Richie never likes talking about her. Craig didn't either. But they both said that the two of you were close. You were the momma's boy." She gave Nick a playful nudge with her shoulder. "Come on, I feel like I don't know anything about her. She's my family too, now."

Nick looked around the bar. "What do you want to know?"

"I don't know. What was she like? Richie said you were always more like her and Richie was more like Craig."

"You could say that. Although, every day I feel like I'm getting more like Craig." Nick gulped down the last of his beer and signaled to Shelley for another. "Case in point." Shelley returned with a fresh beer, and Nick cracked it open.

"Craig told me he used to have a drinking problem."

"Did he now? You two talk a lot?"

"By the time I met him, he was sober. Said after the accident, he never touched a drop. I never saw him drink in the years I knew him."

"Touching," Nick said, dry as chalk.

Lana went silent. She sipped her drink as Nick turned back to the game. Nick took a deep breath and looked back at Lana.

"She was an English teacher," Nick said. "High school English. She liked to write too—short stories, poetry. That's probably where I got in my head I wanted to be a writer. I'm sure you knew that though."

"Richie said she was a teacher and mentioned she liked poetry, but he didn't say she wrote her own."

"Oh yeah. She had a little notebook of poems. I don't think she ever tried to get them published though. I know she was in a poetry club. She loved Walt Whitman. She was always reading him, quoting him. I started writing poetry too. She even gave me notes on the ones she liked and didn't like."

"That's cute."

"It was. Have you ever read Agatha Christie?"

"Who?"

"The author. *Murder on the Orient Express*, *Death on the Nile*, those books?"

Lana frowned and looked up for a moment, thinking. "Oh yeah. I've heard of them. No, I don't think I ever have. I wasn't a big fiction reader."

"She loved her. When I was young, we'd read her books together. And they were these whodunit mysteries, you know, so we would each read a couple of chapters and talk about it and who we thought the killer was and why. Kind of like our own book club."

Nick's voice became more energetic, his face more animated as he relived the memories. "We'd keep notes and stuff: how the murder happened, who the characters were, what they were like if they had a motive, and all the clues we had."

Lana listened intently, her face warm as Nick spoke.

"We'd each give our own theory of what happened and who the killer was. Almost like a presentation."

"Did you ever get it right? Guessing the murderer?" Lana asked.

"Me? Not once. She'd usually figure it out by the end though."

Lana smiled and sipped her drink. She didn't say anything, not wanting to disturb Nick's foray into a peaceful memory.

Nick's eyes went down. He gripped his hands together in front of him, tight. His jaw clenched, and his voice cracked when he spoke.

"When she had her accident—" Nick took a deep breath. "I wanted to fucking kill him. I wanted to wring his neck so badly it scared me a little. Instead, I left. I knew if I stuck around, I would probably kill him. I would never forgive him. But I thought he wasn't worth spending life in prison for, so I left and considered him already dead."

Lana nodded. Nick drank his beer. She sipped her drink and fiddled with her straw.

"Tough to lose a parent like that," she said quietly. "At that age—any age."

"The randomness of it all," Nick said. "It was a day, like any other. A normal night. Then I come home and everything is different, everyone's lives are different—forever. For no reason."

"I'm sorry, Nick. I really am."

"Don't. It's not your fault."

Lana took a deep breath and sipped her drink.

"Let me know where you're staying," she said as she stood. She patted him on the shoulder and waved to Shelley before leaving the Walleye.

Nick stared at his beer. Shelley came over to collect Lana's money. Nick went back to the game. A can-of-corn fly ball ended the top of the seventh inning.

*****

Lana entered the front door of her house. Richie emerged from the hallway. He leaned against the wall with his arms crossed.

"Where were you?" Richie demanded.

"I went to the Walleye," she said as she crossed into the kitchen and grabbed a glass from the cabinet.

"Why?"

"Nick said he would be there."

Lana turned on the faucet and filled her glass. Richie impatiently watched her drink.

"Well?"

Lana wiped her mouth after drinking. "He said he'd stay in a town for a while."

She crossed in front of him and left the kitchen and went into the living room. She sat on the arm of a chair and looked up at Richie.

"Is he going to do it? Steal that car?"

"I don't know, but I asked him to stay in town, and he said he would."

Richie shook his head.

"He's still your brother," Lana said. "You shouldn't have been so hard on him."

"He hasn't been my brother for nine years."

"You want it to be that way for the rest of your life?"

Lana's harsh tone surprised Richie. He dropped his arms and rubbed the back of his head.

"Come on, Lana, you heard him tonight! He's a goddamn criminal! And he's trying to get us to help him! I don't want that shit around you or me. We have enough problems as it is."

"Maybe he became a criminal because he didn't have anyone to depend on. Nobody who could keep him straight. Like, say, a brother."

"So it's my fault now?"

"That's not what I meant."

"He made the choice! Not me! How was I supposed to help him when I didn't know where he was?"

"I'm not saying it's your fault."

"He left us! We didn't leave him!"

"And he came back! What does that tell you? Do you think that maybe he's had enough of that now? Maybe he needs some help to get his life together?"

"Did you not hear him? He was trying to recruit us into stealing a fucking car!"

"He wanted to help us. He was trying to help us."

"Oh, bullshit. You don't know him like I do." Richie paced the living room with his hands on his hips.

"Look," Lana said. "I'm not saying it's a good idea or we should do this. But don't burn the last bridge to the only family you have left! I'm just asking you to give him a shot! Show him what a mistake it is, that he doesn't have to do it, that you'll be there for him!"

Richie rubbed his eyes. He leaned his head back and stared at the ceiling for what felt like a long time. "Fine. I'll give him a chance. But if he does something stupid, if he gets in trouble, gets *us* in trouble, he's out. Forever. I'm not putting up with that shit."

Lana agreed to the terms. She watched her husband pace back and forth. She stuck out her hand toward him. Richie took a deep breath and took it. She pulled him to the chair she sat on. He sat, and Lana leaned on the armrest, resting her head on his shoulder with her arm around his neck. She grazed his right arm with her fingertips.

"We talked about your mom," Lana whispered in Richie's ear. Richie pulled his head away and looked at her. She looked into his brown eyes. He looked straight ahead and rested his head on hers.

"Yeah?"

Lana sat up straight on the armrest of the chair. She ran her hands through Richie's hair, scratching his scalp. "Have you two ever talked about it?"

"No. He was gone before I even got back home."

"I think you two should talk about what happened. I know you don't like to talk about it, even with me, but—"

"I just hate telling people that. Watching that look on their face. Pity. I don't want to see that look on your face too."

She rubbed his head and moved her hand to scratch the back of his neck.

"There's nothing wrong with pity. It means I love you and want to help you. You shouldn't keep anything like that inside."

"I know," Richie said. He leaned forward with his face in his hands. "After it happened, we didn't hear from him for days, then it was only to tell us he was alive, somewhere else. I almost filed a missing person's report."

"Your dad?"

"He had bigger concerns at the moment."

"I'm sorry, baby," Lana murmured. She kissed his forehead and wrapped her arms around his head, pressing it close to her chest as she stroked his hair.

Richie sniffled. He cleared his throat. He wiped his eyes. He looked up at his wife and managed a half-smile. He wrapped his arms around her waist and brought her onto his lap. She put her arms around his neck and rested her head on his shoulder.

They closed their eyes and sat in silence. They were alone with nothing else but each other's measured breathing and soft heartbeats.

5

Sixty-Three Days from the Night

The alarm pierced the still bedroom. Its obnoxious blaring was silenced when Richie's hand slapped down on the digital clock. Lana groaned beside him. Richie slowly gathered himself and sat on the edge of the bed. He could hear morning rain tapping on the window above.

"It's raining," Lana said, facing away from him.

"Uh-huh," Richie mumbled, rubbing his eyes awake.

"Do you need to go in if it's raining?"

"Don't start."

She rolled over as Richie stood up. "I'm just saying, who goes fishing when it's forty degrees and raining?"

"Some people do."

"You can't take the morning off? It's my only day off this week."

"I said don't, Lana!"

She turned back over in a huff and closed her eyes. Richie grabbed a towel and headed toward the bathroom. He stood in the shower, the water spraying his face. He closed his eyes and wondered if he could fall asleep standing in the shower. For a few seconds, he tried, before snapping his eyes open.

He scrubbed up quickly, not bothering to wash his hair. He turned the nozzle to cold before turning it off, letting the freezing water shock him awake. He got out and examined his face in the mirror. He could go another day without shaving.

He quickly brushed his teeth with his dollar-store toothbrush. He threw on some deodorant. He ran his fingers through his hair to shift it to one direction and that was the end of his daily maintenance routine.

He returned to the bedroom. Lana's back was to him and her eyes were closed, but he could tell she wasn't sleeping. He sat on the edge of the bed by her feet, his back to her.

"Sorry," Richie said.

"Don't bite my head off because I want to spend time with you on my day off," Lana said.

"I know. I'm sorry."

"It's okay." She rolled over and patted his back with her foot. "I'm getting lunch with Kimi today. Want me to bring you something?"

"Yeah, sure, thanks." Richie stood up and began to dress. "Don't you two get tired of each other? You work together six days a week and then hang out on your day off."

"We've been together eight years, and I haven't gotten sick of you yet," she said. "Besides, she just broke up with James, thought it'd be nice to take her out."

"Her and James broke up?"

"Yup."

"They were together, like, two years, weren't they?"

"Close to."

Richie threw on some jeans. "She all right?"

"I think so. I mean, she's the one who broke it off. Still, not an easy thing to go through."

"Don't let her talk you into leaving me so you can both be single."

She threw a pillow at him. Richie laughed and tossed it back. He put on a shirt and grabbed a sweatshirt off the floor.

"You're not wearing that sweatshirt," Lana said.

"I'm not?"

"No. You wore it yesterday, and the day before, and the day before that."

"I thought we wouldn't be one of those married couples where the wife dresses her husband."

"We won't if you try even a little. You have five other sweatshirts hanging up in the closet that are clean. What's wrong with those?"

"Fine." He tossed the sweatshirt on the ground and grabbed one from the closet. "Better?"

"Much."

"All right, I'm outta here," he said, grabbing his keys and wallet off the dresser. "Go back to sleep."

"I'll see you for lunch."

"Yup. Love you."

"Love you."

Richie stepped into the kitchen. The rain continued outside. He started brewing some coffee and threw a bagel in the toaster. He leaned on the counter and looked out the kitchen window as he waited. It was so dark from the storm it looked like night. His mind drifted. It drifted to his brother and a car and money.

The toaster dinged, and the bagel popped out. He scarfed down the bagel while the coffee finished brewing. He poured the coffee into his travel mug, a green and gold Packers tumbler that was a gift from Lana. He took a sip and was out the door into the garage and into the same truck he'd driven since high school.

Richie unlocked the front door and entered the dark and bleak Tackle Box Bait Shop. Ever since his dad started dragging him there after school and on the weekend to help out, it'd barely changed. It wasn't large, only a modest-sized one-story building with large windows stretching across its face.

When someone entered its front door, they were greeted by white tile floors and fluorescent lighting. Two aisles of fishing paraphernalia stretched down the left of the door, where worms and minnows were displayed by the back wall. Recently, they've been empty. Too expensive to stock and maintain.

The register rested on the green countertop to the right of the door, where it'd been for decades. Behind the register, the corkboard wall displayed more knickknacks and accessories for every kind of fishing.

As he entered, Richie checked his watch. It was fifteen minutes to seven, which was when the Tackle Box was supposed to open. Richie didn't worry. It barely took ten minutes to set up for the day, and it's not like customers were banging down the door to get in anyway. Richie thought about changing the hours, as he rarely got customers so early, but he was a creature of habit. Even if he did give himself the chance to sleep in on most days, he'd get up early anyway out of routine. Might as well work.

Richie went about setting up the Tackle Box for opening, his wet boots squeaking on the tile floors as he perused up and down the aisles. He drank his coffee and looked outside. The rain continued, pounding the bait shop's large windows.

With the Tackle Box sufficiently ready, Richie flipped the door sign to open. He took his position behind the counter and register with his coffee and newspaper. He sat and waited.

Two hours later, a customer arrived. As the man opened the front door, ringing the bell above it, Richie looked up from his newspaper.

"Hey, Ted," he said before going back to his paper.

"Mornin' Richie." Ted was a middle-aged man with a graying mustache, lean face, and trim figure. Almost every day, he stopped by for one thing or another, sometimes just to chat with Richie. He was dressed in his customary attire: worn jeans, long-sleeve fishing shirt, fleece jacket, and camouflage hat with curled gray hairs poking out from it.

"What's the scoop?" Richie said, sipping his coffee. A half hour ago, he'd gone across the street to grab a fresh cup from the gas station.

"I think I'm gonna grab some line," Ted said, mumbling behind his fingers as they rubbed his hairy upper lip. "If this rain lets up later today, think my sister and I are gonna try to take the boat out later this afternoon. Maybe take my nephew with us. The line I've been using keeps breaking though. I can't figure out why."

"Well, you didn't buy it here," Richie said without looking up from the paper. Ted walked down the aisle toward the fishing line selection.

"How things been?" Ted shouted from the other end of the shop.

"Since you last saw me yesterday? Just great."

Ted mumbled something to himself as his eyes lingered on the fishing line, his eyes darting back and forth over the various fishing lines. "Business good?"

"Better than ever." Richie sipped his coffee and leaned back in his chair.

"You been out fishing lately?"

"Not for a while," Richie said. "I'm here all day and every day. And not all of us have boats to take out when we want to like you, Ted."

Ted approached the register and dropped a spool of fishing line on the counter. "Speaking of siblings, didn't you say your brother was in town? How's he doing?"

"Same old, same old, I guess," Richie said.

"Gosh, I remember when you two were running around this place when your old man ran it, just a couple of tykes causing trouble, making your dad crazy."

"He's fine," Richie said. He picked up the spool. "Ted, what are you doing? This is the most expensive one."

"Yeah, so?"

"So you're smart enough to know it's not worth it."

"Then why do you sell it?"

"For the suckers, Ted, not you."

"I want the most expensive one! Maybe this shit won't snap like the one I got now. Besides, you need the business."

Richie rang up the purchase. Ted dropped the cash on the register without being told the price. Ted noticed the open newspaper on the counter, turned to the sports page.

"What'd you think of the Packers' draft?" Ted asked.

"Who knows? It's all a crapshoot. Guys in the paper don't seem that impressed by it."

"They didn't even have a first-round pick, right?"

"Nah, they traded down, like Thompson always does. Picked some white receiver from Kansas."

Ted scoffed. "I don't trust a white guy as a receiver. Maybe I'm racist, but I just don't. A white tight end? That works. But white wide receivers never pan out."

70

"What about Don Hutson? One of the greatest Packers and receivers of all time."

"Come on, Richie, he played a hundred years ago! They weren't even letting black guys play back then."

"True. What about the little guy on the Patriots? Walker or whatever?"

"Welker. Yeah, he's good, but he's a little guy. Those are the only white receivers worth a damn—the small and quick ones. The kid they drafted isn't that."

"Well, I guess. We'll see." Richie threw the line in a plastic bag and dropped the change on the counter. "There you are, sir."

"Thanks, Rich," he said, gathering his money. "Let's hope this rain clears away now. Say hi to your brother for me."

"I'll see you tomorrow, Ted," he said as Ted headed for the front door.

Richie was alone again. When Ted was gone, he stepped out from behind the counter and walked toward the front windows. It looked like it was going to clear up.

By one in the afternoon, the rain and its clouds had dissipated. The sun had made its appearance and warmed the day into the fifties. Richie sat behind the counter, the shop empty. He read a magazine until he saw Kimi's car pull up.

He tossed the magazine and watched as Lana got out of the passenger seat with a to-go box. She waved to Kimi and entered. She wore tight jeans, a white T-shirt, and a green fleece jacket, her hair tied up in a ponytail. The bell above the door rang as she opened it.

"Hey, lunch is here," she said, holding the to-go box up.

"Beautiful," Richie said. She walked over to the counter and leaned over it to kiss Richie on the cheek.

"I got you a grilled chicken sandwich and some chips, that all right?"

"Sounds great," Richie said, opening the box. He grabbed a chip and popped it into his mouth. "I'm starving."

Lana shed her jacket. "It got hot out there all of a sudden," she said. She stretched her arms out. "They had the heat on in the restaurant, and I felt like I was sweating my ass off. Do I look bad?" she said, showing Richie her armpit.

"Nah, you're good," Richie said, chomping into his sandwich. "Where'd you go?"

"The Landing." She reached over to grab a chip. Richie smacked her hand. "Come on! I only had a salad!"

Richie let her grab a chip. "So how's Kimi? How's she handling the breakup?"

Lana crunched on another chip. "Okay, I guess. She feels more guilty than anything."

Richie took another bite. "I never liked James anyway."

"Why not?"

"First off, he goes by James. Not Jim or Jimmy but James." Lana rolled her eyes.

"Didn't you think he was kind of snotty?" Richie said.

"Yeah, I got that vibe too. You could tell his family's got money."

"I never liked him."

"Me neither. But not like I could tell Kimi that."

Richie ate a handful of chips. "She'll be all right."

"Uh-huh. How's the sandwich?" Richie gave a thumbs-up with a mouthful of chips. Lana looked around the empty shop as Richie continued eating. "How's business today?"

"Oh, you know," Richie said, biting into his sandwich. "Lines out the door. Orders coming in from all over the country. Just another day here at the Box."

Lana propped her elbow on the counter and stared at Richie. Her other hand tapped the counter, her fingernails clacking on the green countertop. Richie stopped chewing.

"What?"

"You talk to Nick today?"

He scoffed. "No."

She stared at him.

"What?" She shrugged. He went back to eating, her eyes still trained on him, beating him down. "Don't do that."

"Do what?"

"Look at me like that. I'm trying to eat."

"Go ahead and eat. I don't know what you're talking about."

"I can't when you're looking at me like that."

"Like what?"

"Like that."

"I can't look at you?"

"Stop, you know what you're doing."

"What am I doing? Since you're the expert."

Richie chewed and looked outside. "I've got nothing to talk to him about."

Lana crossed her arms. "I think you do."

He went back to eating. Lana's nostrils flared. "What?" Richie said. "What do you want from me? I don't see him for years, he comes back and makes an ass of himself and me at our own dad's funeral, I forgive him, I let him stay at our house, and then he tries to involve us in this crime—scheme, whatever. I mean, come on, Lana, we've got enough problems as it is."

"We talked about this. He needs some guidance—some help. No one else is going to give it to him."

Richie shook his head. "Come on. Every day is hard enough as it is without Nick around to fuck things up."

Lana tilted her head. "Every day is hard? Wow, jeez, I didn't know our life was so miserable to you."

Richie put his food down. "That's not what I meant."

"No, excuse me, I had no idea you woke up every day dreading your life with me."

"Would you knock it off? You know that's not what I meant. With our situation, money-wise, we don't need another headache. Nick is another headache."

"Nick is family," Lana said. "And, yeah, things are pretty bad right now, but maybe family is exactly what we—what you—need right now."

"You don't know him."

"I know, you keep telling me that. But maybe you don't either anymore. People change, Richie. At the very least, you could offer your hand to someone who needs it."

Richie went back to eating. She sighed and looked over her shoulder. "I gotta run to the pharmacy, so I'll take your truck back home and pick you up at five." She grabbed her jacket and headed toward the door.

"Love you," Richie said as she approached the door.

"Love you too," she said as she opened the door and left.

Richie watched her get in his truck and drive away. He collected the leftovers and box and tossed it in the trash. He washed his hands and returned to his countertop and his empty shop.

He looked down the empty aisles of the Tackle Box and sighed. He leaned on the counter and thought. He thought about Nick and Lana. He thought about the life he thought he'd have and what it was now. He thought about his and Lana's future. His mind wandered around to Nick.

He thought about Nick and the car.

6

Sixty-Two Days from the Night

Nick's cell phone rang from across the room. He roared an annoyed groan. He threw back the cheap and stained sheets and sat on the end of the bed. He looked at the digital clock on the end table, which caused his mouth to pump out curses like a shotgun.

Who the fuck is calling me this early? he thought. He slapped his hand down on his phone at the table and flipped it open, bringing it to his ear.

"Yeah?"

"Hey, Nick. It's Richie," said the voice on the other line.

"Oh, hey," Nick said. He rubbed his eyes and massaged his throbbing temple. He talked with his eyes still closed. "What's up?"

"Sorry, I probably woke you, didn't I? Sorry about that."

"Don't worry about it, my alarm was about to wake me up anyway."

"Oh. You got somewhere to be today?"

"No."

It was the first time they'd spoken in weeks. In the meantime, Nick had been residing in the shoddy Northern Escapes Motel a few miles south of Sturgeon Bay. It was the only thing he could afford, it being one of the few lodgings in Door County that wasn't a gaudy resort charging hundreds a night.

Richie cleared his throat. "Oh, okay. Well, it's supposed to be a nice day, so Cooper and I were gonna go fishing at Murphy Park. Thought I'd see if you wanted to come. I know fishing isn't your thing, but we'll have beer."

Nick took a deep breath and stared at the cracked ceiling. "How much beer are we talking about?" Richie chuckled, which confused Nick before he realized it was a joke.

Nick found fishing boring, tedious, and even barbaric. Nick knew that Richie knew this, so he must have an alternate reason for the invite. At the very least, it was an olive branch.

Nick accepted the invitation. Richie said they'd be there almost all day, so he could come by any time.

Nick hung up and put the phone back on the night table. As he did, he noticed the half-empty bottle of Kessler's whiskey from the night before. *Dad would be proud*, he thought.

He stared at the ceiling some more. He saw a spider scurry across it. He looked at the clock again. He closed his eyes and prayed sleep would knock him and his headache out.

*****

Richie was right when he said it was going to be a beautiful day. It was unseasonably warm for the peninsula in early May. Before noon, the temperature was already creeping over seventy degrees, a rarity for Door County so early in the summer. Nick could feel the sun coming through the windows as he sat in the back of the taxi. He fanned his shirt. He was regretting wearing jeans and a black T-shirt, but it was all he had that was reasonably clean.

The taxi pulled down the small hill that led into Frank Murphy Park, which sat at the bottom of a valley road populated with farm fields on one side and lake houses on the other. It was not Door County's finest beach park; grass and weeds sprouted from the sand, the playground was rusty, and the sand volleyball court was unkempt.

The park's main feature was the L-shaped pier that jutted out into Green Bay. It was a large pier, standing close to eight feet above the water level, and it was a good fishing spot for smallmouth bass and sometimes even carp. Normally, at least a few fishermen populated the pier daily but few other beachgoers. It was Richie's favorite fishing spot because it was their dad's favorite.

Nick stepped out of the taxi. There weren't many people there. It was still too early in the season. Only a few cars were in the parking lot, and Nick saw only one small family on the beach. On the edge of the pier, he could see two men sitting on plastic chairs with a cooler between them. He walked down the long pier toward Richie and who he assumed was Cooper.

Nick could feel his black shirt absorbing the sun's heat, cooking his torso. His forehead began to perspire. Richie heard his footsteps before he reached them. He turned around, still seated in his plastic chair.

"Hey," he said with a little wave. Nick could tell he felt awkward. He didn't know how he should greet Nick. He wasn't going to give him a brotherly hug after their last meeting, but a handshake also seemed improper. He decided on a modest wave. Nick returned it.

The man sitting next to Richie also turned. Nick immediately recognized that it was Cooper O'Hare. He recognized Nick too and had a much more excited greeting.

"Well, what the hell do we have here? Is that Nick Morgan?" Cooper shouted, putting down his fishing pole. He came up to Nick and wrapped his thick arms around him in a hug. Cooper had no awkwardness about him. If he wanted to hug you, he was going to.

Cooper was always Nick's favorite of Richie's friends. He and Richie had been friends since middle school. Whether it was football, wrestling, or baseball, Cooper and Richie were always on the same team. Cooper was an offensive lineman in his day and a damn good one thanks to his large frame and natural athleticism. In high school, he was more muscle than jelly, but that ratio seemed to have shifted since Nick last saw him. His gut was more pronounced, and even behind his beard, Nick could see another chin, but he still had a handsome face. His relaxed and confident state hadn't changed one bit.

"How you doing, big fella? It's good to see you," Nick said amid Cooper's bear hug. Cooper may have hung out with Richie and the sports-obsessed athletes, but he didn't act like them. He liked everyone, and everyone liked him. He was the guy who could have a forty-five-minute conversation at the grocery store with someone he barely knew.

"Oh, you know me," Cooper said, finally relinquishing Nick. He put his large hand on Nick's scrawny shoulder and turned his face serious. "Hey, I just wanted to say, I'm sorry about your dad."

Nick almost laughed at Cooper's sincerity. He wasn't at the funeral and hadn't heard what happened. But he didn't want to offend Cooper, who legitimately seemed mournful on behalf of Nick. He thanked Cooper flatly.

"I got another pole for you," Richie said from his chair. "Don't have another chair, but you can sit on the cooler."

"Speaking of which, you want a beer?" Richie asked, opening the blue-and-white cooler.

Nick's head still throbbed, but it was dulling by the minute. He looked at his watch and at the cooler full of beers.

"Well, if you insist, okay," Nick said. Cooper eagerly grabbed a beer from the cooler and tossed one to him. Nick cracked it as he took his seat on the cooler while Cooper baited a hook for him as well.

Richie reeled in his line and recast it, the whirring spin of his pole ringing out as the hook set out and plopped down in the greenish bay water.

"I can't remember the last time I went fishing. I'll probably fuck it up," Nick said before taking a sip of his beer.

Cooper said, "It's easy, just aim for the water." He let out a hearty laugh. Nick grinned. He missed Cooper's dumb jokes and relentless joy.

Cooper handed him the pole. Nick took it and tried to remember the technique his dad and Richie taught him when he was a boy. Luckily, the pole made it easy; all he had to do was click a button to release the line and cast. He brought it back slowly, making sure he wasn't going to catch his hook on Richie or Coop. He jerked it forward and let go of the button, releasing the line. It wasn't bad, not great, but pretty decent for the first time in years.

"There you go," Cooper said. Richie also voiced his approval. They sat down, Cooper and Richie in the folding chairs and Nick between them on the cooler.

"So, Nick," Cooper blurted out. "What the hell have you been doing? Where have you been?"

"Ah, shit, man. I've been all around, you know. Just doing this and that to get by."

"Really? Where specifically?"

"Well," Nick started. He cast his eyes out on the shining waves of the bay. He bit his lip. "I went west and hung out there in California for some time. Then I was in Colorado for a good while then I went to St. Louis where I spent most of the past three years and then here."

"Damn, that's crazy. Sounds like you've been busy!" Cooper bellowed. Nick shrugged. "What'd you do in St. Louis? Since you spent three years there?"

Nick cleared his throat. Richie noticed that Nick seemed uncomfortable.

"Oh, nothing serious. Bartended, mostly. Did some temping here and there. Anything for a buck, you know?"

"What about girls?"

"I do all right," he said with a grin. Cooper chuckled.

"You ever get married or anything?"

Nick shook his head. "Nah, that's not for me."

"I hear you," Cooper said.

"What about you, man? What have you been up to?"

"Oh, my dad and I got our own little business doing handyman stuff. Just fixing little things around the house. Sometimes it's pipes, sometimes it's putting in new floors or windows. Us and a couple of guys. We do all right."

Richie butted in. "He's being modest. They only work on big houses and for people who are loaded. Their hourly rate is obscene."

Cooper laughed. "Yeah, rich folks around here don't know how to do anything themselves, so they'll pay whatever to get someone to do it for them. Half the time, it's their summer house, so they're not even there. They don't care about price or anything as long as it's done by the weekend!"

"Sounds like a good racket," Nick said.

"Yeah, I can't complain."

Nick waited a few moments before making a transition in the conversation.

"Have you ever been to that one big log cabin mansion over by Cave Point?" Nick said. "I think the owner's name is Collins or something like that?"

Richie stopped drinking his beer and furrowed his brow at Nick. Nick didn't see him though. His eyes were focused on Cooper, who was mulling over the question.

"No, I don't think so," Cooper said.

Nick tried to hide his disappointment, but Richie could see it.

"Why?" Cooper asked.

"No reason," Nick said. "I just knew someone who knew him, I think. We were kayaking the other day, and I noticed what a gorgeous house it is."

The three turned their attention back to fishing. Richie gave Nick a sideways glare, who raised his shoulders defensively. Nick reeled in his line and recast it. The reel hummed as the line sailed over the water and crashed down with a satisfying plop.

Hours passed and the sun did not let up. The cold beers helped, but they could only do so much. Nick took off his shirt, sacrificing his pale skin to the sun for the little comfort it offered.

"Goddamn, I can't believe how hot it is for just a couple days into May," Nick said. Richie and Cooper both agreed it was unusual.

"Watch, in three days, it'll be forty degrees and raining again," Cooper said.

Nick hadn't had any luck fishing. He'd had a few nibbles but couldn't get anything strongly on the line. Cooper and Richie, however, had each caught a sizable bass, which now resided in the second cooler Cooper brought from his truck.

The sun and its uncompromising rays, however, were becoming unbearable to Nick. He felt like he was baking in an oven with no shade to be found on the large pier. He stood up from his chair.

"Fuck me, it's hot," he said, wiping his brow. "I think I'm gonna take a dip."

Richie looked at Nick in his jeans.

"You bring your suit?"

"Nope," Nick said with a shrug. He emptied his pockets of his keys, wallet, and phone and put them on top of the cooler. He began to take off his shoes when Cooper started laughing.

"I like it!" he said, wiping the sweat off his brow. "Shit, man, I might have to join you. I'm roasting here!"

Cooper sat up, putting his pole down next to him. He began to unbutton his fishing shirt and empty his pockets as well. Richie shook his head and stayed planted in his chair with his pole in one hand and a beer in the other.

Nick, shirtless and in jeans, walked over to the edge of the pier, the opposite side from where they fished. Cooper came up behind him, shirtless as well but with shorts.

"I remember when Richie and I used to do this all the time when we were kids," Nick said to Cooper as they reached the edge and leaned over.

"Yeah, he was telling me about it before you got here," Cooper said. Nick looked back over his shoulder at his brother, who was watching his fishing line intently. They looked at the bay water below. Nick stepped on the metal edge of the pier but retracted immediately; the sun had heated the metal to a scorching temperature.

Although Nick had jumped off this pier too many times to count in his youth, he still felt a slight hesitation. It seemed like a further jump than he remembered. It was about a ten-foot drop to the water, which was only about eight feet deep. It was too dangerous to dive with the possibility of an unseen rock waiting underneath the surface.

Nick focused on how the cool water would feel on his boiling skin, how refreshing it would be to wash away the sweat from his body. He slapped Cooper on the shoulder and backed up a few paces.

"You ready?" he asked with a grin.

Cooper backed up with him. "I'm right behind you, big guy. Richie! You sure you don't want in?"

Richie looked up from his beer and shook his head.

Nick took a stance. He pushed off his back foot, taking off toward the edge. He took two long strides before planting his foot on the metal edge and launching himself as far as he could.

He seemed to hang, suspended above the water. Finally, he felt a breeze as he sailed through the air and toward the welcoming water. His feet struck first, and then his outstretched arms braced his fall into the murky bay.

It was cold—freezing, more like. The bay water clung to its frigid winter temperature as long as it could, and one warm day wasn't going to do much to change it. The air shot out of Nick's lungs like they were popped balloons.

When Nick emerged and was able to gather himself from the cold, he looked up and saw Cooper laughing from the dock. He was howling at Nick's eyes, which bulged out of his sockets.

"How's it feel?" he shouted between cackles.

Nick took a moment to grab a few more deep breaths before swimming toward the ladder.

"Fucking cold!" he cried back. Cooper continued his delightful snickering as Nick climbed. When Nick reached the top of the pier, he shook himself, his hair spraying water like a dog.

"Your turn, Coop," Nick said.

Cooper hemmed and hawed. "I don't know, man. The way your eyes shot out of your head has got me second-guessing!"

"Fucking coward," Nick said. Richie approached with two beers.

"How's the water?"

"You're welcome to try it."

"I'm good here."

Richie looked Nick up and down at his skinny, pale figure. He squeezed his bony arm. "They must not have gyms in California or St. Louis."

Nick wrenched his arm away. "Shut up. Gimme that," Nick said, snatching the beer from Richie's hand. Richie laughed.

"All right, Coop," Richie said. "We're waiting."

"All right, all right," Cooper said. He stepped up to the edge and bent his knees like an Olympic high diver taking position. He swung his arms three times, and on the third time, he let the momentum of his arms carry him forward, and he launched himself with both legs off the pier.

Nick and Richie stepped to the edge and watched Cooper explode into the water. The tower of liquid almost reached them standing above on the pier.

Cooper breached the surface like Nick did, gasping for air with screaming eyes. He spat out water like a whale discharging its blowhole.

"Oh, lordy, lordy!" he howled. Nick and Richie laughed at Cooper gasping for air. Richie went and sat at the edge of the pier. Nick joined him, and they watched as Cooper slowly swam around.

"You know, it's not that bad after a little bit," Cooper shouted to them.

Richie still sat on the edge with his sunglasses and fishing hat on, sipping a beer. He unbuttoned his shirt to let the light breeze caress him a little more. Nick could see sweat stains around the back of his neck and armpits forming.

Nick let the sun's rays dry the water off his skin. He held the cold can of beer to his neck and cheek. He watched Cooper practice his backstroke.

"Remember when we did that polar plunge thing when we were kids?" Nick said to his brother.

Richie laughed. "Yeah, that's right! God, how old were we then?"

"I think ten and twelve because I was in fifth grade and you were in seventh."

"Yeah, that sounds about right. Now *that* water was cold. Middle of February? Jesus, what were we thinking?"

"It was Mom. She guilted us into going with her because she was doing it. Said she didn't want to go alone."

"That's right. God, that was awful," Richie said, laughing.

"Craig wasn't there though."

Richie's laughter halted. "No, that's right. He wasn't."

"It was a Saturday morning. He was too hungover to get out of bed."

Richie sipped his beer. The two brothers fell into a silence. They stared straight ahead at the waves of the bay.

"I worry I'm getting like him sometimes," Richie said.

Nick waved him off. "You're not like Dad."

"That's not what you said before."

"I was just being a dick."

"True. But I think you're more right by the day."

"What's that mean?"

"I'm starting to get it—why he was like that."

"A drunken prick, you mean? You're starting to get that?"

"Angry and bitter at life because things aren't going the way you think. I'm not there yet, but the way things have been going, yeah, I can see how someone can drink like that."

"No, you're like Mom. You always have been. Mom was nice. You're the nice brother. I'm the jerk who's angry at the world and drinks too much."

"Maybe we'll both end up like he was," Richie said.

Nick looked ahead. "Christ, that's a bleak thought."

Richie took a deep breath. "I feel like I'm going to wake up one day and it's going to be thirty years later and I'll be divorced, alone, broke, and a drunk."

"You're too hard on yourself, man."

"I feel like I have to do something before it all falls apart."

Nick glanced at his brother and looked straight ahead. He sipped his beer and said nothing. He let his hook lie.

"So," Richie said after a handful of moments. "How would you do it?"

Nick didn't react. He kept looking ahead.

"Do what?" he said casually.

"Don't bullshit me. You know what," his brother said. He kept his stare on Nick.

"Well, that's a work in progress," Nick said. Richie didn't flinch. "I'm going to need some more time."

"Time for what?"

"Research the house, research him—research everything. Learn his schedule. Do the due diligence. The stuff you do so you don't get caught." He sipped his beer and wiped his sopping wet hair from his eyes.

"So you don't have a plan?"

"I have the makings of a plan—the bones. But the devil is in the details. I never do a job without knowing everything about it, without making sure there won't be any surprises. Surprises are what get you pinched. Or killed."

Richie looked straight ahead. "Assuming we pull it off, we steal this car. Then what?"

"I got a guy, a fence, who can connect us with some buyers."

"What do we do with the car until then? We can't just let it sit in our garage."

"My guy will help with that. He's got stash houses everywhere. He should have one in Chicago."

"How are we supposed to get it to Chicago?"

"I've got a few ideas, but you let me worry about that."

Richie took a sip of his beer. "What would I do?"

Nick looked at him. He shrugged. "I won't know that until I put together a plan. But you're a big guy. Always helps to have a big strong guy on a crew."

"So the muscle?"

"Maybe. Maybe not."

Richie scoffed. "Christ, I can't believe I'm even thinking about this."

"Listen," Nick said, leaning in. "If we're going to do this, you're just going to have to trust me. I've done this before. I know what I'm doing. When I tell you that I—*we*—can pull this off, you have to know that I mean it."

Richie looked out on the horizon and the water. He downed the last of his beer and crumpled the can in his hand and tossed it over his shoulder. He took a deep breath. Nick could see from behind his sunglasses he was squinting, deep in thought. Nick waited patiently. After what seemed like minutes, Richie spoke.

"If I do this...," he started. Nick's chest swelled, but he did his best to remain composed. "*If*," Richie restated. "I do this, it's not for me, and it's not for you. It's for her." He turned back to the water and took off his sunglasses. "She deserves better than what I've put her through." His voice was flat and harsh. "We're in this mess because of me, and if you say this will get us out of it…"

Nick looked ahead. "As good a reason as any."

They sat for a while longer, staring straight ahead in silence.

"All right," Richie said. "Let's fucking do it." He got up and walked back to the chairs. Nick looked ahead and beamed.

His first catch of the day.

*****

DETECTIVE VOGEL. After the funeral, Nick stayed with you, in your home?

RICHIE. That's right.

DETECTIVE VOGEL. Did he stay with you the entire time he was in Door County?

RICHIE. No. About a week and a half after the funeral, I kicked him out.

DETECTIVE VOGEL. Why?

LANA. Drugs. He was doing drugs, bringing it into our house.

DETECTIVE VOGEL. What kind of drugs are we talking about here?

RICHIE. Just marijuana. That's all I saw him doing, but he was smoking a lot of it.

LANA. He drank a lot too.

RICHIE. Yeah, that too.

DETECTIVE VOGEL. Anything else?

RICHIE. No.

DETECTIVE VOGEL. You never saw or suspected any other drugs? Cocaine or anything like that?

RICHIE. No.

DETECTIVE VOGEL. You're sure?

RICHIE. Yes.

DETECTIVE VOGEL. He eventually returned to live with you again, correct?

RICHIE. Yeah.

DETECTIVE VOGEL. How long was he away before he came back to live with you?

RICHIE. I don't know. A little less than two weeks, I think.

DETECTIVE VOGEL. Do you know where he stayed during this period?

RICHIE. A motel in Sturgeon Bay. Northern Escapes, I think it was called.

DETECTIVE VOGEL. Thank you. We can ask them about the duration of his stay. Did you invite him to return to your home, or did he ask?

RICHIE. I offered.

LANA. I asked him to. Richie, that is. To offer Nick to come to stay with us again.

DETECTIVE VOGEL. Why did you want him to come back after forcing him to leave?

RICHIE. Because he's my kid brother. I hadn't seen him in nine years. I didn't want to give up on him.

DETECTIVE VOGEL. Had he stopped his drug use and drinking?

RICHIE. He'd reined it in from what I could tell.

LANA. I thought so too.

DETECTIVE VOGEL. Did he tell either of you what he did during his time away from you at this motel? What he did all day every day?

RICHIE. No. We never really talked about it.

LANA. Me neither.

DETECTIVE VOGEL. What did he do while he lived with you? Did he have a job of any kind?

RICHIE. Sometimes he helped me out down at the Tackle Box.

LANA. I work during the day a lot, or work night shifts and sleep during the day, so I don't know.

DETECTIVE VOGEL. What about the days he didn't work with you at the Tackle Box? What did he say he was doing then?

RICHIE. Nothing, as far as I knew. Just hung out, I guess. He'd stay up pretty late most nights so he would sleep most of the day.

DETECTIVE VOGEL. How did Nick spend his nights? Did he go out a lot?

RICHIE. He mostly just hung out here. We'd watch a movie or the Brewers game or something. Sometimes, we'd go down to the Walleye for a drink or two. Sometimes, he went by himself. But, usually, he'd just stay up late, watching TV.

7

Sixty-Two Days from the Night

Nick dropped his bag and collapsed onto the couch in Richie's living room. He closed his eyes. The day of scorching sun and beer had taken it out of him. His eyelids were heavy, and his skin was sore and pink. His face resembled the color of a lobster. He desperately needed to close his eyes and lie motionless.

Richie was in the kitchen, grabbing a glass of water while talking on the phone. It sounded like he was talking to Lana. It had the cadence of a married conversation. Nick tried to tune it out and sleep.

Although Richie's couch scratched his sunburn, it was still welcoming to sleep on. Nick heard Richie hang up the phone. It sounded like he began to clean some dishes. Nick didn't open his eyes as he shouted toward the kitchen.

"How's Lana?"

Richie looked up for a moment like he'd forgotten Nick had come back with him. "She's fine, glad you're going to be here for dinner." Nick heard his brother walk into the living room. He sat down in a recliner next to the couch and turned on the TV.

"She said she's going to invite her friend over tonight for a bonfire," Richie said. "I'll probably text Cooper too."

Nick opened one eye for a moment. "A little early for bonfire season around here, isn't it?"

"Supposed to be the first warmish night of the year. Why not?"

"Yeah, okay." Nick maneuvered so he lay on his side. "It'll be just like the old days. A big old bonfire with the family."

"Yeah, I guess so."

Nick took a deep breath with his eyes closed. "Tell me about this friend of Lana's."

"Her name's Kimi."

"Kimi," Nick muttered. "She sounds cute."

"Yeah, she's nice. She's Japanese. Well, half-Japanese. Her mom's from there, but her dad's from here." Nick could hear his brother slurp water from his glass.

"Huh," Nick grunted. "How'd that happen?"

"I think she said her dad was in the navy or something and was stationed in Japan," Richie said. "He took her home with him, and they got married."

"That's a nice, romantic story," Nick said. He slid his hand behind a couch pillow, propping his head. A few seconds passed with the only noise being the TV.

"She must be hot," Nick blurted. He opened one eye and saw his brother's confused face. He closed his eyes again. "At least you think she is."

"What?"

"Your voice got a little higher when you mentioned her," Nick said. "You gave me her whole family history. When she talks, you listen."

"My voice did not—," Richie began to say but collected himself. "She's just a friend. Lana's friend. She's cool. They work together, so she's here all the time. That doesn't mean—"

"There's nothing wrong with it," Nick interrupted. "Just because you're a married man doesn't mean you can't think another woman is attractive. As long as you two never *actually*, you know. Unless you already did. Did you?"

"No!"

"Okay, it's only a question," Nick said. "Even if you did, I wouldn't tell anyone." Nick rolled onto his back, wincing as his burned shoulders rubbed against the couch.

"She wouldn't happen to be single, would she?" Nick asked. He opened one eye at his brother.

"I think so," Richie said.

"Don't act like you don't know."

"She is," Richie said, annoyed. "She just broke up with her boyfriend."

"They date for long?"

"Two years, I think."

Nick closed both his eyes again. The announcer on TV whooped at a home run-saving catch.

"Maybe Lana can put in a good word for me," Nick said, his eyes still closed. "I could use a little…"

Richie took a sip of his water. "I'm sure she will," he said.

Nick tilted his head at Richie. "Really?"

"It wouldn't surprise me."

Nick closed his eyes again. Sleep was on the cusp of taking him.

"So how much of the plan do you have?" Richie asked.

Nick sighed.

"Lana's not here, so I think it would be a good time to talk about it."

Nick begrudgingly sat up. "Look, man, I get why you wouldn't want to involve her," Nick said. "But we could use another pair of hands."

"No," Richie said, staunchly. "Absolutely not." He glared at Nick, his eyes unblinking.

Nick took a deep breath. "Okay. How about Cooper? Big guy, handy, and loyal."

"No."

"Why not?"

"I'm not dragging people I care about into this," Richie said. "That's not happening."

Nick rubbed his eyes. He was tired and didn't want to argue with his brother, not after getting back in his good graces today. But he was making it difficult.

"Don't you have friends who you do this stuff with?" Richie asked.

"Not anymore," Nick said frankly.

"So they're all—"

"Retired. In prison. Dead. Yeah." Nick smoothed his hair. "Do I have to explain that the more help we have, the better chance we have of pulling this off?"

"You said that *we* could pull this off. *We*," Richie spat back.

"I meant *we* more in the general sense," Nick said, vaguely waving his hand.

Richie scoffed.

"Okay, fine, I'll try to figure out a way we can do it with just the two of us," Nick said. "But you're making this much harder than it has to be."

Richie leaned back in his chair, satisfied.

"We gotta think of an alibi too," Nick said. "Since I assume you don't want to involve Lana or Cooper by having them lie to the police for us."

"No, I don't," Richie said. "But why would the police suspect us?"

"Cops are dumbasses, but they're not that stupid," Nick said. "I have what you would call a checkered past that included doing things like this. Any robbery or heist that gets reported within fifty miles of my whereabouts, and they'll come looking for me."

"What, are they tracking you?"

"It's a small town, Richie. People talk. I'm sure people have heard I'm back in town, including the cops."

"But you said the car was stolen, right?" Richie said. "So he wouldn't go to the police, you said that."

"That's true, as far as I know. But you can't assume a thing like that. That's how you get pinched," Nick said. "For all we know, he could have the cops in his back pocket."

"Come on, seriously?"

Nick shrugged. "Why risk it?"

Richie shook his head. Nick could see him taking it all in. His face was grave, and regret was washing over it. Nick realized it was going to be hard to keep him committed until it was time. There was no way he wouldn't get cold feet.

"Look, Richie, just relax right now," Nick said, sitting up and reaching over to pat his brother on the knee. "I'll take care of all the planning and shit. Just give me a few weeks, maybe a month, and

I'll figure it all out. When I do, I'll come to you and lay it all out. If you don't like it, if it doesn't feel good to you, you can step away, and it'll be done, over with. Until then, don't worry about it. I don't even want you to think about it. It's only going to drive you crazy with nerves. Let me handle everything for now. Put it out of your mind."

Richie exhaled like a weight was lifted off his shoulders. "Okay, okay, that works. Okay," he said. "What do we tell Lana until then?"

"Just say I'm working down at the Tackle Box or something. She's not home during the day, right?"

"It depends on the day but no, not usually. I guess that could work."

"I'll come with you to the bait shop in the morning," Nick said. "Then, during the day, I'll do my work and you do yours."

Richie seemed satisfied.

Nick curled his hair behind his ears. "Richie, there's one thing that I want to make clear before you even think about this," Nick said. "Even if we pull this all off, everything works and we all walk away millionaires, you and Lana cannot stay here."

"What?" Richie shouted. "I thought the whole point of this was so we didn't have to lose the house!"

Nick put out his palms defensively.

"Yes, exactly. You can pay off all your debts and everything, but then you're going to need to sell the house and move somewhere else if you ever want to spend that money," Nick said. "You don't steal millions of dollars in the town you live in and then live happily ever after there. You understand me?"

Richie looked exasperated. "What about Lana's job? The Tackle Box? All our friends are here. Our life is here!"

"She can get another job, so can you," Nick said. "Or don't! You'll both be millionaires! Just be millionaires somewhere else! Come on, you've lived your whole life here. Don't you want to experience something else? This is the best chance you'll ever get. Go to California, Florida, fucking Europe, anywhere you want!"

Richie slumped back into his chair and shook his head.

"I don't know, man," Richie muttered. "I don't know if Lana will go for that."

"A million dollars can change a lot of minds," Nick said. "If not, well, you're still young, and you'll be rich. You'll have a lot of options out there."

Richie scowled. "No, she's the only reason I'm even thinking about doing this."

"I know, I know," Nick said. "I'm just saying—"

"Well, don't."

"We'll cross that bridge when we come to it," Nick said. He lay back down on the couch. "Now, if you'll excuse me, I have to rest up. I wanna look good when your crush gets here."

*****

Nick sat on the folding chair around the bonfire pit in Richie's backyard. It was twilight, and the sky was a grayish slate of blue with only the North Star shining. The fire began to take shape. The heavy, dark smoke from the twigs and damp leaves Richie used for tinder curled into the sky. The logs crackled and punctured the stillness of the approaching night. There was a breeze, but it was gentle and warm—a night for a bonfire.

Nick shifted his seat back as the fire began to leap into the air. He drank his beer and watched as his brother tended to the fire, doting on it with pricks and pokes and twigs and branches. Cooper had arrived about a half-hour prior and sat on a folding chair to his left. Lana sat to his right, a glass of white wine in her hand.

"Nice job on that fire," Cooper said to Richie. Nick thought of the hundreds of times Richie built bonfires for the family when they were growing up. He loved doing it and would beg their dad to let him start the fire. He always obliged.

"Damn!" Lana suddenly blurted out. "We should have gotten stuff for s'mores!"

"Been years since I had one of those," Nick said.

"Remember next time," Lana commanded Richie. He grabbed the beer he put down to tend the fire and took a seat between Lana and Nick. Nick looked around their backyard, enclosed by trees completely.

"How are your neighbors?" Nick asked.

"They're okay, I guess," Lana said, looking around. "They're not that close, but if you walk in a straight line for, I don't know, two hundred yards, you hit the Eckerts' house. And it's about the same the other way. Those are the Millers." Lana pointed to both ends of her backyard, encircled by a thick tree line.

Nick looked at the dense trees, thinking of how one wouldn't believe there was another house for thirty miles. "They full-time or summerers?" Nick asked.

Lana scratched her chin. "I think the Millers are always here. Eckerts are only here in the summer, so we haven't seen them since fall. Right, Richie?"

"Think so," Richie said with a shrug. "Sounds right."

Lana stood up from her chair and went over to Richie. She sat on his lap, wrapping her arm around his neck. She wore one of Richie's crewneck sweaters. She and Richie talked in low murmurs as Nick and Cooper discussed Cooper and his father's handyman business. It was like this for a few minutes before they were interrupted by lights. They were the unmistakable headlights from a car, moving across the trees and casting long shadows as it pulled down the driveway to the house.

"That's Kimi!" Lana squealed. She put her wine down and jumped up from her chair. She rushed inside the house. When Lana was inside, Nick turned to Cooper.

"Coop, you know this Kimi girl?"

"Yeah, she's usually here when I'm here. She's cool. I like her."

"Lana ever tried to set you up with her?"

Cooper thought for a moment. "No, she's pretty much always had a boyfriend," he said. "Least as long as I've known her."

"Not anymore," Richie said.

"Really? They broke up? They were together for a long time, weren't they?" Cooper asked.

"Yeah, almost two years. She dumped him like a week ago."

Cooper and Nick both turned to Richie with amused looks.

"At least, that's what Lana told me," Richie said, his face turning red.

"Well, if she's single, that's good news for you," Cooper said to Nick.

"Richie keeps talking about what a babe she is," Nick said.

"I did not!"

"It's true," Cooper said, cutting off Richie's protest. "She's kind of a flirt though. Even when she was dating, she would be flirtatious."

"Huh," Nick muttered.

They all turned to see if they could get a better look at Lana and Kimi. Through the windows into the house, they could see Lana walking with Kimi to the kitchen. Nick couldn't get a proper look at Kimi as they stepped into the kitchen.

"How come Lana never set me up with any of her friends? She knows I'm single," Cooper asked Richie. Nick stifled a laugh.

"She doesn't have any single friends, man," Richie said. "You were at the wedding. All her bridesmaids were married or engaged."

Cooper cast his head down, staring at the fire with a noticeable glumness.

"Chin up," Nick said, slapping Cooper on the shoulder. "You'll find a girl. Look at you. You're like a teddy bear. Very huggable."

Cooper stood up. "Now that you mention it, I could use a hug." He spread his arms out wide. Nick stood up.

"Bring it in," he said, wrapping his arms around Cooper.

Cooper squeezed him tight. Nick was taller, by a few inches, but felt tiny in Cooper's arms. Cooper rested his watermelon-sized head on Nick's shoulders like they were slow-dancing at a middle school dance. Behind them, Richie rolled his eyes. Their embrace was interrupted at the sound of the sliding back door opening. They broke away and saw Lana emerge with Kimi following behind her.

"Kimi's here!" she shouted as she and Kimi approached.

"Thank God, some women," Richie muttered in Nick and Cooper's direction.

"Don't listen to him," Cooper whispered in Nick's ear. "He's jealous I never hug him like that."

He winked at Nick, and Nick scratched Cooper's bearded chin.

"Hey, Kimi! How are you?" Richie said, intercepting her on the way to the firepit for a hug.

"Hey, Richie! I'm good! Looks like you got some sun today!" Kimi responded, poking his sunburned nose.

"Oh, yeah, we were fishing all day," Richie said, his sunburn masking his blushing. "Cooper's here too." He pointed toward the campfire. "And that over there is my younger brother, Nick."

Kimi waved to Cooper, who waved back. She stepped over toward Nick and put her hand out. "Nice to meet you," she said politely.

She had a high voice, which wasn't surprising considering her petite frame. She practically disappeared when Richie hugged her and Lana had nearly a foot on her. She couldn't have been more than a few inches taller than five feet. She wore a tank top and beige cardigan with jeans. There was a playfulness to her voice when talking to Richie, almost flirty. Nick could see what Cooper had meant.

Her hair was short, black, and straight, barely reaching her shoulders. The orange light of the fire cast shadows across her high cheekbones and full lips. What grabbed Nick, though, were her eyes. The flames made her brown eyes glow. They exploded past her lashes and tugged at Nick.

"You too," Nick said. He was unsure of what to say next and simply sat down instead. While Nick was shaking Kimi's hand, Lana pulled Richie by the collar as he went to sit down in his old seat by Nick. She guided him to the empty seat next to her, leaving the only available seat for Kimi to sit in between her and Nick. She sat down on Richie's lap. Kimi stepped past Nick and toward Cooper, who rose from his chair.

"Coop!" she shouted, hugging him.

"Hey, darling. You're looking gorgeous as usual," Cooper said, seemingly swallowing Kimi with his large arms wrapping around her small frame.

"Oh, you're such a sweetheart," she said, patting Cooper on the chest. She returned to the other side of the firepit where the only seat left was next to Nick, with Richie and Lana on the other side. As soon as Kimi sat down, Lana shot up out of Richie's lap.

"Oh! I forgot the music inside! Hold on a second," she said before putting her wine down and hustling back inside.

Nick, Cooper, Richie, and Kimi all sat around the fire. They watched the flames leap into the sky and the smoke billow upward. Kimi broke the silence.

"Richie," Kimi said. "I didn't even know you had a brother."

Richie shrugged, embarrassed.

"Well, it's been a while since we've seen each other," Nick answered for Richie.

"Oh, sorry, I didn't make things weird, did I?" Kimi asked.

Richie waved his hand. "No, don't worry. You're fine."

Kimi breathed a sigh of relief. "So how long has it been, then?" she asked, turning her head back and forth between the brothers.

Richie drank his beer and stared at the fire.

"Just over nine years," Nick said.

Kimi's eyes bulged and her eyebrows rose. "Oh," she said. She looked embarrassed and tried to move the conversation forward. "Oh, you must have come back for the funeral," she said to Nick. She turned to Richie. "So sorry about your dad, by the way. I would've come if I could have."

"Don't worry about it. Thanks for covering Lana's shift at the hospital," Richie said.

"Happy to do it." The two shared a smile and took a sip of their drinks. They each went back to staring at the fire. Kimi looked at Nick. "So where do you live then? Are you in Wisconsin?"

"God, no," Nick snorted. He regretted the harsh tone of his rebuke. Kimi chuckled.

"I mean," Nick said. "Wisconsin was never for me. I've kind of been all over: California and Colorado. The past three years have mostly been St. Louis though."

"Wow, that sounds amazing, traveling like that. What do you do?"

"Oh, you know, a little of this, a little of that," Nick said. "Part-time jobs, here and there. A lot of bartending. Some not strictly legal enterprises to help pay the bills."

Richie cleared his throat. Kimi half-laughed, unsure of how serious Nick was. She looked to Richie for confirmation. "He's just kidding," he said. She looked back at Nick. He raised his beer and shook his head to say he wasn't.

Lana came back out with a small, portable orange stereo. She plugged it into an outlet on the porch and stretched it as far as it could go. She scanned through the radio static, searching for a station.

She settled on what seemed to be a nineties station because Hootie and the Blowfish's "Only Wanna Be with You" was playing. Cooper's face lit up at the sound of the music.

"Fuck, man, I *love* Hootie!" he howled in delight. He stood up and started dancing by himself, moving his hips, snapping his fingers, and spinning in place while still holding his beer. Richie ignored him like he'd seen him drunkenly dance a hundred times before. Lana and Kimi laughed and encouraged him. He sang along at a surprisingly loud and high-pitched volume.

"'You and me! We come from different worlds! You like to laugh at me when I look at other girls!'" He wandered over to Lana, still on Richie's lap, and held out his hand. Lana blushed.

"Sorry, Coop," she said.

Cooper moved over to Kimi. "I need to finish this wine first. Next one," she said politely.

Cooper sidestepped to Nick. He laughed and gave Cooper his hand. Cooper yanked him from his chair and embraced him in a waltz position, Nick in the position of the woman. Cooper waltzed Nick around the fire, practically picking him up and spinning him left and right. Nick did his best to keep up.

The song ended, and they were forced to stop. Cooper bowed to Nick, who curtsied back. More applause from the audience.

"Bravo!" Lana shouted.

"Beautiful!" Kimi echoed.

Nick slumped down in his chair. "I think I'm actually out of breath," he said.

"Nice moves," Kimi said.

"That was all Coop. I was just along for the ride."

The radio station went to a series of commercials, and the group was left to sit by the fire without music for a few minutes.

"So," Nick said, "Kimi, you work with Lana?"

"Yup. Been a nurse for about three years now."

"Cool, cool. That's a tough gig." Kimi and Lana both agreed that it was.

"Yeah, it's tough sometimes. A lot of times. All of the time. But I love it."

"Do something you love and you'll never work a day in your life," Nick said.

"That's true, is it like that with your job?"

"Something like that."

*****

After a few hours, everyone at the bonfire had reached some form of intoxication. Cooper was half-asleep in his chair, and Richie wasn't far behind. Nick was tired but felt he was catching a second wind, buoyed by his conversation with Kimi. *She's like Lana*, Nick thought—witty, confident, and honest.

Nick sensed a connection. She shot meaningful glances at Nick and seemed to laugh harder at his jokes and stories. After one story that Kimi laughed especially hard at, Nick noticed how flushed her cheeks were from the wine.

Richie looked at his watch. "Shit. I gotta get up early tomorrow," he groaned. "Why'd you guys let me stay up this late and drink this much? I'm gonna be hungover tomorrow."

"That's the wife's job," Cooper said. "The boys are supposed to get you drunk."

"Of course, blame the wife," Lana said.

Richie tapped Lana to get up from his lap, and he hoisted himself up from his chair.

"Good night, everyone," he said. "Kimi, good to see you. Don't let my brother sweet-talk you all night."

"I'll be right back," Lana said, walking alongside Richie back to the house. "Anybody need another drink?" They all shook their heads.

They watched as Lana and Richie went back into the house. Nick glanced at Cooper, who was on the verge of falling asleep in his chair. His eyelids slowly dropped, and his chin fell to his chest.

"Looks like he's out," Kimi whispered to Nick. They watched him in silence a few more seconds and could hear a slight snore emanate from him. They both quietly laughed.

It was only Nick, Kimi, and the unconscious carcass of Cooper. For a minute, they listened to the fire and the music. Kimi snacked on a bag of chips. She tilted the open bag toward Nick. He took a handful. Kimi's phone buzzed. She took it out of her jeans and flipped it open.

"Lana texted me," she announced.

"From inside? Why?" Nick asked, crunching into a chip.

"She wanted to know if she should come back out or let us be *alone*," she said with emphasis. Nick looked at the house and back to Kimi, who was looking at him with a tilted head.

"Your call," Nick said. He crunched on another chip.

She looked at her phone and bit her bottom lip.

"A little privacy wouldn't hurt," she said. Nick could hear her fingernails clicking the phone's buttons. When she was done, she put it back in her pocket. She pointed at the small circular table next to Nick. "Can you bring that over here?"

Nick stood up and picked up the outdoor glass table and placed it in front of Kimi. "Thanks," she said. As Nick set the table down, she reached into her other pocket and dropped a small, plastic baggy on the table. She looked up at Nick.

Nick recognized the white powder. "Is it that kind of party?"

"It can be." Nick looked at the bag and back to her. "I like a little pick-me-up before, you know."

Nick waved his hand. "None for me. I don't do that stuff anymore." He went and sat back down in his chair.

"You sure?"

Nick reached into his jacket and pulled out a glass pipe and a silver grinder. "Yeah, I've got my own party favors."

"Suit yourself. You got a credit card or something?" Nick reached into his pocket and grabbed his wallet. He tossed his driver's license to Kimi on the table.

She opened it. "Wow, someone seems to be doing pretty well," she said, admiring the wad of cash wedged inside the wallet. Nick shrugged. She pulled out his driver's license. "Nicholas Craig Morgan. Born: March 12, 1981. Six feet tall, one hundred and seventy pounds. Pretty good. Nice zit, by the way."

"Hey, come on!"

Kimi giggled and put down the wallet. She took his driver's license and used it to chop the cocaine into a line on the table. Nick poured the ground bud from his grinder into the pink glass pipe. As Kimi pressed her nose down on the table, Nick raised his pipe to his lips with his lighter.

As Nick exhaled, coughing slightly, Kimi rubbed her nose and sniffled. She rubbed some leftover powder on her gums and put the bag away.

"A nurse who does coke. Tsk, tsk. You should know better."

Kimi rubbed her nose. "I know, I know. I used to only do it in college, but then sometimes I'd be in the last hours of a twelve-hour shift and needed something to get me through it." She sipped her wine.

"Hey, no judgment from me. You gotta do what you gotta do." Nick took another hit from his bowl. "Does Lana do it too?"

"No. Never. She's a good one. Most use *something*. She just gets by with coffee and attitude. I don't know how. She doesn't even know I do it. I mean, I've told her I've done it but not that I still do it. And I'd like to keep it that way."

"I'm no snitch."

"Good."

Nick took another rip and emptied the remaining ashes in the grass. He put the pipe down on the table and sipped his beer. He pulled out his cigarettes and lit one and took a deep inhale as he leaned his head back, staring at the cloudless, speckled sky.

Kimi shifted her chair toward Nick so she faced him. Her eyes were as bright as ever and she smiled, showing off her straight, white teeth. She raised her legs, stretching them and resting them on Nick's thigh, one ankle on top of the other.

"Can I help you?" Nick said, ashing his cigarette.

"You can," she said ominously. "I'm about to be vibrating with energy. Could use somewhere to put it."

Nick took a drag and looked at the trees, thinking. Nick placed his hand on her ankles, running his fingers up and down her calf. "I've got another idea."

Kimi followed his gaze toward the trees. "I'm not fucking in the woods."

Nick laughed. "Not that."

"Then what?"

Nick turned to her with a wicked look. "I'm thinking about doing a little work."

8

Sixty-One Days from the Night

The sunlight from the two windows above her bed finally woke Lana. She checked the clock: just past ten. She felt glad she had slept in but also felt a twinge of guilt that Nick and Kimi had probably woken up before her.

She sat up and stretched. She grabbed her slippers and walked softly out into the hallway and the living room. She figured Nick must also be sleeping until she heard the sizzle of cooking in the kitchen.

She went into the kitchen to see a stack of pancakes piled on a plate in the middle of the small kitchen table, and Nick hovering over the stove with a pan in his hand and a bowl of batter next to him.

"Smells good in here," Lana said loud enough for Nick to hear.

"Well, good morning, sunshine," he said. "Pancakes are on the table, and there's more coming, so eat up. There's coffee too."

Lana opened the cupboard above the sink and grabbed a plate, then two more for Kimi and Nick. "It's been a while since someone else cooked breakfast in my kitchen," she said as she sat down, placing the plates around the table.

"I don't have many useful skills, Lana," Nick said. He flipped a pancake. The plop and sizzle of it echoed in the kitchen. "But I can make some pretty damn good flapjacks."

Lana grabbed two pancakes from the plate and the bottle of syrup next to the stack. It was unopened. "Did you buy syrup?" she asked.

Nick turned around and came over to the table, pan and pancake in hand. He slid it off and onto the pile in the middle. "Well, yeah. I wanted to make pancakes, but you didn't have any syrup, so I went to the store early this morning. Got some orange juice, coffee, milk, and a few other things. It was no big deal, only a short bike ride."

"You biked?"

"Yeah," Nick said, returning to the stove. "Richie woke me up this morning when he left for work. I couldn't fall back asleep, so after a while, I just got up. I wanted to make pancakes, but there wasn't any syrup. I found a bike in the garage and went to the store."

Lana stared at Nick with curious fascination. "You're crazy," she said with a shake of her head. "But thanks anyway."

"No problem. It was nice, to be honest, a little early morning ride. It almost made me want to become a morning person." He turned off the stove, his pancake duties done. He sat down at the table with Lana and stabbed a pancake with his fork and brought it to his plate.

Lana cut up her first bite and stuffed it into her mouth. "Verdict?" Nick asked. Lana gave a thumbs-up while she chewed. Nick looked satisfied as he poured syrup on his pancakes.

"So," she said. "What'd you and Kimi do when we went to bed?"

Nick gave her a sideways glance as he chewed his pancake, reading between the lines of the question. "Not much. Just hung out," he said, sipping his coffee.

"Huh." She cut another bite of pancake. "I saw her asleep in your room."

"I slept on the couch. I offered her my bed."

"How very gentlemanly of you," Lana said. "Did you offer her anything else?"

"Lana."

"What? I'm just wondering if I have to change the sheets."

Nick shook his head and cut into his pancakes again, ignoring the question. Lana stared at him impatiently.

"Well?"

"Well, what?"

"Come on, did you guys do it or not?"

"No," Nick said. He sipped his coffee. Lana frowned.

"You don't like her?" she asked as she took another bite.

"How do you know I said no? Maybe she doesn't like me."

"Sounded like she liked you when she texted me to give you guys some privacy. Unless you screwed it up after that."

"I think she was just messing with you."

"Kimi wouldn't joke about that. Not to me," Lana said. She was about to say something else when they heard a bedroom door opening. Lana turned to see Kimi emerge from the hallway.

"Morning, baby girl!" she said in her sweetest voice. "Come get some pancakes."

Kimi's hair was strewn about and her eyes barely opened as she walked into the kitchen. She yawned.

"You guys aren't as quiet as you think," she moaned. She poured herself a cup of coffee. "Please, don't let me stop your conversation." She sat down at the table and grabbed some pancakes.

"I was just wondering what you guys did when I went to bed last night," Lana said. Kimi grabbed a pancake and put it on her plate. Nick grabbed one too.

"Nothing, really," Kimi said, matter-of-factly. Lana looked to Nick for confirmation, who nodded with a mouthful of pancake. They returned to eating. After finishing another pancake and chugging the last of his orange juice, Nick belched, to the dismay of Lana.

"Kimi said you guys work the night shift tonight," Nick said to Lana.

"Yeah, unfortunately," Lana groaned. "We weren't supposed to, but some other nurses asked us to cover for them. Seven to seven, twelve hours."

"Yikes. I don't know how you do it," Nick said in Kimi's direction, who scowled at him. Lana caught the exchange.

"I need some milk for these," Kimi said. She stood up and went into the fridge to grab the milk.

"Kimi, what happened to your jeans?" Lana asked.

Kimi stopped. "What?"

Lana pointed at her pants. "The whole back of your pants are covered in mud," she said, scratching dried mud off her legs.

Kimi's eyes darted wide open. She glanced at Nick and then back to her jeans. "Oh, yeah, I just slipped and fell in some mud last night. You know I'm a big klutz after a few drinks."

"Ah, man, that's awful you could ruin those jeans," Lana said, continuing to pat dried mud off.

"Don't worry about it. I don't want to get mud on your floor."

"Lemme help you there," Nick said, reaching his hand out toward Kimi's backside.

Lana smacked it away. "Hands to yourself. I have some sweatpants you can borrow, and you can take those jeans off and we can wash the mud out," Lana said, standing up.

"No, really, it's fine," Kimi said. "It's probably best I just go home and wash these and try to get some sleep." Kimi put down her coffee and grabbed her cardigan and purse from the living room.

"You sure?" Lana said. "You don't want any breakfast?"

"No, thanks, that's all right. I'm feeling kind of nauseous anyway," Kimi said, making her way to the door. "Give my best to Richie! Nick, nice to meet you. Lana, I'll see you tonight, love you!" She closed the door behind her before Lana could say another thing.

"Bye," Lana said, standing in the kitchen, dumbstruck. "What was that?"

"Don't ask me. She's your friend."

Lana sat back down and crossed her arms. "Did something happen last night?"

"No. Besides Kimi falling in some mud." Nick cut into his pancake. Lana's eyes didn't leave him.

"Look," Nick said with his mouth full. "Give me the evil eye all you want. It won't change anything." Lana kept staring, her eyes boring holes into Nick's skull. Nick finished his last pancake and stood up from the table.

"I'm gonna take a shower," Nick said, piling his dish into the sink. "I told Richie I'd meet him at the bait shop. Don't worry about the dishes. I'll clean them later."

"How are you getting there?"

"I'll just bike."

Lana stared at Nick.

"Okay," Nick huffed, avoiding her gaze. "I'll be in the shower."

He walked past Lana and out of the kitchen with his eyes down. Lana watched him walk past and down the hallway into the bathroom. When he closed the bathroom door behind him, she turned forward and held the hot cup of coffee in both her hands.

"What the *hell?*" she whispered to herself.

*****

The next day, there was a knock at the front door of the Morgan home. Nick was the only one at the house awake. Lana had returned from her twelve-hour shift at the hospital a few hours ago and had passed out. Richie was at the Tackle Box. Nick had gone with him in the morning but biked back to take a nap after a long night of recon at the Collins mansion. Before he could sleep though, the knock came.

Nick stood up in a huff, prepared to tell whoever it was to get lost. He opened the door and was surprised to see a familiar face.

A Door County sheriff stood on the stoop.

"Good morning," the sheriff said stiffly. For a few moments, Nick said nothing. He rattled his mind for a name to the face he knew. He found it.

"Holy shit. Deputy Kucharski, is that you?" Nick asked.

"Yes. Hello, Morgan," Kucharski said. "It's Sergeant Kucharski now. This is Deputy Peterson. Do you have a minute? We have a few questions we'd like to ask."

"What's this about?"

Kucharski cleared his throat. "The night before last, a neighbor of yours reported seeing people breaking into and leaving a nearby house. We're canvassing the neighborhood and seeing if anyone saw or heard anything suspicious. Do you have a minute?"

"I didn't see or hear anything. There you go. Have a good day." Nick went to close the door, but Kucharski's hand stopped it.

"Nonetheless, we'd like a word, Morgan." He pushed the door open. "If you wouldn't mind. We can do this here, nice and easy, or we can do this at the station, where it won't be so nice. Now, we don't want to do that, do we?"

Nick tilted his head at the older sheriff. "Okay, sure. I enjoy helping our brothers in law enforcement. It'll give us a chance to catch up!"

The sheriff politely smiled.

"Let's talk on the back porch. And be quiet, okay? My sister-in-law is sleeping, and I don't want to wake her up." He stepped aside to let them in and pointed them toward the backyard deck.

Nick noticed how Kucharski looked the same as he remembered him. The stocky sheriff had to be in his fifties now. He had a larger gut than before, but he had some leftover strength from his younger days. Perhaps the only significant difference was his jet-black hair, which he always kept cropped short. It was a little thinner on top and almost completely silver now. His thick mustache held some color but was graying too. His nose was still massive and his eyebrows long, but there were more pronounced wrinkles on his forehead. Despite his promotion, he still wore the same brown uniform with a beige tie.

They went out to the deck and sat on the small patio chairs around the table. It was a chilly morning, in the high forties. Nick grabbed his jacket and stuffed his feet into his boots before following them outside. The wind was cold, but the sun was warm on his skin.

"Can I get you guys something to drink?" Nick asked from the door as the two lawmen stepped out onto the porch. "Water? Coffee?"

"No. This will only take a minute, Morgan." Nick joined them on the porch. He circled the glass patio table and took a seat on the other side. Kucharski removed his sunglasses and hat.

"Wow, look at you, Phil," Nick said as he kicked his feet up. "A sergeant now. Congrats. You know, you were always my favorite school cop. Excuse me, school resource officer. I know you always hated that term. Cop."

"Thank you, Morgan," Kucharski said curtly. "If you don't mind, I'd like to get straight to the matter at hand."

"Jesus, look at your hair," Nick muttered. "You used to have a really good head of thick, black hair. Now, you look at least twenty years older. I guess that's the stress of the job, eh?"

Kucharski breathed through his nose. "Morgan, I wanted to ask you—"

"You used to look like John fucking Wayne in that sheriff's uniform."

"Enough!" Kucharski grunted. "Morgan. I don't have time for your bullshit, okay?"

"Of course, I apologize. Nostalgia's a funny thing." Nick drew out his cigarettes. "Mind if I smoke?" Kucharski said nothing but took out his notepad and a pen. "Ain't it funny? Ten years ago, you'd kick my ass for smoking."

Kucharski began to ask a question before Nick interrupted him. "Surprised I didn't see you at the funeral," Nick said. "For the old man. You two were pretty close, weren't you?" Kucharski looked up from his notepad. His jaw clenched. Nick could almost hear his grinding teeth."

"I was there."

"You were? Huh, I didn't notice you. Must be because you were out of uniform! That's right, you and Craig coached baseball together, didn't you?"

"That's right," Kucharski said. "My son Danny was the same grade as Richie, and they always played baseball together. Craig and I coached Richie and Danny's baseball teams for almost ten years, all the way to graduation. Craig was a good man. Not right, a man's last day on Earth going like that."

"I never liked Danny."

Nick turned his attention to Deputy Peterson, who stood behind Kucharski, his arms clasped behind him, his sheriff's hat and black aviator sunglasses on. He stared at Nick, stone-faced.

"But you're right, that wasn't right of me to do that at Craig's funeral. But most things aren't right," Nick said, keeping his eyes on Peterson. "You sure I can't get you boys anything?"

"I was proud of Richie that day, standing up for his father," Kucharski said. "At least Craig had one proper son."

"I wasn't that bad back in the day."

"If it wasn't for the respect I had for Craig," Kucharski snarled, "the favors I pulled for him, you would've been expelled. Probably in juvie, hell, jail. Looking back, I regret not bringing the hammer down on your ass."

"You're obsessed with the past, Phil. Think about the here and now. I'm different now."

"You don't look different to me."

"What are you so ornery about? The funeral?" Nick scoffed. "Come on, Phil. You knew the man. You drank with the man. Hell, half the time we found Craig drunk at the Walleye, you were passed out next to him. You telling me you never let him drive home knowing full well he couldn't see straight?"

"Don't you dare!" Kucharski growled. Deputy Peterson shifted for the first time, quickly glancing at Kucharski before going back to staring at Nick. "We're not here to talk about your father, God rest his soul."

"Indeed."

"I have some questions for you."

Nick leaned back with his cigarette in his mouth. "I'm waiting to hear them."

"Deputy Peterson," Kucharski grunted. "Help yourself to some coffee. Inside." Peterson hesitated. Nick shooed him away with his hand.

"Grown-ups are talking."

Peterson momentarily stayed still but, eventually, did as he was told and turned toward the door.

"And don't wake Lana, all right? She just got off a twelve-hour shift," Nick said as Peterson went inside. He turned back to Kucharski when he was gone. He bobbed his eyebrows. "Finally, we're alone."

"Okay, Morgan," Kucharski said, tapping his pad with his pen. "Now, we both know we don't like each other—"

"Whoa, hey," Nick said, cutting him off. "Where's that coming from? We've known each other for a long time! I've always liked you."

"Shut up!" Kucharski said. His gruff voice vibrated with menace. "I'm going to ask you some questions, and you're going to give me the truth, or I swear to God I will haul your ass in and throw you in a cell today."

Nick ashed his cigarette. "Fire away."

Kucharski put his pen to the paper of his notepad. "Where were you Saturday night, the third?"

"I was here," Nick said, ashing his cigarette. "We had a bonfire that night. You can probably still smell it in my hair." Nick grabbed a curl of his hair and whiffed it. "Takes forever to get that smell out."

"You should try washing it. You were here all night?"

"Correctamundo."

"Who else was here? At this bonfire?" Nick took another drag. He leaned his head back and exhaled.

"My brother Richie, his wife Lana, and our friends Cooper O'Hare and Kimi." Kucharski scribbled furiously on his notepad.

"What's Kimi's last name?"

"I don't know."

"You don't know?"

"We met that night."

"Does your brother or Lana know her last name?"

"Probably."

"We'll need that information."

"I don't see why."

"You don't have to."

Nick took another drag of his cigarette. Kucharski wrote some more notes in his pad. "Were you and others drinking that night?"

"Do we look like Mormons to you?"

"Any drugs at this party?"

"Oh yeah, it was a real rave. LSD, coke, pills, heroin, speed, crystal. Richie went nuts after he took an eight ball to the dome," Nick said, tapping his temple and clicking his tongue. Kucharski glared from behind his eyebrows as he wrote in his notepad. "No, there were no drugs. Jeez, lighten up, Phil."

"What time did everyone arrive and leave?"

Nick took a deep breath. "Cooper came around seven, I think. Kimi about an hour after that. Richie and Lana went to bed around midnight, maybe later. Cooper left around an hour later. Kimi slept over."

Nick could hear Kucharski's pen scribbling from across the table. "When your brother and his wife went to bed, what did you, Kimi, and Cooper do?"

"Nothing really. Cooper fell asleep in his chair. Kimi and I just talked. Waited for the fire to go out."

"During this time, did you see or hear anything unusual?"

"We had music playing pretty loud, so we couldn't hear much."

"Do you have the phone number and address of this Cooper O'Hare?" Kucharski asked, flipping a page from his notepad.

"No. I'm sure you guys got a phonebook."

Kucharski huffed and looked up from his notepad. He closed it. He put it back in his breast pocket along with his pen.

"Are you familiar with the Eckert family?"

Nick shook his head. "Not really. They live up the road, don't they? Think Lana mentioned them one time. Haven't met them yet."

Kucharski leaned back and interlocked his fingers, resting his hands on his gut. "A neighbor reported last Sunday night that he saw movement and people inside the Eckert home, even though the family was in Illinois at the time. Mr. Eckert later confirmed some valuables were missing."

Nick looked displeased. "Boy, some people just don't have any luck at all. They get a nice summer house for the family, and it gets busted into. To have your stuff, your cash, your wife's jewelry stolen like that, it's just bad luck," Nick said. "It's like your nose. A fucking schnozz like that is just bad luck."

"I never mentioned cash or jewelry was taken."

"That's usually what thieves steal, right?"

Kucharski leaned forward on the table. "Is there anything you'd like to tell me now, Morgan?"

Nick looked around as if Kucharski were talking to someone else. He pointed at himself, vexed. "Me? What would I have to say?"

"You think I'm stupid? You're barely back in town for the first time in a decade and within a couple of weeks, the house next door to where you're staying gets robbed."

"That's right, I forgot. Everything that happens in this town is my fault, right? What'd you do while I was gone? Did you find another poor kid to pin all your problems on?"

Kucharski pulled out his notepad again and flipped it open. "I looked up what you've been doing since you left. Looks like you've stayed busy."

"You know what they say about the devil and idle hands."

Kucharski squinted at the pad. "Multiple petty larceny charges, all in California. Public drunkenness, possession of a controlled substance, forgery of documents, breaking and entering, and the coup de grace: assaulting a Los Angeles police officer. That one got you two years in an L.A. prison and a year of parole, including counseling and rehab. Frankly, I don't know how you got off so easy."

Nick took a drag and looked away, uninterested. "To be fair, I didn't assault him. I bit him. And I was high, so I don't remember doing it. I'm sure I had my reasons."

"Can't say I was surprised to see you spend time on the inside," Kucharski said, putting away his notepad.

"That's very sweet of you, Phil."

"Since you got out of prison, though, you've been clean. Not so much as a parking ticket."

Nick flicked his cigarette butt off the porch and held out his palms. "Inspiring, don't you think? I'm a shining example of the rehabilitating wonders of the penal system."

"You wanna know what I think?"

"No, but I'll bet you tell me all the same."

"I don't think you're any different from the punk you were back in the day. People like you don't change. You can't help yourself."

"Thank you, Phil. You'd make a great rehab counselor."

"This time, though, you fucked up," he said, leaning forward. "You came back here with a record. I so much as get a *shred* of evidence you broke the law, and you're done. You're going back inside."

Kucharski leaned back in his chair and crossed his arms. A grin spread over his face. "You got greedy, Morgan. You saw a nice, empty house down the road, and you just couldn't help it. You made off with a couple of thousand dollars' worth of property and thought

114

you had a nice little score. But this time, your pops isn't here to bail you out. It's just me."

Nick scratched his beard and took a deep breath, seemingly deep in thought. "What was stolen?"

Kucharski eyed him with suspicion. "I won't reveal details of an open investigation."

"Investigation?" Nick chuckled. "Jesus, this little town. Someone rips a couple of bucks off a guy and the police are all over it."

Kucharski said nothing. Nick cleared his throat.

"If you told me exactly what was stolen, I could help you. I know a few people in this line of work. I could ask around," Nick explained. "We could work together. Wouldn't that be something, Phil?"

Kucharski huffed. "All you need to know is that enough was taken to warrant a felony charge. A felony charge with your record? You're fucked."

Nick curled his hair behind his ear. "Don't you get tired of this, Phil? Every time some trust fund prick loses their Rolex and calls the cops demanding an investigation? These fucking rich people, Phil, they're not like you and me. We work for a living, and we barely get by while they cruise around on boats worth three years of your salary. People like us should stick together, not always be fighting each other."

Kucharski took a deep breath. "Morgan, my advice to you right now is to confess and get ahead of this."

Nick looked offended. "Confess? Why would I do that? You said so yourself. I've been clean. I've been living a straight life. I've turned over a new leaf."

"So it's just a coincidence then? All of this happening just a few doors away from you? It's all one big coinkydink, huh?"

"Coinkydink," Nick repeated. "That's so Wisconsin. I love that."

Kucharski maintained his relentless stare. Nick straightened his jacket.

"It's a strange world, Phil. Coincidences happen all the time, don't they?" He took out another cigarette. "And your idea to come down here and scare a confession out of me is just sad. It's beneath you, honestly. Kindergarten cop bullshit."

"You won't get another chance like this," Kucharski said. "Confess and maybe there's a deal for you with less jail time."

"You'd do that for me, Phil?"

Kucharski said nothing.

Nick leaned back in his chair, his hands in his lap. "I appreciate the offer, but I'm going to have to pass since, as you know, I didn't do it. So unless you got an arrest warrant, I think I'm done talking to you." Nick leaned over the table and put his hands together like they were about to be cuffed and pointed them at Kucharski. "Well?"

"Soon enough," he snarled. He stood up in a huff, knocking his chair backward. He put his sunglasses and hat back on. He put his hands on the table and leaned forward, bringing his face close to Nick's.

"I'm going to wipe that fucking smirk off your face, Morgan. And I will enjoy it."

"Jesus, your nose is even bigger than I remembered."

Kucharski snorted like a bull and walked to the sliding door. Before he opened it, he turned back to Nick. "Don't leave town," he said. He went inside the house to grab his partner and they left. Nick looked through the glass door until he could see them leave. He listened to the patrol car as it rolled over the gravel driveway.

Nick leaned forward onto the table and took a deep breath. He massaged his face and curled his hair back behind his ears. He rolled his head, stretching his neck. "God fucking dammit," he mumbled to himself.

"Was that the cops?" Lana yelled. She stood at the threshold of the sliding door.

Nick jumped in his chair. He cleared his throat and tried to make his voice sound calm and reassuring. "Lana," he said, slowly standing up as if approaching a wild animal. "Before you say anything, let me just say: you have nothing to worry about."

"Nick," Lana fumed, stepping out onto the patio and slowly cornering Nick like a predator would with prey. "Why the *fuck* were the cops at my house?"

"Now, I see how, from your perspective, this looks bad," Nick said, his palms raised.

"Nick!"

"Okay! Apparently," he started, clearing his throat, "there was a robbery at your neighbor's house, the Eckerts, two nights ago. And the cops, considering my record, think that I was involved in it somehow."

"Did you?"

Nick looked away and puffed out his cheeks.

"Nick!"

"Yes! Yes, I might have helped myself to a few things…"

"Jesus Christ!" Lana shouted. She started pacing back and forth. "Why? Why would you do that?"

"In my defense," Nick said. "I was high and wanted to impress a pretty girl."

"Do you think this is funny?"

Nick bit his lip.

Lana stepped forward and hit Nick. She flailed her arms, smacking Nick in the shoulder and the back as he covered up to protect himself.

"Hey! Hey! Come on!" Nick pleaded. Lana eventually ceased. She paced back and forth on the patio as Nick retreated to behind the table.

"Lana, relax! Look at me. Hey! Look at me! Do I look worried?" he asked, patting his chest.

Lana glared at him. "What happened? What did you do?"

"Well, it was after you and Richie went to bed. Cooper was passed out in the chair. Kimi and I were talking—"

"You dragged Kimi into this?"

"Dragged is a strong word."

"Jesus, Nick! Do you know the trouble she could get in? She could lose her nursing license! Not to mention going to jail! This could ruin her life!"

"Lana, Lana, Lana, please just listen to me, okay? All we did was go in, swipe a few things they wouldn't miss, and leave. We were careful. I made sure of it. There's nothing connecting us to this!"

"A few things they wouldn't miss? Clearly, they fucking did, Nick! They called the cops!"

"It was a neighbor. Apparently a neighbor saw some movement in the house or something, which is just bad luck. If it wasn't for that, they never would have even thought they were robbed."

Lana squeezed her temples and shook her head.

"The point is," Nick said, "that they have no evidence it was me and Kimi! That was just Kucharski trying to scare me! That dickhead has wanted to nail me since I was fourteen."

Lana paced back and forth, her face in her hands. "So what happens now?"

"Nothing," Nick said. "You don't have to know anything."

"I want to know! No more secrets in my house!"

"Okay! I'll get rid of the stuff and that'll be the end of it."

"How can you be sure?"

"This is not my first time."

"Oh, that's great. That's *exactly* what I want to hear."

"Lana, I know it was a mistake, I admit that. It will never happen again, I swear to you. It was a drunk mistake. But me, you, Richie, Cooper, and Kimi are all going to be just fine. I swear to you."

She put her hands on her hips. "Richie's going to kill you."

Nick winced. "Does he need to know?"

"Are you kidding? Yes! I'm not going to lie to him!"

"I'm not asking you to lie! Just don't tell him! If he doesn't ask, it's not a lie!"

"Nick, he has a right to know. This is his house. You're his brother. You need to tell him."

Nick groaned. He slumped into a patio chair.

"He'll kick me out, you know that." Lana pursed her lips. "And you don't want that. As mad as you are right now, you want me to stay, I know you do. And I want to stay too. Richie and I are starting to get along. This was just one stupid mistake that had nothing to do with him. He doesn't need to know this."

Lana rubbed her face. "Fine," she said. "I won't tell him, but I'm not going to lie to him."

"That's fine. If he asks you or me, I'll come clean, I swear. But please, give this a chance to blow over. I promise you it will. In a week, you'll forget all about it."

Lana looked at the trees blowing in the wind. She shook her head and looked at Nick.

"I'm going back to bed."

*****

DETECTIVE VOGEL. What about the Eckert situation?

RICHIE. Eckert situation? Do you mean our neighbors?

DETECTIVE VOGEL. Yes. Back in May, around the time you say Nick returned to living in your home, they reported a robbery. Sergeant Kucharski here questioned Nick himself about it.

RICHIE. I have no idea what you're talking about. Do you?

LANA. I was sleeping when Nick was questioned, but yeah, I found out about it after.

RICHIE. You didn't tell me?

LANA. Nick assured me he had nothing to do with it. He said it was just a cop he had a history with, one who had it out for him.

SERGEANT KUCHARSKI. And you believed him?

LANA. Yes.

RICHIE. You still should have told me!

LANA. I was going to, but then nothing happened after, so I assumed he was innocent.

SERGEANT KUCHARSKI. Still sure about that?

LANA. Is that important right now?

DETECTIVE VOGEL. I apologize for Sergeant Kucharski. So Nick told you he had nothing to do with it?

LANA. Yes.

DETECTIVE VOGEL. And you had no reason to suspect him?

LANA. No.

DETECTIVE VOGEL. Okay. Did he ever mention any friends he was going to see? Did he have any friends or associates over at the house?

RICHIE. Associates?

DETECTIVE VOGEL. Anyone he associated with.

RICHIE. No, he didn't have any friends or associates outside our friend group.

DETECTIVE VOGEL. Who were you some of your friends Nick would associate with?

RICHIE. I wouldn't say they associated; they just hung out. My friend Cooper O'Hare and my wife's friend Kimi Roberts.

DETECTIVE VOGEL. Was this a romantic or physical relationship between Nick and Kimi?

RICHIE. Not as far as I knew.

LANA. No, I don't think so. They were just friends.

DETECTIVE VOGEL. Did Kimi ever mention a friend of Nick she met
or heard him talking to or talking about?

LANA. No. You'd have to ask her, I guess.

DETECTIVE VOGEL. We will.

9

Thirty-Six Days from the Night

George Collins enjoyed the first moments of every day. The bleary seconds that immediately followed the severing of dreams, night-mares, or blank sleep were special to him. Many despise those seconds, ring out curses at the blasted alarm clock disturbing their peace. Not George.

George didn't need an alarm. He trusted his body to know when to wake, and for fifty-plus years, it hadn't failed him yet. He greeted each morning with a smile. This morning was no different.

George woke up alone, as was his norm. He wasn't a hermit by any standard. He socialized with friends and girlfriends almost every day and was known for throwing incredible parties for the peninsula elite. Rarely, though, did any of them spend the night at Chateau de Collins or share the morning with him. No, the early hours were his and his alone.

The morning sun had crept over the horizon. George's house and its windows faced west, allowing the morning light to gradually flood in through the large windows that hovered over his bed as his eyes slowly opened. He sat on the edge of his king-sized bed, whip-ping the silk sheets off his nude body. He rose and walked over to the French doors that led to the small balcony attached to his bedroom.

He stepped onto the hanging. The cool morning air goosed his skin. He gripped the railing, closed his eyes, and inhaled. He filled his lungs with the morning spring air. He smelled the grass, slick with the morning dew, and listened to the chirping birds.

His house, perched atop the corner of a small cliff, offered immense views of the seemingly infinite Great Lake, its usually raucous waters in an eerie morning calm. Its mirror-like surface reflected the shadows of the trees as the sun rose behind its horizon.

George said nothing. He never did during his morning embrace. His voice would taint the natural order and upset the harmonious balance. No, he simply consumed it through his senses. He took one last breath of the sharp air before returning inside.

With the Door County air still in his lungs, George prepared for the rest of his day as he always did. His morning exercise was first. This could be different each day as George had no specific workout regimen or routine. Some days he'd use the stationary bicycle. Occasionally he'd use the StairMaster, and other days he'd swim laps in his underground pool.

Today, he chose the elliptical. He'd been using it more over the past year. He didn't like it at first—he thought it was a machine reserved for senior citizens who had bad backs and weak knees and exercised only under doctor's orders. It wasn't a machine for George, who, for his entire life, had maintained the trim and cut figure of an athlete, a shining example of scrupulous dieting and punishing workouts.

But George was no longer in his twenties, thirties, or even forties. He was on the back nine of his fifties, and he began experiencing aggravating pain in his right knee three years prior. It was hard for him to accept at first—he flat out ignored it for two years. Eventually, it became too much to ignore, and George realized he couldn't pound out the miles running on the treadmill or pavement anymore.

His doctor told him it was a lack of cartilage in his knee, and if he continued to push it, he'd be walking with a cane soon. He could have elected surgery to insert artificial cartilage, but George wouldn't do it, not until he had to. His doctor recommended switching to the elliptical or swimming for cardio, as well as simple daily stretches and physical therapy. George reluctantly obliged, weaning himself off the treadmill and into the water and softer exercise equipment.

So George went through his daily stretches for his knee and hopped on the machine he resented for its representation of his mortality. After forty-five minutes, he stepped off with a towel and water bottle. He wiped his brow and patted his face before gulping down the water and moving on with the rest of his morning.

His daily appointment with the sauna was next. The sweat lodge was his favorite room in his sprawling log cabin mansion. The wooden room was tucked in the corner of the gym, and he never missed his daily reservation with it. He liked to make sure to sweat any remaining alcohol or other substances out of his system before beginning the day. It was important to start each day as fresh as possible.

After a half hour, he emerged from the sauna with perspiration dripping off him, feeling cleansed. He returned to his bedroom and jumped into his shower that featured an aerial rain-shower head, letting the water cascade over his body and carry the sweat off of him. He spent only a few minutes there, diligently scrubbing and washing, but not overstaying. He didn't like wasting time, even in the shower.

After drying off, he stood in front of his bathroom mirror, which took up the entire wall above the sink and began his maintenance routine. He started by shaving with his single blade razor, the kind he'd used since he was fifteen.

He made a shaving lather in his vintage apothecary mug and dabbed it on his face with his special boar shave brush. Then, he made sure the single blade razor was sharp, sometimes sharpening it on the spot if needed. He shaved deliberately. He carefully carved around his silver goatee that covered his upper lip and chin. He prided himself on his facial hair's flawless lines.

After that, his tweezers went to work on his eyebrows and nose. His unibrow was especially prominent, and it took daily pluckings to keep it from becoming a distraction.

Next, George washed his face. George previously performed this endeavor in the shower, but recently he read an article that claimed it was better to do it after a hot shower, as the pores open up more. He used a special exfoliating daily scrub that a recent female conquest turned him on to. He'd been using it every day for about six months and was ecstatic about the results. His tan and soft skin was one of his proudest achievements.

After a quick wipe of lotion over his arms and legs, George prepared his hair. These days, his onyx hair had more salt than pepper, but it still held the same thickness as when he was in high school. He smoothly rubbed the seventy-dollar pomade he had gotten from a salon through his hair. He grabbed his fine-tooth comb and brushed it straight back. He liked the pomade because it held strong, but not too much. He wanted to look sophisticated but didn't want to have the crusty-haired look of a Wall Street suit from the nineties.

Thus concluded the maintenance portion of his routine. He threw on his silk, navy robe and proceeded downstairs for breakfast. The first meal of the day was significant for George. It was usually the only meal he ate alone between lunch with friends and dinners with girlfriends, and he enjoyed treating himself with exquisite food and peaceful contemplation.

Before the cooking began, his espresso came first. He picked up his home machine a couple of years ago on the recommendation of an Italian friend of his, and although it may have been expensive, he couldn't quibble with the years of delicious morning espresso it gave him. Plus, he enjoyed the process of making it—the measuring of the coffee grounds, the steaming of the milk—routines put his lively mind at ease.

An omelet was his preferred breakfast selection as of late. He went through streaks of various recipes he experimented with weeks at a time until he found the one that hit the right notes for his palette. Today was an egg-white omelet with spinach, feta cheese, Italian seasoning, and parsley. Simple but delicious.

While he cooked his omelet and drank his espresso, he listened to the only jazz radio station in the area. George always listened to jazz while cooking. The atonal melodies and wandering piano and saxophone fit his culinary focus.

Once the omelet was ready, he poured himself a glass of orange juice and decorated the plate with fresh fruit he procured from the farmer's market every weekend. On this day, he chose half of a grapefruit as his appetizer while his omelet cooled.

While he ate at his large kitchen island complete with granite countertops, George brought out his laptop to check his email. Most of it was meaningless junk mail and spam, hardly worth even a glance. On rare occasions, there was a business matter George had to attend to or an invitation for a social gathering.

Next, it was time to check the daily planner and calendar. George kept his planner with him everywhere, a practice he began when he was a young man and continued to this day. Like his email inbox, there was rarely anything of importance written down since his semi-retirement. In the past, George's days would be filled with dozens of notes, reminders, and appointments written in code. The pages could barely contain all the notes needed for Collins to stay on schedule. Now, the majority of the notes were date night or sailing lesson reminders.

Once breakfast was finished, George returned to his master bathroom. He flossed first, then brushed with his two-hundred-dollar toothbrush with rotating bristles. Then, he used mouthwash to cap off his cleaning program. All of this fastidious care was worth it. His teeth were gleaming and immaculate pearls, another point of pride for George.

Finally, it was time to dress. In his spacious walk-in closet, George perused his shirts, pants, jackets, and more to find what spoke to him that day. Since he stepped away from his work, he'd relaxed his strict professional style. He even came around to wearing shorts, which he never did while in Miami, even on the hottest summer days. He enjoyed displaying his toned calves for the world.

Today was going to be another warm one. He decided on some khakis and a blue-and-white striped Ralph Lauren polo shirt. Shorts would be better, but then he wouldn't be able to wear his ankle holster. He put his Tissot Chronograph watch on his right wrist and a gold bracelet on the other. He grabbed his Ray-Ban Wayfarer sunglasses to finish the outfit.

George, as he always did, went to the front door and grabbed his newspapers, waiting for him on his front step. He had reached the final part of his daily morning program. It's recommended to wait at least a half hour before drinking coffee after using mouthwash, so

George chose to spend that time reading the papers on his deck while smoking the day's first cigarette. He sat on the same lounge chair he always did and looked out on his kingdom.

All was well. The sun had fully made its entrance onto the clear blue morning sky, and its rays were beginning to bake the Earth. The shade from the nearby umbrella and consistent breeze kept George cool though. He took out his silver cigarette case holding his cigarettes and plucked it from its place. His trusty lighter sparked and away he went.

George closed his eyes and inhaled, embracing the smoke in his lungs. He exhaled. He opened the papers.

After perusing the large papers such as the *New York Times*, the *Washington Post*, and the *Miami Herald*, George turned his attention to local news. The *Green Bay Press-Gazette* was the closest "big city" news periodical in the area. There were very few articles or stories of consequence in it, but he read it daily regardless. He enjoyed the quaintness of the news in these parts. He liked to embrace the community he resided in, even if he didn't quite understand it and its residents fully. He did his best to understand what was on his neighbors' minds.

It was usually around 8:30 a.m. by the time George finished his cigarette as well as his reading of the paper. He checked his watch: 8:22. It was time to prepare his thermos of coffee.

By 8:29, Collins was sitting in his Jaguar, his vestibule of coffee tucked neatly into the cup holder. He opened the garage door and started the engine. Before exiting, George took a moment to check his glove box. His snub-nosed .357 revolver rested in its usual spot.

George pulled out of his garage and down his long, gated driveway leading to the secluded road. As he pulled out onto the road, he made sure the black gates behind him closed and sealed off the entrance.

Despite an open contract on his head worth millions, George had become relaxed and complacent in his semi-retirement. He did not see the gray and rusted truck emerge from an abandoned trail among the trees and follow him.

*****

When George returned to the Ephraim Yacht Club later that day after a brief excursion to the store for cleaning supplies, he was greeted by his friend Jon, throwing his hands up in annoyance at the sight of him.

"George! There you are. I was just talking about you!"

George stepped inside the modest building and into the lounge room where Jon sat at a table filled with loose papers and folders in front of his laptop. George dropped his bags of supplies on the table.

"Me? Who could you possibly be talking to about me?"

"Ah, it was this kid, kind of hippy-looking fella. You know, it's funny," Jon said, petting his walrus mustache. "He came in about, oh, five minutes after you left for the store and left barely a minute before you stepped right through that door. Shit, you probably saw him on your way in."

"No, I don't believe I saw anyone," George said as he moved toward the wooden shelf housing the lounge games. "You up for a game of dominos, Johnny boy?"

"Ah, what the hell? I'm not doing any work anyway." He cleared off the table as George brought over the box of dominos and poured them onto the table.

"Why were you talking about me with this hippy kid?" George said, shuffling the dominos.

"We didn't just talk about you," Jon said. "He was asking about the club and some of the boats that dock here."

"Did he mention me by name or did you?"

Jon thought for a moment. "Ah, I think he noticed your boat, and I mentioned your name."

"*The Lone Wind?*" George collected his dominos.

"Yeah, at least I think he did. Either way, I was just telling him about it and some of your escapades."

"I see," George said. The game began, and they started laying down dominos in quick succession. "Whaddya say, Jon, the usual? Five dollars a game?"

"Hell!" Jon snorted. "I'm already down thirty-five bucks to you. I gotta start getting lucky soon."

They played a few minutes with only the patter of the dominos on the wooden table before George spoke again.

"What'd he want? The kid, that is," George said.

Jon laid down another domino. "I'm not exactly sure," he said without taking an eye off his dominos. "Ah! That's right, he was looking for a charter—a boat and captain that would take him and his family out on the water for a weekend. He mentioned your boat because it's the biggest."

"Hmm."

"I told him a few names that would probably be up for that, you know, at the right rate."

"Doesn't he know there are businesses that do that sort of thing? Why'd he come here?"

"Ah, he said he wanted a real sailing pro, someone who could also teach him how to sail. He heard we do lessons and stuff here, I guess."

"Who'd you tell him to contact?"

"Well, he sounded adamant that he needed a big boat with space for all the people. I said he could try asking you, but you're pretty busy on the weekends, especially if it was going to be a holiday weekend like the Fourth since you've always got your big shindig fundraiser. Sorry, George, don't mean to tell people about your business. I don't know when to shut up."

"No apology needed, Johnny boy. Everything you said was true. It sounds as if you two had quite a lengthy conversation."

"I suppose so. Kind of a weird kid. A little hinky."

"Did you give him my number?"

"No, I didn't want to do that. I told him to stick around, told him you'd be back soon, but he left in kind of a hurry."

"Hmm. You get his name?"

Jon tilted his head. "I guess I didn't. Least, I don't remember."

George laid down his last domino. "Looks like your tab is up to forty."

*****

Six minutes before George's return to the yacht club, Nick hustled across the street where Richie's truck was parked, out of sight. He watched as he saw Collins's car pull back into the yacht club. He made sure he wasn't seen and grabbed the notebook sitting on the dash. He opened and furiously began scribbling down notes under the George Collins heading at the top, concentrating on every morsel of information he had gotten from Jon.

Avid sailor. Teaches lessons. Owns largest sailboat in the club. Called The Lone Wind. *Hosts big Fourth of July party every year at the country club.*

He stared at the last bit. He tapped the eraser of the pencil against the notebook. An idea came to him. He closed the notebook and tossed it inside the glove compartment. He started the engine and gripped the wheel. He glanced at the glove box.

He put the truck in gear and drove home.

10

Thirty-Three Days from the Night

The Sunday night cookout became a tradition at the Morgan house during Nick's residence. Every Sunday night, Kimi or Cooper or sometimes both would join the Morgan clan for a buffet of grilling food: cheeseburgers, baked beans, fresh corn, salad, pies, and a litany of other dishes. This night, only Kimi could make it. The night was warm and gentle.

The group was becoming close. As Nick promised Lana, the Eckert situation seemed to have blown over, with no more harassment from Kucharski or any other law enforcement. With the sheriffs off his back, Nick was able to continue his recon of George Collins and was nearing completion of his plan that seemed too simple to be true.

Richie continued to lie to Lana about him and Nick's plan. Her suspicions, though, continued as she noticed a change in Richie. He seemed to look at her differently lately; his eyes were always distracted, and when they did look at her, they looked guilty. She planned to keep the drinks coming and set a trap.

Lana and Kimi each had the day off, and Lana invited her friend for a day of kayaking and lounging at the Murphy Park beach. She was also a tool of Lana's plan—to distract Nick. The two got along so well Richie and Lana both assumed their relationship had become physical in secret.

As the group prepared to sit down at the table inside the Morgan dining room, Nick and Richie's bloodstream was adequately fortified with alcohol while Kimi kept Nick focused on her. Lana was chummy all night long, serving the food with laughter and eagerly refilling drinks.

The group stuffed themselves with food, hungry from their drinking. After a few minutes, they came to a collective stop, exhaling at once as if exhausted by the feasting. Lana looked around the table.

"I don't know about you guys, but I think I'm ready for that pie," she announced. Groggy eyes from Nick and Richie met her. Kimi, though, beamed.

"Oh, yes! I brought a cherry pie for dessert! I'll get it," she said excitedly, getting up from her chair and heading into the kitchen.

"I'm stuffed as it is. But," Nick said as he rubbed his stomach, "there's always room for cherry pie. Especially a Door County cherry pie."

Richie looked up from his plate at Nick. "You used to devour those pies. Lana, you wouldn't believe it," he said with a laugh. "I don't know how you stayed so skinny all the time. If there was a pie in front of you, no one else was getting a bite."

"Cherry is my favorite too," Lana said. "Richie prefers pumpkin, but Kimi knows I like cherries."

On cue, Kimi appeared with the pie in hand and more plates and silverware for everyone. "Oh, Kimi, you're such a sweetheart," Lana said.

Kimi waved her off as she began to cut slices. "Oh, it's nothing. You guys are always feeding me. It was the least I could do. Momma always taught me to never go anywhere empty-handed." She handed out slices. She handed Nick his plate, their fingers grazing in the handoff. Kimi cut a slice for herself and sat down.

"Well, dig in, everyone!" Kimi said. The group did not need encouragement. Nick attacked his pie like it was his last, ignoring his full stomach to enjoy the fruity and sweet taste of glaze and cherries. No one talked as they ate.

When he was done, Nick began telling a story to Kimi as they sat on the other end of the table of Lana and Richie. The opportunity was now.

"Hey, Richie," Lana said, her voice barely a whisper. "I was driving around Ephraim the other day, and I could've sworn I saw your truck."

Richie choked down his pie. He glanced at Nick, but his face was turned away from him, toward Kimi. "Ephraim? My truck? Really?"

"Yup," Lana said, taking a bite of pie. "Had a missing hubcap on the front-right tire and everything. What were you doing in Ephraim in the middle of the day?"

Richie cleared his throat. "Ephraim? What day was this?"

"Yesterday."

"That was me," Nick cut in. Richie and Lana turned to see Nick staring at the two. "Yeah, yesterday? I borrowed Richie's truck for the day and was around Ephraim for a little bit."

Richie exhaled. Lana stared at Nick, slightly annoyed.

"Oh. What were you doing?"

"Nothing really," Nick said with a shrug. "I just wanted to see some of the old sights, you know? We always went to Ephraim when we were kids. I wanted to see if Walter's Ice Cream was still there. Still is. Their milkshakes are the best."

Nick's lie was smooth and easy. Lana looked at her husband, who averted his eyes. "Huh," she said. She took a sip of her wine. Kimi frowned across the table.

Lana fiddled with the pie on her plate with her fork. "Was following George Collins part of your little memory trip too?"

"How'd you know about that?" Richie blurted out before Nick could say anything. Nick dropped his silverware.

"Goddammit, man, she didn't know until you just told her!" Nick said, exasperated. Richie looked at Lana in confusion. She smiled.

"Seriously though, how'd you know?" Nick asked.

"I'm not an idiot," she said. "I was there too when you told Richie your plan to steal that car. Plus, Richie's been weird the past couple of weeks. I figured if you were sneaking around with Richie's car, it probably had something to do with that. I just didn't think Richie would be stupid enough to go along with it!"

Nick frowned, annoyed that he'd been found out so easily. "We were going to tell you."

"Tell me what? When?"

"When we were ready. When it was all ready," Richie said.

Lana glared at her husband, then at Nick, who lowered his eyes. "So you're really going to do it?"

Silence emanated from the table.

"Jesus Christ," Lana muttered and dropped her face into her hands.

"Nothing's been decided," Richie said. "I was just letting Nick, you know, gather information, and then he was going to—"

"What?" Lana snapped. "Give some kind of presentation? A PowerPoint on the pros and cons of grand larceny?"

"Listen, let's all just—," Nick started.

"If you tell me to calm down, I swear to God I'll wring your skinny neck."

Nick cleared his throat. "Okay, so the idea was I was going to put it all together and show it to Richie. And a couple of days ago, I did."

Lana turned to Richie, staring him down. She didn't ask a question. She didn't have to. Richie lowered his eyes. "It sounded like a pretty good plan."

"For fuck's sake," Lana muttered. She stood and stormed to the kitchen.

"Lana, wait!" Richie shouted after her, getting up from the table and going into the kitchen. Nick and Kimi were left alone at the table. They could hear Lana yell at Richie from the kitchen.

"So that's it then?" Lana shouted. "I get no say? I mean, why would I? I'm the one who'd end up completely fucked if you ended up in prison!"

They heard some mild protesting from Richie, but it was quickly drowned out.

"How could you just keep this from me? Lie to me for—what— weeks? To not include me at all? How could you lie to me like that? Tell me!"

Nick cringed. He turned to Kimi. "I could use some fresh air." Kimi emphatically agreed, and they quickly rose from the table and headed toward the back door.

They stepped outside, and each took a deep breath as if they were being suffocated inside. Nick moved to the edge of the porch and leaned on the wooden railing. The sun began to set behind the tall trees.

Kimi stood next to him. They looked out at the silhouettes of the trees and the flaming gold sky behind them. Nick took out his cigarettes. Kimi held out her hand. He put a cigarette in it and lit it for her before lighting his.

They both took a drag and exhaled the smoke. For a few seconds, they enjoyed the sound of the chirping crickets in the grass.

"So," Nick said, "you're probably wondering what's going on."

"I don't think I've ever heard Lana yell at Richie like that."

Nick looked over his shoulder. "It'll be all right. She'll calm down."

"You sure about that?"

"She's smart. She knows Richie doesn't do anything unless it's for her."

"What's he doing for her?"

Nick blew out the smoke. "Something extremely stupid that could get them both very rich."

"What, are you trying to get him to rob a bank with you?"

"Don't be ridiculous. Banks are way too hard."

Kimi stared. "Jesus, you're serious."

Nick shrugged. "It's a long story. But you'll hear about it, eventually."

"Why's that?"

"Because you're part of it. The plan."

"Me? No. No. Whatever the fuck you're trying to do, I'm not interested."

Nick smoked his cigarette without a word.

"Why would you think I'd want to be part of whatever this is?" Kimi asked, exasperated.

"You love Lana. You want to help her and them. You could get rich too."

Kimi looked over her shoulder at Lana and Richie through the glass door. "You're going to help them?"

Nick looked at her from the corner of his eye. "That's right."

Kimi looked again over her shoulder. She blew smoke. "Safely? No one gets hurt? No one winds up in jail or whatever?"

Nick turned to Kimi, leaning on the railing. He looked at Lana and Richie inside.

"I can promise you one thing: if it means I spend the rest of my life in prison, nothing will happen to those two. Or you."

Kimi looked into his green eyes. After a moment, she looked away, seemingly satisfied, and stared straight ahead again. She looked out and absorbed the sky and the trees. Nick did the same, and they listened to the still night.

*****

Richie and Lana were left alone. Lana paced back and forth in the kitchen, her hands rubbing her forehead. Richie stood at the threshold of the kitchen. He nervously wrung his hands.

"I was going to tell you," Richie finally said. Shame filled his voice and engulfed his words. "Eventually."

"Eventually? Are you fucking kidding me?"

"We're not going to be able to talk if you're going to be like this."

Lana laughed. "If *I'm* going to be like this?"

Richie thought she was going to shout more, but she collected herself. She closed her eyes and took a deep breath. She sat back down at the table and stared at her husband.

"Please explain it to me so I can understand. Because, right now, I'm trying. I am really, *really* trying, and I'm at a loss," Lana said, throwing up her hands in resignation. "How could you even consider this, and how could you not tell me? How could you lie to me like this? You're not a criminal, Richie, and you're not a liar, so I don't even know who you are right now."

Richie buried his face in his hands. "I don't know," Richie began. "I thought—"

"Thought what?"

"That I could make things right!" Richie shouted. "That maybe I could fix *all* of this."

The outburst surprised Lana. Her demeanor softened. Richie's face was desperate and frustrated. She'd never seen him so vulnerable and upset. Lana leaned back. She looked into his eyes. Richie turned away and left the kitchen into the living room. Lana followed him.

"I know you blame yourself for our problems," Lana said as they reached the living room. "But I don't know how many times I have to tell you—it's not your fault! Everyone's hurting right now. No matter what happens, we'll get through it. And we'll get through it *together*, not going behind each other's backs and lying!"

"That's an excuse," Richie said, standing in the living room, his voice hard. "Fuck excuses. I don't care what's going on out there. All I care about is what I can control."

"This wasn't in your control either. We both made mistakes. We didn't know that it could come to this."

"Do you remember what I promised you?"

Lana frowned. "Promised me?"

"When I asked you to marry me. That night. When you said yes. Afterward, what I promised you. Do you remember?"

Lana stepped closer to him, her voice low and soft. "You promised that we would be happy." Her breath caught in her throat. "With a nice house and beautiful kids."

"I'm sorry. I broke that promise."

"No, you didn't," she said forcefully. She stepped closer to him. "We *are* happy. At least, I am, because I'm with you. And I'd be happy with you if we lived in a box on the street."

"But I wouldn't!" Richie shouted. It startled Lana. She turned away. "I don't mean I wouldn't be happy with you. I mean I could never be happy knowing that's the life that you had to live so you could be with me!"

Richie slumped down in the chair.

"I can't keep failing," Richie said. His voice cracked. "I can't keep fucking up. I need to do *something*. I don't want my own wife to be a martyr, to suffer through life because she chose me."

He gathered his breath and looked up at her. "You're the best decision that I ever made. But I can't shake this feeling that I'm the worst mistake you ever made…"

Richie put his face in his hands and rubbed his eyes. Lana looked down. She took a deep breath. She kneeled in front of him. She grabbed his hands and looked into his red eyes.

"You're not a mistake. And you never will be."

"Even if I do this?"

She sighed. "Even if you do this."

"So—okay?"

"Okay."

Richie reached down and hugged Lana, picking her up in his arms. She hugged him tightly, resting her cheek on his shoulders. As they embraced, she whispered into his ear, "But I'm not letting you do it without me."

Richie held her out in front of him. "What?"

"If you're doing this, so am I." She stood up and walked to the back door.

"No, no, no," Richie said, chasing after her. "No, Lana, I'm serious. It's too dangerous!"

She stopped in front of the glass door and turned around to look at him. "If it's not too dangerous for you, then it's not too dangerous for me."

She grabbed the handle to slide open the door. Richie's hand grabbed hers and stopped it. She stared at him. They remained like that, their eyes locked. Richie broke first, letting go of the door.

Lana opened it. "Inside," she barked to Kimi and Nick. She stepped away from the door and let Nick and Kimi enter. They avoided eye contact as they entered. They awkwardly stood between Richie and Lana.

"We're in," Lana said, her arms crossed.

"*We're* in?" Nick asked.

"No," Richie said.

"Yes," Lana said.

"Lana—"

"I'll go to the cops," she said matter-of-factly. The room stopped. "What?"

"If you try to do this without me, I'll go to the cops. Or I'll tell this Collins guy myself. Either way, you're not doing this without me. So accept it now or call it off."

Richie scoffed. Nick bit his lip and looked at his brother, hiding his giddiness. "If it matters at all, I vote aye." He looked at Lana. "We could use her."

Lana smugly grinned at Richie. Richie shook his head. "Looks like it's settled," Lana said.

Nick clapped his hands. "Beautiful! We're all in agreement." He circled to the other side of the table, standing over it. "It's already been a long night. I'll go into the details tomorrow."

"We work the night shift tomorrow," Lana said, gesturing toward Kimi. "Seven to seven."

"Okay," Nick said, thinking. "We'll meet you both for breakfast then, afterward. My treat."

"Wait," Lana said. "Both of us?"

"Kimi's in too."

"No, she's not," Lana said emphatically.

"Yeah, I am," Kimi said.

"Kimi," Lana said. "No, you don't. This has nothing to do with you."

"It's about you and Richie, so yes, actually, it does."

"Kimi, I love you, but this is—"

"I'll go to the cops," Kimi said.

Nick laughed.

"I'm serious," Kimi said. "It's like you said, Lana. You're not doing this alone. If you try to do whatever this is without me, I'll tell the cops."

"You don't even have anything to tell them," Lana said.

"I heard the name Collins," Kimi said. "I think that's enough."

Lana shook her head. "Goddammit," she muttered. Kimi blew her a kiss.

"It's settled then," Nick said. "Day after tomorrow, breakfast powwow."

Nick swiped the keys to Richie's truck and ushered Kimi through the living room as she grabbed her purse and coat on her way out the door. Lana and Richie were left in the living room, dumbfounded. Richie looked at Lana.

She threw up her hands in exasperation and went into the kitchen.

11

Thirty-Two Days from the Night

The clouds made a dreary morning. Nick could feel the inevitable rain as he sat on a wooden bench in front of Fred Karlsson's Swedish Restaurant. On the outside, Fred Karlsson's was an unremarkable building; its dark oak walls gave the impression of a European hideaway, the kind one would find in a Scandinavian town no one's heard of. In case anyone forgot its heritage, Fred's tall wooden sign with bright yellow letters and a Swedish flag reminded them.

No one came to Fred Karlsson's for its sign or its wooden walls adorned with knickknacks or even its food. They came for the goats.

Nick admired the lush green grass that coated its roof. By the time they'd arrived, the goats were already grazing on Fred's roof, snacking and lounging. Nick and Richie watched them as they waited for Lana and Kimi.

"Doesn't seem very fulfilling," Nick muttered. "Hanging out on a roof all day."

"They're goats," Richie said.

"What, goats don't like to run around and stuff?" Nick said. "I thought goats liked to climb mountains."

"Mountain goats climb mountains," Richie said. "Those are regular goats. The kind you'd see on a farm."

"Either way, if there's goat stew or some shit on the menu, I'm calling PETA."

Richie rolled his eyes. He recognized Kimi's compact car pull into the parking lot. "They're here," he announced. Nick looked and saw them too.

"Okay, remember: they just got off a twelve-hour shift. They're going to be exhausted and grouchy," Richie said out of the side of his mouth as Kimi and Lana exited the car. "Trust me, don't act chipper. Don't ask how work was because they don't wanna talk or think about it. In fact, don't even try to make conversation. Just say hello, and let's get some coffee and food in them first. Don't take too long to order either."

"Should I not look them in the eye?" Nick asked. "Jesus, good thing I'm not wearing any red."

Lana and Kimi approached sullenly, their heads down and their gait drooping. Their feet plopped on the pavement, and they seemed to strain for each step. As they approached, Richie put his arm around Lana. "Hey," he said in a low voice.

"Hey," Lana replied with more grunt than speech. That was the extent of the greetings as they all walked together toward the entrance of Fred Karlsson's. Kimi greeted Nick flatly. Nick heeded Richie's advice and kept quiet.

"God, my feet are killing me," Kimi said. Nick stopped in front of her. He hunched over, offering his back.

"Allow me, my lady," he said. Kimi's weary face laughed, and she hopped onto Nick's slim back and shoulders. He carried her piggyback into Fred's.

Richie held the door open as Nick walked into Fred's with the petite Kimi on his back. He strode up to the waiting hostess standing behind her podium in the famous Karlsson's Dirndl uniform: a long white Scandinavian dress and a tight green bodice with decorative yellow stitching. Naturally, she had long blond hair and a pale complexion that paired well with the Swedish decor.

"*Guten morgen*, Fraulein," Nick said. "Table for four, please."

The young girl beamed. It was the kind of smile service workers make five hundred times a day or were scolded by a manager. She reached below the podium for some menus.

"A private corner, if that can be arranged. *Danke*," Nick added.

Kimi whispered in his ear. "You know you're speaking German, not Swedish, right?"

"I don't think she minds."

The smiling hostess beckoned for the group to follow her as she led them past the gift shop and into the dining room. It was surprisingly small but stuffed to the brim with square tables carved with Scandinavian drawings and art.

This early there were only a few other guests, but Nick wondered what this place was like when it was packed in with hungry tourists. He felt sympathy for the servers in their ridiculous dresses.

He carried Kimi to the table before letting her down. She pinched his cheek in thanks and sat down. The hostess obliged Nick, seating them at a table in the corner halfway across the room from any other patrons. She placed menus around the table. Before she left, Nick whispered in her ear.

"If you could keep the tables around us empty while we're here, we'd appreciate it," he said, slipping cash into her hand.

"No problem, sir," she said.

The group sat at the small corner table. Nick and Richie sat across from Lana and Kimi. They sat in moody silence. Lana held her head but looked in danger of falling asleep at any moment. Kimi looked slightly better, but the bags under her eyes were heavy and dark. Nick and Richie took wide looks around the room, taking in the Scandinavian decor and architecture.

"Quite a place," Nick observed out loud.

"You know," Kimi said, "I've driven by this place probably a hundred times but never been inside. It was always just that place with the goats."

"The breakfast is supposed to be good," Nick said.

"Thank God," Lana muttered.

Another grinning, Swedish-clad server emerged. She announced her name as Kaitlyn and eagerly welcomed the group with the uniform smile.

"Hello, Kaitlyn," Nick said.

"How is everyone doing this morning?" she asked. The table responded with various grunts and mumbles.

"Kaitlyn, darling, we need your help," Nick said, beckoning her to him. She leaned down. "Those two heroes over there just got off a twelve-hour night shift at the hospital, so they're going to need the best, strongest coffee you've got back there. We'll all take some, stat."

Nick winked at her. Lana rolled her eyes.

"Of course! I'll get that right away and give you folks a minute to look at the menu," she said heartily before exiting.

"She's cute," Nick mentioned to the table.

"Dress doesn't look too comfortable," Kimi added.

"Imagine if you two had to wear a dress like that all day at work," Nick said.

"Patients would probably be happier to see us," Kimi said. Lana laughed lightly.

The table fell back into silence as they waited for the coffee. Kimi rubbed her eyes. Lana yawned. They all combed through the menu. Nick's stomach grumbled while reading about the pancake breakfast.

Kaitlyn returned with four coffee steins. She laid them down and poured the steaming hot coffee. Nick's stein had art depicting Swedish boys and girls climbing a mountain.

"Are we ready to order or would you like a minute?" Kaitlyn asked as she finished pouring coffee for Nick.

"We're ready," Nick said without polling the table.

After everyone ordered, Nick beckoned Kaitlyn over again.

"Put everything on one check, sweetheart," he whispered. She beamed and promised to before leaving. The group wordlessly sipped their coffee and admired their steins. Nick scratched his beard. Kimi massaged the back of her neck.

"Well, thanks for breakfast, Nick," Kimi said, breaking the silence. Nick waved her off.

"Don't thank him yet," Lana muttered from behind her mug.

"What?"

"He's just buttering you up before the, you know," she said.

"Let's eat first," Nick said, throwing away the topic.

Kimi looked indifferent. She took a sip of her coffee before resting her head on the table, using her arms as a pillow, and closing her eyes. The group fell back into their quiet until the food arrived.

*****

144

A little over a half hour later, Nick flicked his cigarette butt into the nearby garden and reentered Fred Karlsson's through its heavy wooden door. He strode inside, his eyes lingering on two waitresses as he made his way to their table. Kaitlyn arrived at the table at the same time as him.

"Anything else I can get you?" she asked, holding a pot of coffee.

"Yes, could you refill everyone's coffee, sweetheart?" Nick asked as he sat back down at the head of the table. He beckoned Kaitlyn to come in close again. "We're going to be talking privately for a little bit, so could you give us some space? I'll signal you when we're ready."

"Of course!" Kaitlyn said. She took her coffee pot and Dirndl dress and moved onto another table. Nick looked at his table. He studied their faces. They all looked at him with anticipation.

Lana looked back at him. "Well? Are we going to do this?"

"What are we doing again?" Kimi asked.

"It'll all make sense in a second," Nick said. He took a deep breath. "Okay, so I'm going to tell you all something that is extremely—how should I put this—clandestine."

Nick cleared his throat. "Right. Well, before I say anything, I need it understood by everyone here that nothing said leaves this table. Forever, I mean. You take this shit to your graves."

The table silently agreed.

"I'm fucking serious. I need all of you to say you understand."

They all verbally agreed.

"Okay, good. I'm sorry for getting serious, but this is serious business." Nick took one more look around. No patrons or servers were within earshot.

"I want everyone to understand that I am not forcing anyone to do anything. If anyone doesn't like what they're hearing, they can leave and forget anything was ever said."

"Okay," Kimi mumbled.

Nick leaned forward and lowered his voice. "This is the plan for one night's work in which we each walk away with one million dollars."

Nick explained the mark. He described George Collins and the stolen 1948 Talbot-Lago Sport Coupe that was sitting in his garage.

He explained its history, how it was stolen in New Orleans years ago, and how it hadn't been seen since. Until now.

Nick took a breath and let his words hang for a minute.

"This is about a car?" Kimi asked. Nick confirmed. "And you two are on board with this?" she said to Richie and Lana. Richie nodded. Lana shrugged.

"If Richie is, I am."

"Jesus," Kimi said, looking away. "I mean, are you even sure you can do this? Do you know what you're doing?"

"Yes," Nick said resolutely.

Kimi sipped her coffee.

"Now," Nick said, "I don't want to misrepresent what this is. This is a serious crime. A felony. If things go bad and we get busted, we're talking about doing time."

Nick let that hang over the table. They each looked down, thinking.

"Shit," Kimi said.

"I'm telling you this because I don't want it to seem like I tricked you or anyone else at this table into doing something dangerous. Because this is dangerous, I'm not hiding that." Nick cleared his throat. "But I think the upside is worth it. The exposure is low, and the risk is mitigated due to the circumstances. We're talking about up to four million dollars, maybe even more, split four ways for one night's work."

The group silently contemplated.

"So what's the plan, then?" Lana asked.

Nick reached into his back pocket. He pulled out a folded, glossy card, about the size of a mail envelope. He opened it and held it up to the group.

"We attend Mr. Collins's famous Fourth of July fundraiser at the luxurious Egg Harbor Golf and Country Club."

*****

Nick was finished. He sipped from his stein and surveyed the table. They sat in silence, digesting the plan. Nick waited; he wouldn't be the first to speak.

146

Kimi cleared her throat. "Huh. Maybe it's me, but it all seems pretty easy."

"You're right to think so. Getting in and getting the car is, frankly, no sweat. The trick is transporting it out of there to a safe place as fast as possible, without raising any alarm. And we need to make sure there's no way it can get tied back to me and, by extension, all of you."

"Which is why we're going to the party—er—fundraiser," Lana said.

"Exactly," Nick said. "If anyone asks, we'll say we were at the party that night, confirmed by our invitations, our valet tickets, and dozens of unbiased witnesses who we talked to that night."

"But only Lana and I will be at the party all night," Kimi said.

"Correct. You're going to be our alibis. Anyone wonders where Richie and I were, you'll be there to confirm we were there. And others will confirm you were there."

"You do make it sound easy," Lana said. "Which makes me think there's something you're not telling us."

The table looked at Nick.

"I'm not holding anything back. I don't do that. That's everything." He leaned back and sipped his coffee. He put down his stein and leaned forward toward Kimi. He raised his eyebrows as she bit her lip and reflected.

"I don't know. All of this for a car?" she said.

"Don't think of it as just a *car*. Think of it as a stack of cash—millions of dollars sitting in someone's garage. Not tucked away in some safe or behind a giant vault door. It's sitting right in someone's garage with just a flimsy door standing between us and it."

"Damn."

"Kimi, I don't think you should do this," Lana said.

"Let her make her own decision," Nick said.

"I am. I'm just telling her what I think. She's *my* friend, after all!"

"Well, why don't you let *your* friend say what *she* thinks first before telling her what *you* think she should do?"

"She can do whatever she wants. She knows that! I don't want her sitting and thinking I'm asking her for a favor or something."

"Well, you're already leading her toward a decision! Let her decide without any pressure!"

"Without any pressure? You're telling me you haven't been pressuring her?"

"What have I done to pressure her?"

"Both of you, stop!" Richie scolded, raising his hands between Nick and Lana. "Keep your voices down! This is Kimi's choice, and we all know she can make whatever decision she wants. Kimi, go ahead."

She twiddled with her thumbs some more and looked at the ceiling. "You know," she said, "I work hard. I work really fucking hard. I love my job, and I love helping people, but a lot of the time, it feels like it doesn't matter. It feels like no matter what I do, I can't get out from underneath my student loans, I can barely afford an apartment I share with a roommate, and I've been driving the same piece-of-shit car since college. I'm getting close to thirty, and I have almost nothing saved up. I don't know if I'll ever be able to afford a house. Honestly, I deserve better. I bust my ass, and I'm good at what I do, and what I do is important. Maybe that makes me selfish."

The table stayed silent.

"So yeah. Fuck it. I'm in."

Nick rapped his knuckles on the table. Lana looked disappointed but hid it when Kimi looked at her. She reached over and grabbed her hand.

Nick waved across the room. "Kaitlyn, sweetie! We're done here. I'll take the check." He turned back to the table. "Congratulations, everyone. You're going to look back on today as one of the best of your life."

Richie cleared his throat. "So about this party. It sounds pretty exclusive."

Kaitlyn appeared with the check and black booklet in her hand. Nick took it and thanked her. He pulled out his wallet.

"That it is, brother of mine," Nick said. He dropped a wad of cash in the booklet and gave it back to Kaitlyn. "I don't need any change, honey, thank you."

"So how do we get into it? We won't be able to just walk in."

Nick tapped the invitation in the middle of the table. "That won't be a problem. I already got this one, stole it out of a guy's mailbox, someone I knew George would invite. Notice anything about it?"

The group leaned forward over the middle of the table, studying the black invitation.

"There's no name on it," Lana said.

"Good eye, Lana," Nick said. "All I gotta do is make a few copies of this bad boy and we're good as gold."

Richie picked up the invitation, feeling its glossy coating. "I don't know, looks pretty expensive. You can't just copy it on a printer or whatever."

Nick took the invitation and put it back in his pocket. "Trust me, it won't be my first forgery."

"What if there's like a list at the door?" Kimi asked.

"Nothing a few bills can't fix. Look, this isn't the president's ball with the secret service. It's just going to be a couple of seasonal workers barely making minimum wage. They won't care. Richie and I will rent some tuxedos. You girls will throw on some expensive dresses, and who wouldn't want to let in a handsome group like ourselves in?"

Lana shrugged. "I guess that makes sense."

Nick looked at Kimi. "All right, then. It's a date."

12

Miami, Florida
Seven Years, One Month, and
Eleven Days from the Night

Bill and Ezra Cook waited. They stood next to the semitruck without speaking a word. Ezra yawned—he was tired from the drive from New Orleans. Bill, on the other hand, was fresh from the nap he took on the way.

Bill checked his watch. A little past two in the morning. A light glinted over the watch. He looked up to see the headlights of Frank Buccinello's Cadillac pierce through the windows. It was empty besides the two of them. It'd been the meeting location for numerous exchanges between Bill and Frank over the fifteen years of their working relationship. As he waited, Bill approximated that twenty million dollars had changed hands within these dirty concrete walls.

Bill took out his pack of cigarettes and offered one to Ezra. He declined. Bill lit his cigarette and waited. He noticed it was raining outside. There was a knock, a pounding on the door. Bill looked to Ezra, who jogged over to the door. Bill dropped his cigarette and stomped on it.

Ezra opened the door to Frank standing in the rain, trying to shield himself with a black bag over his head and another one slung over his shoulder.

"Christ!" he yelled when the door opened. "Fucking hurricane out there. How you doing, Z?" He walked in and dropped the bags.

When he saw Bill, he beamed and held out his arms. "There he is! There's my Billy boy!"

"Frank!" Bill said with his permanent grin. The two embraced. Frank shook Bill in his arms.

"Where is she? Is she here? Where's my lady Joan?"

"Ezra! Bring Joan out, would you?"

Ezra jogged over to the semi, pulling out a ramp behind it. Frank rubbed his hands in anticipation. "I'll tell you, Billy, you've outdone yourself this time. You don't know how long I've been waiting to get my hands on this girl."

"Frank, trust me, she will exceed all your expectations," he said. Frank patted him on the shoulder as they watched Ezra get into the back of the semi. Frank looked around.

"Christ, they're not here yet?"

"Who, your brothers?" Bill said. "Angelo and Little Henry should be here soon. I called them right after I called you."

"Ah, fuck them, the lazy pricks."

They heard the engine ignite. Its roar echoed through the empty warehouse. Frank was happier than Bill had ever seen him. He began cackling in delight as it slowly backed down the ramp.

He ran to the purple-and-silver masterpiece, his arms out wide and laughing the whole way as Ezra brought it down and parked it with the engine idling.

"Look at her!" Frank yelled as she came to a stop. Frank circled her as Ezra got out. "Goddammit! Look at this French fucking beauty!"

He howled and whooped as he inspected it. He peered inside the interior as Bill approached the 1948 Talbot-Lago Grand Sport Coupe.

"Billy!" Frank said. For the first time, Bill saw he was at a loss for words. He grabbed his face and planted a big kiss on his cheek. Bill laughed.

"Go on now, Frank, get inside! She's been waiting for you!"

Frank slowly got into the driver's seat, tentatively taking a seat. "*Madone,*" he cooed as he ran his hands over the steering wheel. Bill came up and closed the door for him. He leaned in through the window.

"How's she feel?"

"Like a million bucks."

"Well, hopefully a little more than that," Bill said with a wink.

"Hell, Billy, I'd give you anything for this baby. Take my fucking house. I don't care!"

Bill laughed. "Nonsense, we had an agreement."

Frank didn't seem to hear him. "You know they had one of these at the Le Mans! Can you believe that? Something like this going a hundred miles per hour, trading paint with another racer?"

Bill smiled. "Of course, you've only told me that about a hundred times, Frank."

Frank laughed. He smelled the interior. "Goddamn, this is the most beautiful thing I've ever been in."

"I won't tell your wife you said that."

Frank cackled. "You know, this is exactly the kind of car my old man would've loved." He ran his hands over the dashboard and passenger seat. "It's classy, elegant, dignified, you know? They just don't make them like this anymore."

Bill concurred. Frank looked at him and started laughing again. "Billy, you beautiful Yiddish-speaking, potato-eating Mick-Jew bastard!"

Bill forced his face blank. He pointed to the manila envelope on the dashboard. "Frank, do me a favor and grab that folder there."

Frank handed him the envelope. Bill grabbed it and stepped back to let Frank open the door and get out. Frank turned and put his hands on his hips as he admired it more.

"How'd the job go? Any trouble?" Frank asked.

"None at all. Some casualties, but nothing exorbitant."

"You think the heat's going to be bad for this?"

Bill shook his head. "I don't believe it's anything to concern yourself with. I wouldn't recommend any joy rides around town anytime soon. But give it some time, and you'll be fine."

"Ah, don't worry about that. I'm not stupid," Frank said. "This is for retirement. One day, when my kids are out of the house, I'm going to move to Italy, back to the mother country. I'm gonna drive this thing all through the entire country—up and down the coast and through the mountains and vineyards. God, I can't wait! Who knows, I might even take my wife."

They both laughed. Bill looked at Ezra and gestured toward the bags Frank brought. "That sounds beautiful," Bill said. "I'm considering hanging things up myself."

Frank frowned. "Really? I can't say I blame you. You're not getting any younger."

"No, I am not."

"You got some money saved up? What am I saying? You're a Jew, of course you do!"

Bill gritted his teeth. "I've got a nice little nest egg. In fact, I believe this job will put me over the top. Push me on my way out."

"Shit, so you're going to do it? Hell, I hate to see you go, Billy. I can trust you more than half the morons in my crew."

"I appreciate you saying that, Frank. I've always enjoyed our business relationship. There are just a few things I need to do before leaving."

"Where are you gonna go?"

Bill pondered for a moment. "I'll do some traveling. But I have a mind to settle north, in Wisconsin. My father grew up there before relocating us down to Florida when I was a boy. I have some fond memories of that place from my childhood."

"Are you fucking crazy? People up there retire and move down here, not the other way around!"

Bill chuckled. "Florida doesn't need another retired Jew. No, I could use some good old-fashioned Midwestern niceness."

"Ah, you're crazy, Billy. I couldn't stand those winters. It gets down to fifty here, and I won't leave the house."

"I don't mind the cold."

"What about Karen? She into this idea of yours about retiring and going north?"

"She won't be a problem."

Frank folded his arms across his chest. "What about sailing? Isn't that what you're always doing? How are you gonna do that up there?"

"Why, Frank, are you forgetting about the Great Lakes? You can do plenty of sailing up there. Can go from Chicago to New York if you wanted to. All the way up through Canada."

"Huh, I didn't know that."

Bill turned and looked at Ezra, who was counting the money from the bag. "Everything in order?" Ezra gave him a thumbs-up. He grabbed the bags and brought them over to the semi. Bill turned back to Frank. "Well, Frank, it looks like this is it."

Bill stepped to his side, placing himself between Frank and the door. He grinned. "All that's left is this." He handed the manila envelope to Frank.

Frank furrowed his brow. "What's this?"

"It's for you. A little parting gift. I wasn't sure if I'd see you much after this."

"Oh, Billy boy, you shouldn't have."

"Think nothing of it. It's only a little token of gratitude. I wanted to show you how fondly I've enjoyed working with you after all these years."

"Billy, you just got me a fucking car! You shouldn't be giving me more gifts!"

Bill scoffed. "Oh, that's just business." He tapped the folder Frank held out in front of him. "This, my friend, this is personal. This is from the heart."

Frank thought he registered an edge to Bill's voice but pushed it aside. Bill's warm eyes and shining teeth were disarming, and Frank opened the envelope.

"You're a good guy, you know that, Billy?" He pinched his cheek like he'd done a hundred times. Bill hated it.

"You always call me Billy, Frank," Bill said. "Even when I've explained I prefer Bill."

"Ah, I'm sorry. I'm a creature of habit. It won't happen again, okay?" Frank opened the folder and pulled out its contents. They were eight-by-ten glossy, black-and-white photographs. Frank's face went cold.

"Bill," he said, his head shaking. "What is this?"

"Why don't you recognize it, Frank?" Bill said, his face still shining. "That's you and my wife, isn't it? You and Karen. They're lovely photographs, don't you think? I'm partial to this one, the one with Karen on her knees. The use of shadows is exquisite."

Frank swallowed. "Look, Bill, I don't know who gave these to you, but I swear to God—"

Before Frank could finish, a bullet exploded through his back and out his stomach.

The blood sprayed on Bill's face as Frank collapsed, dropping the photographs and clutching his abdomen.

Ezra stepped forward, pistol in hand. Bill took out his handkerchief from his back pocket—the one with his initials emblazoned in gold stitching—and calmly wiped Frank's speckled blood off his face. Frank shrieked profanities.

"That almost went through him and hit me," Bill grumbled at Ezra.

"Sorry."

He wiped his face clean and placed the handkerchief back in his pocket. He examined his shirt, which was also splattered with blood that had previously resided inside Frank Buccinello's torso. He shook his head, dismayed.

He looked down at Frank, writhing in pain. "Where were we, Frank?" Frank clutched his abdomen and screamed, choking for air in between squeals. "Ah, yes," Bill said, kneeling. "You were making a declaration, a promise guaranteed in the name of God."

Frank coughed blood.

"Bill, I swear to God…" He coughed more blood. It was beginning to pool under him.

"I wouldn't be so cavalier about using his name right now, Frank," Bill said. "In a few moments, you will be meeting him, so I wouldn't blaspheme. That's what you were about to do, no? Lie?"

Frank propped himself up on his elbow and did his best to slide backward, toward the door. "You're fucking crazy!" he did his best to shout. "You'll burn for this! They'll peel your fucking skin off!" He slid backward more. He left a trail of blood as he crawled.

Bill stood up and looked down at Frank, disappointed. He clasped his hands behind his back and stepped toward Frank, following the crawling, dying man. His voice was steady and flat.

"Don't take this personally, Frank, but I never enjoyed your company," Bill said. Frank coughed blood. He turned onto his stomach and did his best to crawl faster, but his hands were slick with blood, and they slipped on the concrete floor.

"I never found your cute little Jewish and Irish jokes that funny, your manners are appalling, and your overall personality is, to be honest, disgusting."

Frank crawled. Bill followed.

"Now, of course, I'm used to this kind of ribbing for the most part. I'm able to turn the other cheek—for you especially, considering how well you paid for my services. But as you seem always to do, you overstepped your boundaries. You were greedy, and, worst of all, you were careless."

Frank pushed himself to all fours and vomited blood. Bill grimaced, pulling out his handkerchief again and bringing it to his nose. Frank dropped and rolled himself onto his back. His eyes darted back and forth on the ceiling. Bill held out his hand. Ezra gave him the gun. Bill leaned down over Frank's face.

"Frank, please, stay with me for a moment," he said, snapping his fingers. Frank's eyes moved to Bill's face. Recognition came over them. They became furious.

"There we are," Bill said. He held the gun in both his hands, his elbows resting on his crouched knees. "Frank, I need you to understand your situation and why this is happening."

Frank tried to shout but only more blood came out.

"Refrain from caterwauling for a moment, please. You know I'm not some bloodthirsty murderer, out for vengeance for an insignificant slight. To be honest, I find the whole ordeal of murder *unseemly*. I don't like to perform such acts unless necessary."

Bill clutched Frank's face.

"Look at me, Frank. You're going to die here. You will die on this filthy, cold, concrete floor in this run-down, empty warehouse, surrounded by no one except your enemies." He saw fear replace the wrath in Frank's eyes. "I need you to understand why it has come to this, Frank. You must understand that this is no one's making but your own."

Bill took a deep breath. His eyes darted around, then back to Frank.

"You crossed the line, Frank. You defiled my wife and my marriage. Not only is your death your fault but hers as well. Karen was a lovely woman. I will miss her."

Bill leaned in closer and lowered his voice to a whisper.

"Your wife will be a widow. Your children will be fatherless. Your brothers and mother will bury you in a closed casket. Do you know why?"

Bill waited as if Frank had any capability of answering.

"Because it will be days before they find you, Frank. We'll discard your corpse in the back, like any other trash—out of sight but exposed, so the sun and rain can get to you. Your carcass will be a bloated, disgusting mess. The animals will come for you. Maybe the birds will even peck out your eyes. Wouldn't that be something?"

Frank tried to take deep breaths, but he only ended up inhaling his blood. Bill gently patted his chest.

"I want you to think about that right now, Frank," Bill said. "I want your final thoughts to be of your body wasting away in the hot Florida sun while I take your precious car, the one your daddy would have loved, and live out the rest of my life in utter bliss. Please, think about that now, Frank."

Bill dropped Frank's head. It landed on the floor with a loud *thud*. He stood up and pointed the pistol at his body and pulled the trigger. He pulled it again and again until the magazine was empty and all that came out was a click.

Bill took a deep breath. Ezra came over and handed him another handkerchief. Bill wiped the pistol before dropping it on what remained of Frank Buccinello.

"What do you want to do with him?" Ezra said.

"Brother, you know I don't like repeating myself," Bill said, still standing over the remains of Frank. "Bring him out back for nature to do its part."

"You want to just leave him here?"

"We'll be gone by the time they find him—if they do at all."

"Bill, you know I'm always with you, but this is a lot. This might be too much."

Bill looked at his brother like they were in grade school again and he was asking silly questions about girls.

"You worry too much, Ezra," he said. "Angelo and Little Henry may be brothers, but they hate each other. With Frank gone, those knuckle-dragging morons will go to war over who takes his crown. They won't have time for us. They won't even know it was us. Even if they do, by the time the war is over, their organization will be a shell of itself. Their competition will finish them off for us. Did you bring what I asked?"

Ezra reached into his jacket pocket and pulled out another envelope. "Yeah, I got it all here." Ezra handed him the envelope. "It's all in there: passport, driver's license, social security card—everything. What about the car?"

"Seriously, Ezra, you must work on your listening. It's coming with me."

"Okay."

Bill opened the envelope and skimmed through its contents. He picked out the driver's license and held it up, examining it in the light. "Huh—George Collins."

"What? You don't like the name?"

"No, it's quite all right. It'll just take some getting used to, I suppose. What's your name?"

"Stephen Thompson."

"A nice name. Where are you heading after dropping off the car?"

"Canada. Maybe even Alaska. I've always wanted to see it."

"I'm sure it's lovely. A shame we won't be brothers in our next lives. You'll visit though, right?"

"Of course. Your plane tickets for the morning are in there. I guess I'll get this thing on the road right away. Where should I take it?"

"Meet me in Milwaukee. Call me when you're a few hours away."

Ezra agreed, and Bill closed the folder and slapped it with his hand. "Excellent." He put his arms around Ezra and hugged him. "Drive safe, brother. When I see you, it'll be in Wisconsin."

They broke off their embrace, and Bill turned to leave out the front door where his car waited for him. Ezra went about cleaning his brother's mess, as he always seemed to do. He moved the body. He made sure nothing was left behind that could be traced to them. He drove the 1948 Talbot-Lago back onto the semi. He hopped into the cab and mentally prepared himself for the twenty-three-hour drive and started the engine. In ten minutes, Bill—now George—and Ezra—now Stephen—were gone.

All that remained was the corpse of Frank Buccinello.

13

Twenty-One Days from the Night

"Nice ride," Nick lied from the passenger seat of Kimi's car. He scanned the interior with its stained upholstery and cheap plastic.

"Thanks," Kimi said.

"So they're meeting us there?"

"Yeah, Lana said Richie's going to pick her up when she gets off from her shift, but they'll probably be a little late, so we should go there now to make sure we keep our reservation."

"Do we need a reservation?"

"The Friday night fish boil is supposed to be a big deal there. It gets slammed."

Nick reached into his pocket and pulled out a tin case. He opened it and pulled out a joint. He ran it lengthwise under his nostrils, breathing in its aroma. "You wanna work up an appetite?" he asked, holding it on display. "Rolled them this morning."

"Do you carry around your little stash of weed everywhere you go?"

"Never know when the opportunity may arise. Come on, you're not working tomorrow." Nick lit up. He puffed on it twice before passing it to Kimi. She reluctantly took it. She exhaled, billowing clouds into the car. She coughed vociferously—wet, chunky coughs.

"Uh-oh," Nick said, retrieving the joint. "We got some virgin lungs over here."

"Shut up," Kimi said between coughs. "It's been a while."

"Sorry, I don't have any coke for you this evening."

"I don't do that anymore."

"You quit?"

"The last time I did it, I almost wound up in jail for robbing a house, so, yeah, I thought it might be time to kick the habit."

They smoked and listened to the radio for the rest of the drive. Nick held the joint up to Kimi's lips so she could smoke while keeping her hands on the wheel and eyes on the road. They said nothing, allowing the music to fill the silence.

*****

Kimi stared at the waitress as if she'd spoken a different language to her. Nick could see her cognizance dulling—her mouth agape as the gears in her head turned.

"Yes," she finally said to the waitress, a middle-aged woman with graying brown hair and a dirty apron. She held a pen to her notepad and waited.

"What would you *like* to drink?" she said in a politely impatient tone.

Kimi dropped her eyes to the drink menu she held. Nick could see her eyes daunted by the choices. "She likes wine. Just bring us a bottle. A white, whatever your favorite is," Nick jumped in. The waitress turned to Nick, almost startled that there was someone else at the table. She jotted into her notepad and left. Kimi exhaled like she'd been holding her breath.

"You okay, Cheech?" Nick asked.

"Yeah, yeah, I'm fine. Sorry, I'm fine," Kimi said, rubbing her eyes. "I get spacey when I smoke. I feel like a million thoughts come into my head, and I can't focus on any one thing. Like, when she asked me if I wanted something to drink, I couldn't decide if I wanted a beer, a cocktail, or wine or maybe even water, and then I thought that I was taking too long to decide, and she noticed and thought I was crazy or on drugs, and then when I looked at her, I could only see that big mole on her forehead, and I wondered if she knows how distracting that mole is, and I thought, of course she does—it's on her face—and on and on and on."

Nick had also noticed the mole and agreed it was captivating.

"God, did I embarrass myself? Did I look stupid?"

"You're fine, relax," Nick said.

Nick fanned himself. They sat outside at a table on the edge of the Waterfront's seating area. It was sticky warm, a thick humidity blanketing everyone.

Kimi removed her cropped camo jacket to reveal a red, white, and blue tank top underneath. She closed her eyes and began to take deep breaths, her chest swelling and depressing as her lungs filled with air. Nick watched for a moment before averting his eyes when he realized he was staring.

She opened her eyes.

"Better?" Nick asked.

"Much." She looked around like she was seeing the Waterfront for the first time. She looked at the wooden deck and all the other tables surrounding them. There was hardly a single open table.

To their right, thirty feet of dying grass led to a sand beach looking out at the bay where the sun was taking its time setting. On the beach was what looked like a giant stone cauldron, encircled by burning logs.

"So that's the boil, then?" Kimi said, gesturing to the large pot sitting on the beach. A man sweating through a T-shirt tended to it, dropping more logs around the stone kettle, fanning the fire.

"Yeah," Nick said. "If I remember right, they bring it to a boil, add some potatoes and onions and whatever, then throw in the fish. And that's it. You've never been to one?"

She shook her head. "Been to plenty of fish fries, never a fish boil."

Her eyes lingered on the flaming logs and giant kettle. They watched as another man joined the fire tender next to the kettle. He was chubbier and had a goatee and also was sweating through his shirt, a red University of Wisconsin T-shirt. He held a tub filled with ice and what looked like fish. He dropped it on the ground, and the two chatted, occasionally peeking into the kettle between words.

Kimi's phone rang. The sudden noise made her jump in her seat. She fumbled through her purse before coming up with it. "It's Lana," she said before flipping it open.

The waitress appeared as she answered, holding two wine glasses in one hand and a bottle in the other. She turned to Nick, lowering her voice.

"Would you like to try it first? I think it's good, but I don't want you to buy an entire bottle of something you don't like, right?" she said, putting down one glass and pouring a small tasting into it. Nick took the glass and drank it in one gulp.

Nick didn't have the taste buds for or interest in judging wine, but he could feel the anxious eyes of the waitress on him. She wanted him to be ecstatic, enthralled by the wine, as if she'd stomped the grapes and bottled it herself. Nick gave her a flat smile.

She poured the wine into Kimi's glass with a hint of disappointment. Nick thanked her, and she left. When she left, Kimi closed her phone and returned it to her purse.

"She said we should go ahead and eat because they're going to be pretty late." She saw the glass of wine in front of her like a desert traveler spotting a lush oasis. She grabbed it and took two deep gulps. "Damn, that's good. My mouth is so dry."

"They're still going to be awhile?" Nick asked.

"Correct. Oh, look! They're putting the fish in!" she said, pointing to the beach as the two men dropped the fish into the boiling cauldron. She took another sip of wine. Nick drank his.

Kimi turned back to Nick. She sighed. "I don't want to keep up this charade all night. I'm too high for it. They're not coming and never were. It was always just going to be you and me."

Nick raised his eyebrows.

"Don't get too excited. It was a favor for Lana."

"A favor?"

"Yeah, she just wanted a little privacy for her and Richie. They haven't had a night alone together since you moved in." She put her wine glass down and fanned her sweating neck and chest.

Nick huffed. "She could have just asked me to leave them alone. I would've understood. Could've just gone to the Walleye and got drunk by myself."

"Maybe that's what she was worried about."

"What's wrong with that?"

"Wanted to make sure you wouldn't get in any trouble."

"So you're my babysitter for the night?"

Kimi took another sip of her wine. "Don't be so pissy! You're on a date with a dime-piece like me and you didn't even have to do anything."

"So this is a date, then?"

"Not really. I mean, you're not getting lucky tonight, sorry to tell you. If you want to, you can pretend it's a date. I won't stop you."

Nick shook his head, and Kimi giggled, snorting a little bit as she did. They turned their attention back to the beach. There was a commotion behind them as people began to gather around the railing to get a better look.

"What's happening?" Kimi asked, craning her neck to see the flaming kettle on the beach as the two sweaty men encircled it.

"I think they're about to throw the kerosene on," Nick said.

"Kerosene?"

"When the fish are about done, they throw kerosene on the fire to get the fish oils to boil over. Makes a huge flame, it's a whole big thing—kind of the grand finale of the boil."

They trained their eyes on the kettle, which now had a thick layer of bubbling foam on top of it. The first sweaty man approached the fire with a red cup. He tossed the liquid at the base of the kettle and its burning logs. The fire burst, exploding into the air in a furious blaze. The two men drifted back, shielding their faces with their arms. Even thirty feet away, Nick and Kimi could feel a gust of hot air whoosh over them.

They could see the foam spill over the cauldron and onto the ground. A few seconds after the inferno erupted, it returned to its crackling state. The crowd oohed and aahed at the combustion. The audience applauded.

"Huh," Kimi mused as she watched the two men on the beach slide a long metal pole through the two rings attached to the top of the kettle. They gingerly hoisted it up and away from the logs and toward the side of the restaurant, taking small, hurried steps to keep from tipping the boiler.

The two dropped into silence. Kimi's eyes still looked like they were in a trance. When she picked up her wine to drink, she gripped it like it could leap out of her hand at any moment.

She put the wine down and looked around again. She turned back to Nick, looking at him from behind her sunglasses. "So it's almost the big day. What is it now, three weeks from today?"

"Uh-huh."

"Everything looks good? On track?"

"Mhmm."

"Are you getting nervous?"

Nick picked up his glass and swirled the white wine inside it. He didn't care for it. It was tolerable but too sweet for his liking. "Not at all."

"Ooh, Mr. Cool Guy."

"You get used to it. After you do this kind of thing for a while, it's only another job. Clock in, do what you gotta do, and clock out." He looked west. "Weather guy said we'd get a big storm later tonight. But I don't see any clouds."

"So this is what you do? I mean, for money. You always do this kind of stuff?"

Nick tightened his lips. "More or less."

"How does someone get into that line of work?"

"Why, you thinking of a career change?"

"No. Although for what I get paid, it doesn't sound too bad. I'm just curious."

Nick grabbed the bottle and poured himself another glass of mediocre white wine. He looked at the bottle: a Riesling from a local winery.

"How does anyone get into any career?" Nick sipped. "You meet some people, you start doing work, and next thing you know you've been doing it for years and now you don't know how to do anything else."

"So what'd you do? Hold up banks with a gun and a mask like you were some cowboy?"

Nick shook his head. "There was a little of that in the beginning. But banks are tricky. A lot of security, a lot of cops, and a lot of heat. You can get a whole task force dedicated to bringing you down if you do it too much."

"Okay, not banks. What then?"

"Houses. Mansions. Cars."

"You robbed houses?"

"The right houses. The ones that got jewelry sitting around and a safe with some cash in it. Sometimes, you can rip more off a house than a bank."

"That's hard to believe."

"If you know what you're looking for and stay smart. Houses aren't like banks. They got some security systems and all that, but there's no armed guard by the door. You stake a place out properly; you find its weaknesses; you find out when they're away, on vacation or something; and you can get a nice score with little to no heat."

"So these were families?"

"Some of them. Listen, these weren't working-class Joes and Janes. These were people with vacation homes, yachts, expensive cars—which can also be nice scores."

"So you were like a jewel thief—a cat burglar," Kimi said with a laugh.

"Not what I would call it, but I guess, in a sense."

Kimi's face turned serious. "Do you ever feel bad afterward? Stealing from people?"

"No," he said cavalierly. Kimi raised her eyebrows.

"These people aren't going bankrupt from what we take. Half the time, they don't even realize anything was stolen. They just think they lost it. Even when they do, they got insurance that pays out. Sometimes for more than it was even worth. They don't lose sleep over a necklace worth a few hundred bucks or one watch from the collection that goes missing. Shit, even if it's a car, it just gives them an excuse to buy a new one."

"I guess that's one way to look at it. Very cynical, but one way."

"You disagree."

"It sounds like rationalizing to me."

"Maybe."

Kimi ran her finger around the edges of her wine glass. "Have you ever hurt anyone?"

"What do you think?"

Kimi took a deep breath. "I don't think you like hurting people. You're not a psycho."

"Or I'm good at hiding it."

"But I imagine you had to get your hands dirty at some point. On some job."

Nick looked away and pursed his lips. "You do what you gotta do to survive." He drank his wine.

"You never actually answered my first question."

"There've been so many. What was it?"

"How'd you get started?"

Nick took a deep breath. "I was in LA doing whatever to make a buck. Small-time hustling shit here and there. I met some people." Nick sipped his wine.

"That's it?"

"Basically. You fall in with a crowd, tag along with a crew, and then that's all you do."

Kimi sipped her wine. "Ever get busted?"

"I spent two years in prison, although that wasn't for getting busted."

"What was it for?"

"Fighting a cop. Well, biting a cop, to be more specific."

Kimi laughed. "You *bit* a cop?"

"At least that's what they said. I don't remember. I was pretty fucked up. I denied it, but I'm pretty sure I did it."

"So what about when you got out of prison? Did you go back to your old ways?"

"Nah, not really. I went to Colorado to connect with this guy I knew who could get me a job as a bartender as long as I helped him get his small business off the ground. This was in Boulder. But once I was on my feet, I cut it off with him. Went straight—was just a bartender for a little bit. It was all right."

"Sounds like there's a 'but' coming," Kimi interjected.

"*But* I moved to St. Louis a little after that, and I started to need more money, more cash than a bartender can earn. So I reconnected with some old friends, made some new ones, and got back into the swing of things. We did some good work. Made some good money. It was a fun time. But in that business, it only takes one bad day."

Kimi studied Nick's face. "What happened?"

Nick looked around at the families enjoying their evening, drinking and laughing. Young kids ran around the tables and on the large swath of grass beyond the deck, playing tag and races.

"I'll spare the details. All you need to know is that a job went bad. *Very* bad. And I had to do some things. To survive. For my friends to survive."

Kimi tried to compose her face. "What'd you do?"

"Some people had to die."

Kimi lowered her voice. "You killed someone?"

"I defended myself. It was me or him."

"Jesus," Kimi muttered. She drank her wine. "Who was he?"

"Does it matter?"

"No. I guess not."

Nick smoothed his hair and rubbed his face. "Hard to sleep after that. Hard to do anything. The only time I didn't see his face was when I was high, so that's the only thing I did. I didn't leave my apartment for weeks. Finally, it got to the point that if I didn't leave, I'd blow my brains out. So I came home."

Kimi rubbed her front teeth with her tongue. She thought they felt different than usual. "Shit."

Nick sipped his wine and wondered how long the food would be.

"I thought you said you came home because of this job—that you heard about it from a friend?"

"A friend of mine specialized in stolen cars, and this one was like his white whale. He obsessed over it for years, and he finally found it. Imagine my surprise when he said it was in my hometown. He was putting together a crew to get it. I was the first person he wanted because I knew the place. That was before that night—" He cleared his throat. "He wasn't as lucky as me."

Kimi waited for Nick to continue.

The waitress with a dirty apron and middling taste in wine appeared at the table. "How are we doing here?" she asked. Kimi, frustrated at the interruption, told her they were fine curtly. "Okay, well, the buffet is ready, so make sure you get up there and get some good fish while it's hot!" Kimi shooed her away and waited for Nick to continue.

"I'm starving," he said, stepping up from his chair. Kimi frowned but followed. They entered the buffet line, which already stretched around the entire deck.

At the buffet, they each grabbed freshly boiled Lake Michigan whitefish, steam still rising from it. They took generous portions along with potatoes, onions, lemon wedges, coleslaw, rye bread, and a slice of Door County cherry pie for dessert.

Back at the table, Nick prepared his meal, squirting lemon juice over the whitefish and spreading the butter on his potatoes and bread to melt and soften. Kimi did the same, but she moved at a more deliberate pace. She looked distracted, Nick noticed, like her mind was still turning over the details of Nick's story.

She looked at Nick before taking her first bite. "*Itadakimasu!*" she said, chomping into the fish.

Nick laughed. "What's that?"

"It's just a Japanese thing you say before eating. My mom would always say it. *Itadakimasu!*"

"What's it mean?"

She thought for a moment and stabbed her fork into her lettuce. "Literal translation is, 'I humbly receive.' It's like bon appétit.

"Ah," Nick said, biting into the whitefish. "So you speak Japanese, then?"

Kimi wavered. "Mostly with my mom. But she always tells me it's not so good. If I ever went to Japan, they'd probably notice or know I'm not from Japan, you know?"

"Have you ever been to the motherland?"

"Have you ever been to—wherever the fuck your family's from? Ireland or whatever."

Nick laughed. "No, but I have no idea where our family's from. You, at least, have a mom that was born there, right?"

"Yeah."

"So have you been to Japan?"

"No. I never really wanted to, or had the money, for that matter."

"What about family on your mom's side? Are there any still back in Japan?"

"Well, yes. My mom has—or *had*—a whole family, but they were pretty pissed she married an American, a soldier no less, and left with him to America. They kind of disowned her. At least, that's what I think happened. She doesn't talk about it."

"Damn, that sucks. I'm sorry," Nick said.

"Don't worry about it. I never got the feeling she wanted to go back—my mom. I think she always wanted to leave."

"I get that."

"It's funny, my dad would speak better of Japan than my mom. He loved talking about his time there. She barely ever did."

"I think that makes sense. That's where he met your mom, fell in love, and all that."

"True. It's funny how that works. My American dad has nothing but good memories, and my *Nihonjin* mom barely ever talks about it."

"*Nihonjin?*"

"Japanese word for Japanese."

"Ah." Nick scooped into his baked potato. "So Lana speaks French and you speak *Nihonjin*. I'm starting to feel dumb around you guys."

"It's actually *Nihongo*, the Japanese word for the language, that is. *Nihonjin* is the word for its people. But, yeah, quite cultural, aren't we? I've been trying to teach Lana bits of *Nihongo*, and she's doing the same with me for French. She's gotten pretty good, mostly phrases and slang. Better than I am with French."

"Can you teach me some?"

"Like what?"

"Anything. Something to impress people at dinner parties."

Kimi pondered, looking in the sky as she chewed. "Well, you know *itadakimasu* already—and *Nihongo* and *Nihonjin*. Let's see. Oh! A good slang one that you can use all the time is *yabai*."

"*Ya-bai*," Nick repeated, sounding it out. "What's it mean?"

"It used to mean 'bad' or 'dangerous,' but it's kind of taken on a different slang meaning. It's a bit of a catch-all. It can still mean 'awful,' but it can also mean 'beautiful' or 'delicious.' You have to figure it out from the context. It's kind of hard to explain, now that I think about it."

"Huh. *Yabai*."

"That's probably not a good one. But say, for instance, if I liked the food, I could say, 'This food is so good. Really *yabai*.' Or if you didn't like it, you could be like, 'Ugh, this fish is *yabai*.'"

"Well, for the record, I do think this fish is really good, very *yabai*."

"It's one of those slang words that if you say it all the time, older people will think you're an idiot."

"When I'm in Japan next time, I'll keep that in mind." He bit into his fish. "How about some phrases?"

Kimi tore a bite out of her bread. "Well, now you can accurately say: *Sukoshi Nihongo wo hanashimasu*." Nick sipped of wine and parroted the phrase back. Kimi repeated it multiple times to help him.

"What's it mean?"

"I speak a little Japanese."

They both laughed. Nick bit into his rye bread. "So you've got a Japanese mom and a Wisconsin dad. That must have been an interesting childhood."

Kimi drank her wine. "I guess. My mom's not that different from other moms, I think. She has her little cultural customs and traditions she passes onto us, but she's like any other protective mom, I think."

"Growing up around here must have been quite…different."

"What do you mean?"

"I grew up here too, Kimi. In high school, I could count the number of minority students on one hand. In the whole school, not just my class."

Kimi shrugged. "Yeah, you get used to it. Actually, you don't. I don't know why I said that."

"You put up with a lot of shit?"

"You know how kids are, especially teenage guys. Yeah, I heard some shit."

"Sorry."

"It really wasn't *that* bad. I heard 'chink' a few times, but it was mostly dumb jokes. Everyone would assume I was the best math student or that my parents were forcing me to be a doctor."

"I guess they weren't far off."

"I guess, but my mom was never like that. She wanted me to do well in school and was tough sometimes, but she wasn't the tiger mom you always see in movies or TV."

"What about your dad? Goes to Japan to serve and comes back with a wife? Sounds like an interesting guy."

She smiled. "He is. He's the funniest guy I've ever met. That's how he got my mom—he made her laugh even when she barely understood English."

Nick smiled, and they went back to quietly eating for a few moments.

"Ah, I just remembered what I've been meaning to ask you. Is Kimi a Japanese name or is it short for Kimberly?"

"It's Japanese. The story goes that before my older brother was born, they couldn't decide whether to give him an American or Japanese name—you can figure out which side wanted which. So they came to a compromise: Dad got to come up with first names for the boys. Mom got first names for the girls. And they switched when it came to middle names. That's why my brother's name is John Kazukia Roberts."

"Seems fair. What's your full name?"

"Kimi Elizabeth Roberts."

"Very pretty. Kudos to your parents. Does it mean anything?"

"It means 'beautiful story' in Japanese."

"That fits."

Kimi rolled her eyes. "What about you? What's your middle name?"

Nick dropped his eyes to his food. "Eh, just Craig. Nothing special."

Kimi drank her wine. They fell into a comfortable silence. They listened to the idle chatter of the patrons around them, the wind against the trees, and the crashing crests on the beach. Nick poured more wine for both of them.

Kimi finished her meal, licking her fork clean of the glaze left-over from the cherry pie. She put it down and drank her fresh glass of wine. She eyed Nick as he ate, rubbing her tongue against her cheek. She tilted her head and looked at the sky like she'd just remembered something.

"What about the girl?" she asked.

"What?"

"The girl. The one you moved to St. Louis with."

He frowned. "I don't know what you're talking about."

"Oh my god. There is a girl!"

Nick's face twisted.

"I was goofing around, but there really was one! Look at you. You're blushing!"

"Shut up," Nick muttered from behind his wine glass.

Kimi leaned forward, resting her elbows on the table, staring at Nick as he looked anywhere but her eyes, her white teeth beaming at him.

"She must have been pretty special to move from Colorado to St. Louis for."

"I'm a hopeless romantic, so what? What's wrong with that?" Nick said. He bit into his pie.

"Nothing at all," Kimi said, her face still gleaming as she leaned back in her chair. "So what was she like? Was she pretty?"

Nick thought for a moment. "You remind me of her. I mean, she wasn't half-Japanese, but still."

"Well, she must have been gorgeous. So what happened? Where is she now?"

"Still in St. Louis."

"And...?"

"And what?"

"Did you two break up? Did you just dump her on your way out of town?"

"We reached our expiration date."

"She dumped you, didn't she?"

"Kicked me to the curb."

"Can't say I blame her after what you just told me."

"I couldn't either."

Kimi sipped her wine. She licked her lips. "Did you love her?"

"I think this is getting a little too personal."

"Oh, come on. You'll tell me about all the crimes you committed but you won't tell me about the girl you loved?"

Nick bit into the last piece of his pie. The crust crunched in his mouth and the cherries squished, releasing more juices. "All right. Yeah, I did."

"Aww."

"What about you?"

"Did I love her? No, I can't say I did."

"What about your ex-boyfriend Richie was telling me about? What was his name?"

"James."

"What about him?"

Kimi looked at the beach. "No, I don't think so."

"Why not?"

"I don't know."

"Yes, you do."

Kimi looked out at the bay. "He was one of those guys, you know? Handsome, good job, really nice, good family, ready to settle down."

"Sounds like a catch."

"He was. He is. He's just so"—Kimi collected her breath—"fucking boring."

Nick nearly snorted wine out his nose.

"That sounds mean, doesn't it?" Kimi said.

"Hey, sometimes the truth is."

Nick took out his pack of cigarettes and lighter. He offered one to Kimi. She took it. Nick lit hers before lighting his own. She leaned her head back and exhaled. She looked around and then back at Nick.

"I had to end things before he proposed, which I knew he was about to do. That would've made things worse."

"Well, at least you gave him that mercy. How long did you two date?"

"About two years," she said with a wince.

"Well, better than twenty years from now with a divorce and a kid."

"I guess."

"Besides, it was probably the best two years of his life."

"Enough with the sweet talk, buddy. I see what you're doing."

"What am I doing?"

"Getting me to talk about this stuff, making me feel vulnerable so that you can come in with your crooked smile and soft words. Not to mention all this wine."

Her words were beginning to slur together, and her movements were loose, abrupt. Nick blinked his eyes and realized he was feeling the same way.

The waitress appeared again. "How was everything, guys?" Nick and Kimi sang their praises of the fish and pie. The waitress eagerly accepted them as if she'd caught, filleted, and cooked the fish herself. She asked if she could get them anything else as she took their plates. They assured her she couldn't and that they'd simply take the bill.

"It's too hot to smoke," Kimi said, putting out her cigarette. She looked around and took a deep breath before turning back to Nick. "So you're not nervous at all about the thing?"

"I already told you, no. Sounds like you are though."

Kimi leaned her elbows on the table. "Maybe a little. Sorry, I'm not some hardened criminal like you."

"Ouch," Nick said. "Don't worry, you'll be fine. I promise. You know what you're gonna wear?"

"A dress I wore to a wedding last summer. I've been looking for an excuse to wear it again. Never thought it'd be for a situation like this. What about you?"

"I picked out a very nice tuxedo the other day. I think you'll like it."

"It better be nice if I'm gonna be on your arm. I have standards in this town to live up to."

"I'll do my best. Do you know what you're gonna do with your money? I mean, besides take care of the problems you mentioned before?"

"I don't know," she said, running her finger over the rim of her wine glass.

Nick ashed his cigarette. "You know, they're going to leave here when it's all done. Lana and Richie."

"Yeah, I figured," Kimi said, dejected.

"You okay with that?"

"Fuck no! It's gonna suck, living here, working here without her."

Nick laughed. "I'm sorry about that. But a million dollars is a lot of money. You can go somewhere else, start fresh."

"Yeah, maybe. I could use a fresh start."

"Don't we all."

The waitress finally appeared with the check. Nick took out his wallet and dropped cash on the table. He checked his watch.

"What about you?" Kimi asked. "What're you gonna do with your cut?"

"Well, I assumed you and me would run away together." She laughed. Nick looked around. "It's still pretty early in the night. We should give Richie and Lana some more alone time. Wanna go to the Walleye for a nightcap?"

Kimi looked at the beach and bit her lip.

"Sure, we could do that," she said. "Or we could go back to my place and open another bottle of wine. My roommate's gone for the weekend, so we'll have the place to ourselves. We can drink and hang out, watch a movie or something."

Nick weighed the idea in his head. "If I didn't know any better, I'd say you were trying to get me to go home with you."

Kimi rolled her eyes. "Come on, don't make this hard."

Nick thought about a joke but bit his tongue. "You've had a lot of wine. We both have."

"So? We're two attractive, drunk people. Sex is a natural conclusion."

"That is a good point."

"What's the matter? You don't want to? Something wrong with me?"

"It's not that," Nick took another drag. "I don't want things to get weird, you know? You're friends with Lana. We see each other all the time. We're working together now."

Kimi huffed. "We're not getting married here. It's one night, hanging out, nothing more." Kimi looked at her watch. "I'm sure Lana and Richie would enjoy having their house to themselves for the night."

"That would be the courteous thing to do."

"Well?"

Nick ashed his cigarette. "At the very least, I can make sure you get home all right."

"I knew you were a gentleman."

They got up from the table and left the Waterfront. Nick called a cab as they walked to the parking lot with Kimi under his shoulder and her arm around his waist.

"This is a pretty fun night. A *yabai* night," Nick said. "I use that right?"

"I don't know. I'm too drunk."

14

Twenty Days from the Night

Thunder roared through the Morgan home and snapped Richie and Lana awake like a hail of gunfire ripping through their bedroom. Their eyes shot open, staring at each other for a moment.

"Jesus," Richie muttered.

Lana breathed heavily, the shock of the thunder and sudden wake still gripping her as if she'd woken from a nightmare. After a few seconds, she started to laugh. Richie did too.

"Quite the storm," Lana said, still lying on her stomach under the covers, naked from the night before. Richie agreed. He lay on his back and propped his hand behind his pillow. He stared at the ceiling and watched flashes from lightning dance shadows across it. Lana slid closer to him and rested her head on his broad chest.

"What time is it?" she said.

Richie draped his arm around her shoulders and glanced at the digital clock next to the bed. "Almost nine."

"I can't remember the last time we had a morning like this. Where neither of us had to get up early or go anywhere, where we could just sleep in, together."

"Me neither."

She closed her eyes and listened to the rain on the window. "Did you hear Nick come in last night?"

"I don't think so. I was a little distracted though."

She reached up and flicked his nose.

"Ow."

"I'm glad you took the morning off," she said.

178

"No one's fishing in a thunderstorm, right?"

She smiled. She started to get up.

"Where are you going?" Richie said, grabbing her arm.

"I'm gonna make some coffee. I'll be right back."

"Come on, stay here," Richie said, holding on.

She laughed and wrenched her wrist away. "I will be right back. I promise." She stood and threw on a robe before opening the door. She looked back before walking into the hallway. "Don't move."

Lana tiptoed down the hallway. She stopped by the guest room, Nick's room. The door was open a crack and she peeked through. No Nick. She opened it wider to confirm he wasn't there.

"Hmm."

She stepped into the kitchen and started the coffee. She stared out the window at the steady rain as it brewed next to her. She stepped toward the living room mirror. Her hair was a nest.

She returned to the bedroom with two steaming mugs. Their bedroom remained in darkness from the storm, as if the day hadn't started. Richie propped himself up against the bed's headboard. "There she is." Lana handed him his coffee and sat on the edge of the bed near his knees. "Thank you."

"You're welcome." They sat in silence for a while, drinking their coffee and listening to the rain and thunder.

"So," Lana said. "You think Nick spent the night at Kimi's?"

"Maybe. I hope so."

"You hope so?"

"Otherwise he's probably in jail or passed out in a ditch somewhere, so yeah, the best hope is he stayed the night at Kimi's."

Lana slapped him in the arm. "You're hard on him."

"I know him."

"Uh-huh. Do you think they've done it before? Like behind our backs?"

Richie sipped his coffee. "I don't know. Does Kimi even like him like that?"

"Yeah! Are you blind?"

"I don't know."

"Obvious to me."

"You think she wants to hook up with him?"

"Yeah."

"How do you know?"

"She's said so."

"Oh. Why?"

"Are you kidding?"

Richie sipped his coffee. "No…"

"Nick's a good-looking guy."

"You think so?"

"I mean, yeah. He's got nice long hair, a good beard, skinny, and tall enough. He's got the whole bad boy vibe. Some girls like that."

"All right, I get it."

"Aw, are you jealous?"

"No."

"I think you are," she said, needling him in the ribs.

"Stop it, come on. I got coffee here!"

Lana laughed. Richie did too despite trying to look angry. They stopped when they heard the front door open.

"Ope, speak of the devil," Lana said.

"I guess it was nice while it lasted," Richie grumbled.

Lana patted his leg. "I'm hungry, so I might as well make some breakfast," she said, standing up.

"All right," Richie said. "Hey, put something on before you go out there."

Lana looked at the robe she was wearing. "I am wearing something."

"I mean, it's only a robe. It's not really—"

"Are you serious?" Lana said with a laugh. "I mention that your brother's handsome and now you don't want me walking around in a robe in my own house?"

"I'm just saying…"

"Come on, Richie, have a little faith," she said, leaving the bedroom. She walked down the hallway and into the living room to see Nick in the kitchen, grabbing some coffee. "Good morning!"

Nick looked up as he poured into a mug. "Hey, morning. This coffee's good, right?"

"Yup, just brewed it."

"Perfect."

Lana walked into the kitchen. "Long night?"

"A little too much wine."

"Ah." She opened the fridge. "I'm gonna make some breakfast. You like breakfast burritos?"

"Oh, Lana, you are a saint."

"It'll probably be about twenty minutes."

"No problem." Nick looked out the window. "Helluva storm out there."

"I know," Lana said, pulling out burrito fixings from the fridge. "The thunder this morning woke Richie and me up. I don't know if I've ever heard it so loud. Must be close."

Nick picked up his coffee and went toward the door to the garage. "I'll be in the garage."

Lana frowned and watched him open the door into the garage. She heard the garage stall door open. "Huh," she muttered to himself.

Richie appeared in a white T-shirt and boxer shorts with his cup of coffee.

"He wakes," Lana said. Richie rubbed his eyes as he entered.

"Where's Nick?"

"In the garage."

"The garage?"

"Mhmm."

"What's he doing?" She shrugged. Richie thought for a moment. "Ah, I bet I know." He walked to the door.

"Breakfast is ready in twenty," Lana shouted after him.

Richie stepped into the garage to find his brother sitting in a folding chair, looking out into the waterfall of rain pounding the gravel and grass through the open stall.

"Well, look at this," Richie said.

Nick turned. "Hey, morning, champ."

Richie grabbed another folding chair from the wall and brought it over to Nick. "This looks familiar," he said. He folded the chair and sat down with his coffee. "Remember we used to always do this with Dad?"

"Yeah. I was thinking about drinking beer with him, in the garage, watching a storm like this."

"I had my first beer with him doing that."

"Really? When?"

Richie sipped his coffee and thought. "I was fourteen, so it must have been the summer of ninety-three? I think."

"Where was I?"

"I don't know. Inside, I guess. When was yours?"

"I was seventeen, and it was at the Walleye. Remember, Mom sent me to pick him and Uncle Luke up, and they bought me a beer."

Richie smiled, and the brothers sipped their coffee and watched the storm as thunder rolled.

"So how was your guys' night?" Nick asked.

"Good. We grabbed some dinner at the Mariner. You remember that place? It was nice. Went to the Walleye afterward, had a few drinks. Yeah, it was pretty good."

"Good."

"What about you? You have fun on your date?"

Nick looked sideways at his brother. "We did, but not in the way you're referring to."

"Nothing happened?"

"Nothing. We had dinner and a lot of wine. We went back to her place, drank some more, smoked a little, and I passed out on the couch."

"Hmm. Did she want to?

"Yeah, I think so."

"But you didn't."

"It'd just complicate things. Sex. Especially with Lana's best friend and a *colleague* of ours now. We don't need that kind of shit right now. Better to stay focused."

"That's very professional of you."

"I know. I hate it."

"Well, I'm impressed you had the willpower."

"It wasn't fucking easy, I'll tell you that."

"I can imagine."

"I'll probably need to take a timeout to my bedroom to release some tension."

"Okay, I don't need to hear that."

"Excuse me, not all of us have a hot wife ready to go every night. I'm just across the hall, and your walls are pretty thin."

"It's not every night."

"Almost."

"All right, I regret bringing it up."

Nick chuckled, and they went back to watching the storm. Richie drank his coffee. Nick rubbed his temples, trying to relieve his headache.

They heard a door open. Lana entered the dark garage, still wearing her robe and slippers and carrying her steaming cup of coffee.

"Hey, how are we doing out here?"

"Just fine, darling," Nick said. Richie smacked his leg. "What?"

"Breakfast will be ready soon."

"Thanks, hon," Richie said.

Lana stood behind Richie and rubbed his shoulder and watched the rain with them.

"So, Nick, how was your night?" she said.

"You're too late. Your husband just got done interrogating me."

"I did not."

"I'm just curious. What'd you do after dinner?"

"Went back to her place and drank some more. A lot, actually. I passed out."

"Where'd you pass out?"

"On the couch."

"Alone?"

"Yes, Lana, alone. I slept on the couch. She slept in her bed."

"Hmm." She stared at the rain.

"Is there something you'd like to say?" Nick said.

"I guess I'm a little disappointed."

"How's that?"

"Well, I'm proud of Kimi for resisting your charms. No offense, Nick, but Kimi deserves a more serious man."

"No, none taken. Why would I take offense to that?"

Lana socked him in the shoulder. "Still, it would have been cool if Kimi and I were sisters-in-law."

Nick guffawed. "What, you thought we'd hook up, and at breakfast I'd get down on one knee?"

"No, Nick. Things lead to other things. You'd be so lucky. Kimi's the real deal."

"You're not wrong."

"Maybe when you grow up, you'll find a nice girl to settle down with," Lana said, reaching over and pinching his bearded cheek. He smacked away her hand. Lana giggled. "All right, I gotta check on the food. I'll give ya a shout when it's ready." She patted Richie on the shoulder and tousled Nick's hair as she left.

Richie watched Lana leave. When she did, he turned back to Nick. "She thinks you got a girlfriend back home or something. That's why you won't make a move on Kimi."

Nick sipped his coffee and stared at the storm. "Not for a while now."

Richie stared straight ahead. More lightning followed by thunder shortly after, rumbling through the garage. "What's her name?"

"Cassie. Cassie Hendricks."

"Sounds cute."

"You don't know anything about her besides her name."

"Cassie's a pretty name."

"Uh-huh."

"Are you gonna go back to her? When this is over?" Richie asked.

Nick clicked his tongue. "I don't know. I don't think she ever wants to see me again."

"Bad ending, huh?"

"Yeah."

"That's no reason to give up."

"Maybe it's for the best. Even happy stories can have sad endings."

"Whatever the fuck that means," he mumbled under his breath.

Nick smirked. The two brothers went back to leering at the storm. They watched as the water cascaded off the edge of the open stall.

"I'm trying to think of the last time we hung out, just the two of us, before you left," Richie said. It surprised Nick. He thought about it.

"Yeah, you're right," Nick said, looking through the rain to the swaying trees. "Must have been before you left for Whitewater. Even when you came back in the summer from college, you were always working, and I was doing, you know, my own thing."

"Christ, eleven years," Richie muttered. "Some brothers we are."

Nick felt a pang of guilt. He pushed it aside. "We had some good times though, right? Before you left? Before I left?"

"It was more of you getting me in trouble than us hanging out," Richie said with a smirk.

"Hey, that's what brothers do. One of us had to be the bad influence, and it sure as hell wasn't going to be you," Nick said.

Richie agreed. "Some people don't get along, even if they're family," Richie said. Nick looked at his brother out of the corner of his eye. He waited for an explanation. "It wasn't anybody's fault you and Dad didn't get along. Some people just don't mix, like water and oil."

"Or beer and liquor."

Richie scoffed. "Look, I know Dad drank. A lot. He was an alcoholic. He lived in Wisconsin all his life. Whaddya want from him?"

"We're making excuses now? We're blaming the whole state?"

"When was the last time you went a day without a drink?"

"Yeah, maybe it's in the blood." He sipped his coffee. "You gotta admit, even when he wasn't drinking, he was still a prick. Can't blame it all on the booze."

"Yeah, he wasn't very fun to be around. I know that. But that doesn't mean he didn't love you. I mean, how many times did the cops bring you home on a Saturday night and he got you off with a warning?"

Nick began to count on his fingers, raising each finger multiple times. "A few."

Richie gathered his breath. "I'm not saying he didn't make mistakes—of course, he did—but he got better. You may not believe it, but he did go sober, and he got better. So I forgave him. I forgave

185

him as I forgave you, for leaving. At least Dad tried to be better." A lightning strike flashed across the sky. "He didn't give up and bail."

Nick rubbed his cheek with his tongue. He sipped his coffee.

"Sorry," Richie said, his voice calm. "I thought that needed to be said."

"No, it's okay," Nick said. "You're right." Nick took a deep breath. "That's good you forgave him. I'm glad, I really am. I wish I could too, sometimes."

Richie sighed. Nick sipped his coffee. "I thought about coming home. I really did. A couple of times. But I just couldn't. The idea of coming home and Mom not being there…" He shook his head. He ran his hands through his hair. He took out his cigarettes and lit up.

"Plus, I knew he had you, which made staying away easier. I could always count on you to be the good son."

"I get it," Richie said as his brother exhaled smoke. "I do. But you weren't just a son, you were a brother too. And that night I lost you too."

Nick took a drag. They stared straight ahead at the rain.

"I'm sorry, Richie," Nick said. He couldn't look at his brother. "I really am."

"It's okay."

Nick took another drag. "I think all the time what my life, our lives, would be like if it never happened. If Mom was alive."

Richie clenched his jaw. "Me too."

A heavy silence fell over them with only the patter of rain filling it.

"You know, we never really talked about it," Richie said. "The accident. That night. By the time I got home from Whitewater, you were already gone."

"I know."

"Well, what happened that night?"

"You already know."

"Not from you. You were there."

"So? Why do you want to know?"

"I think I have a right to know."

Nick sighed. He took one more drag of his cigarette before flicking the butt into the storm. The rain extinguished it.

"I was at Tyler's that night," Nick said. "It was around midnight, and I got a call from the police. Told me Mom and Dad had been in an accident and said to come to the hospital. Tyler drove me there. When I got there, this doctor started telling me about Dad's condition and all this stuff they were doing and blah blah blah. Then I asked about Mom." He cleared his throat. "She was already gone. Dead on impact. I didn't even see her."

Nick cleared his throat and wiped his eyes.

"Cops were there. Started asking me questions. 'Do you know if your father had been drinking?' and shit like that. I knew it. I knew right there. The drunk fuck. He killed her. Probably had a case of beer, got behind that wheel, and killed her."

Nick stared at his coffee. "I told Tyler to take me home. I packed a bag and went to the bus station. And that was that."

He looked into the storm.

"How did he not go to jail?" Nick said suddenly. "He's driving drunk and someone dies. How is that not manslaughter? It should be fucking murder!"

Nick composed himself. Richie took a deep breath.

"He was below the limit."

"What a bunch of horseshit."

"There was a deer."

Nick scoffed. "Is that what he fucking said? A deer?"

"A witness confirmed it," Richie said softly. "A driver behind them saw it too. He was drinking that night, but he wasn't over the legal limit. Now, if he'd been stone-cold sober, maybe he could've seen it in time—brake fast enough or avoid it or something. I'm not saying he's off the hook, but that's why he got a slap on the wrist. They just fined him and sent him to AA. That's where he got sober."

Nick shook his head. "Fucking bullshit."

"I wanted to kill him too," Richie said. "It wasn't just you. I didn't talk to him for a long time after that. Almost two years."

Nick looked at his brother. Surprised.

"It's true. I felt like you did: he wasn't worth my time. But he kept calling me and calling me and showing up. I finally gave him a chance. He was sober. He stayed dry. As far as I know, he didn't touch a drop after that night."

Nick sipped his coffee and stared straight ahead.

"I know you don't want to hear this," Richie said. "But it's true. He changed. He worried about you. A lot. He always said you'd come back, eventually. But he wanted you to come back on your own. He always thought you'd choose to come back and then you two would talk. He wasn't going to force you to forgive him. Hell, I don't think if he ever really forgave himself. He just wanted to talk to you."

Nick bowed his head and rubbed his eyes.

"He just wanted the chance."

Nick put his coffee down. He buried his face in his hands. His shoulders began to shake like he was sobbing. Richie reached over and patted his brother's leg.

"It's okay. It's okay. You're here now."

Nick sniffled. He wiped his eyes, his hair hanging over his face. Richie stood up and pulled his brother up too and wrapped his arms around him.

"It's okay, Nick. It's okay."

"I'm sorry, Richie, I'm sorry," Nick said, his voice muffled in Richie's shoulder.

"It's okay. It's okay."

"I should've never left. I never should've left you."

"Shh. Shh. It's okay."

Lana opened the door. "Hey—"

Richie held up his hand. He kept hugging his brother. Lana went back inside.

He held him a while longer, his little brother in his arms as the rain went on.

15

One Day from the Night

Nick stared out the window of Richie's truck as he, Richie, and Lana made the drive to Cedar Pine Resort in Egg Harbor. Nick gawked at the lawn decorations; the flags; and red, white, and blue bunting that littered every house and business as they passed through the patriotic harbor town.

Most of the drive had been in silence with only the radio. Lana cleared her throat.

"This is nice," she said. "Family drive to see the fireworks. Shame Kimi or Cooper couldn't come."

"Yeah," Richie said. He was about to say something but realized he had nothing else to say. Lana looked at Nick, distractedly watching the scenery go by.

"Nick?" she said, nudging him.

"Huh? Oh, yeah. Just like the old days," he said before going back to staring out the window.

As they got closer to the resort, they began to see cars parked on the tree-covered road leading to the entrance of the resort. Going to Cedar Pine for the fireworks show was a yearly tradition for many families on the peninsula, including the Morgans.

"Gonna be a miracle if we find a parking spot," Richie bemoaned.

"Maybe you should drop us off out front and find a parking spot like a good husband," Lana said. Richie drove down the entrance to the resort and toward the grass clearing where onlookers staked out spots for blankets and chairs.

"Good man," she said as Richie parked the truck and the two got out. Nick grabbed the cooler from the truck bed, and Lana grabbed the blankets. Richie drove off with the truck, searching for a spot.

Walking to the grass clearing on the north side of the resort that overlooked the pier and Egg Harbor, Nick was awash in nostalgia. In the decade since his last visit, little to nothing had changed. Kids ran around playing games near the towering trees with sparklers in their hands. The parents drank beer and wine, and the kids guzzled sodas.

"Nothing's changed here," Nick said as they walked into the grass clearing.

"Would you want it to?"

Nick thought for a moment. *No, I suppose not.*

Lana found a spot near the front in the grass adjacent to the stone wall that overlooked the rocky shore and the resort's pier. The sun was almost settled for the evening, slowly going down behind the trees and brushing the sky with pink and orange.

Lana laid out two blankets on the grass. Nick plopped down the cooler and opened it. He handed Lana a beer and grabbed one for himself. She sat on the blanket, her legs crossed, and looked around, content.

Nick sat down and drank his beer, looking around silently.

"Are you okay?" Lana asked him.

"Fine. Why?"

"I don't know. You've been a little weird lately. Kind of quiet. Not like you."

Nick sipped his beer. "Have I? Must be nervous about tomorrow."

"I thought you said you don't get nervous about jobs anymore?"

"Well, I never did one with my family."

Lana smirked. They went back to silence and listened to the music play behind them.

They looked at the small stage and band set up behind the clearing in front of the trees. "Even the band's the same," Nick said.

"Really?"

"Basically. Four dudes in Hawaiian shirts playing the oldies." Lana looked closer. He was right. The four band members were all older, portly gentlemen wearing loose-fitting and colorful Hawaiian shirts. There was a drummer, two guitars, and a saxophone.

"They sound good."

"I can guarantee you they'll play 'My Girl.' Every year they play 'My Girl,' without fail." He gulped his beer.

"Every year?"

"Every. Single. Year."

"Well, it is a good song."

The two sat and listened to the band play Van Morrison's "Brown Eyed Girl" and people-watched for the next ten minutes or so as they waited for Richie. Lana pointed out a group of high school girls, five of them huddled together near the rock wall, chatting. Nick pointed to a group of high school boys about thirty yards away from the girls, also huddled together. Each group tried to subtly put on for the other.

"Look at this, a little high school drama playing out before us," she said. "High school boys and girls. I miss those days."

"Yeah?" Nick said. "I bet you had a lot of boys chasing after you, asking you to go to the dance."

Lana rolled her eyes. "Actually, no. I had, like, one boyfriend all throughout high school. Lasted like a month."

"Yeah, right."

"It's true! I was a late bloomer. And I was shy."

Nick scoffed.

Lana ignored him. "I feel like I should warn the girls. Tell them not to do it. High school boys aren't worth it."

"You're right about that." Nick drank his beer.

Finally, Richie arrived from parking the car. Nick got up from the cooler and tossed him a beer.

"Thanks. Hopefully, I won't get towed. Nice spot." He cracked his can of beer and took a big gulp. He sat down on the blanket next to Lana. She grabbed his arm and draped it around her shoulders. Nick went back to sitting on the cooler. He took out his pack of cigarettes and lit one. Richie frowned at the smell of the cigarette.

Lana pulled out a deck of cards from her hoodie's pouch.

"Come on, let's play some Michigan Rummy."

"All right, we don't have a pen and paper to keep score," Nick said.

"We can remember our score in our heads. Honor system."

Lana shuffled the deck and dealt the cards as the three sat in a circle on the scratchy blanket. After a couple of rounds, Nick was close to winning. He was waiting on another eight, but it wasn't coming.

Nick put down a ten of spades. Richie picked it up. Lana growled. Richie pondered what to lay down. He laid down a six of hearts. Lana grabbed from the deck. She laid down a seven of diamonds. Nick drew from the deck and laid down a queen of spades.

Lana dropped her head. Richie snatched up the card. "Gin!" he said and laid down his hand.

"Goddammit, Nick!" Lana said.

"What?"

"You were feeding him spades the whole game! You didn't catch on that he picked up every single one?"

"Whatever," Nick said and dropped his cards on the blanket.

"Don't be a sore loser," Richie said to Lana. "Come on, it's your deal." Lana stood up and stretched her back.

"Nah. I wanna walk around a bit," she said. She looked at Richie, who stood up. Nick remained sitting on the cooler, drinking his beer."

"All right, I gotta pee first," Richie said. "I might grab a hot dog too. Anyone want anything?"

Neither did. He disappeared into the crowd toward the old resort. Lana looked down at Nick. "Come on, take a walk with me," she said. Nick begrudgingly got up. They walked toward the edge of the lawn where the stone wall overlooked the pier and harbor below. Lana sat on the wall and stared out into the harbor. Nick stood behind her and drank his beer.

"Never get tired of it," Lana said.

"What's that?"

"The sunsets. Can't beat a summer here."

Nick agreed.

Lana pointed down below to the harbor, packed with boats of every kind. "Look at that boat—or yacht, I should say—at the end over there." Nick followed her hand to a black-and-white fifty-foot yacht tied off on the end of the nearest dock.

"Wow," he said.

Music started playing again. The band, which had taken a short break, started again. The soft chords to Eric Clapton's "Wonderful Tonight" echoed through the air.

> It's late in the evening; she's wondering what clothes to wear.
> She puts on her makeup and brushes her long blonde hair.
> And then she asks me, "Do I look all right?"
> And I say, "Yes, you look wonderful tonight."

Lana began to hum along, slowly bobbing her head back and forth to the melody. Nick sat down on the wall. Lana noticed how miserable he looked. The bags under his eyes were heavy, as if he hadn't been sleeping much. She already knew that. Over the past week, she'd gone to bed before Nick and woken up to him already up almost every day.

"Come on," she said, putting her beer down on the wall and standing up.

"What?"

"Dance with me. It's a good song."

"You're kidding."

"You've been sulking all night. Come on, have some fun," she said, grabbing his hand and pulling. Nick reluctantly put his beer down and followed.

She led him a few steps out into the grass where there was a small clearing amid the dozens of other blankets other families had laid out. No one else was dancing. Nick noticed eyes come over them as they walked past and took a position in the center of the grass clearing.

Lana placed her right hand on Nick's left as she stretched it out, placing his other arm around her back. She placed her left arm on his shoulder as they began to sway back and forth to the music.

"We're the only ones dancing," Nick muttered.

"So?"

"I can't believe you dragged me out here."

"Would you stop? You've been a sour puss all week. What's the matter with you?"

"Nervous, I guess."

"Well, we don't have to do it."

"No, we do." The forcefulness of his voice made Lana glance at him. "I mean, it's the right thing to do."

"Well, stop being weird then. You're supposed to be the confident one. The one who's done this thing before. You're making everyone else anxious."

They continued swaying to the music. Nick looked over Lana's shoulder to see Richie approach their blanket with a bratwurst.

"Here comes your husband," Nick said.

"Does he look jealous?"

"Definitely."

She looked over her shoulder and waved at Richie. He gave a half-hearted wave and sat down with his brat. Lana looked at Nick, whose eyes were looking out in the distance, as if deep in memory.

"Are you thinking about her?" Lana asked. "Is that why you've been so weird?"

"Who? Kimi?"

Lana rolled her eyes. "No. You know who I mean."

"No. Why is everyone so curious about my love life?"

"Makes you seem like a real person."

And then she asks me, "Do you feel all right?"

And I say, "Yes, I feel wonderful tonight."

Lana hummed along. "So were you?"

"This song might have reminded me of her, a little bit."

194

"Aww."

"Shut up."

Lana giggled. "Oh, Nick, you're cute. You can pretend to be the brooding jerk, but you're just sad about a girl you miss."

Nick shook his head and looked away.

"Have you talked to her at all lately?"

Nick took a deep breath. "No."

"You think you should? You know, before tomorrow?"

"I'm regretting this dance."

Lana kept up her penetrating gaze. It made Nick squirm.

"I don't know, maybe."

"Are you going to tell me her name?"

Nick exhaled. "Cassie."

Lana beamed a satisfied, cocky grin. "I like that name. She sounds pretty."

"She was—is. Smart too."

"Doesn't sound like it if she dated you." Nick fake laughed.

"Hilarious. She was a lawyer—going to be a lawyer. She's graduated law school by now."

"Wow, a pretty lawyer. Sounds like a real catch."

"She was."

"So what happened?"

"Nothing really. Didn't work out."

Lana scoffed. "Bullshit. 'It didn't work out.' What does that even mean?"

"Not all of us are lucky enough to find our soul mate at a frat party." Lana pinched his neck. The song winded down to its end. The guitar struck its last chord and let its sound vibrate and fade away.

Nick and Lana broke off to applaud with the rest of the audience. They saw Richie walk toward them. Lana turned to Nick and gave a playful curtsy. "Thank you for the dance, good sir." Nick smirked and bowed like a gentleman before Richie came between them.

"I'll be the one dancing with my wife from now on," Richie said.

Nick stepped aside, presenting Lana to him. "No arguments here. She talks too much for me."

Lana slapped Nick's arm as he returned to their blanket on the grass. He reached into the cooler and cracked open another beer as the band started up again.

The front man for the band came to the mic. "Okay, folks, the fireworks will start in a few short minutes, but before that, we're going to leave you with one more song. We saw a few dancers out there, but I think we can get a few more, so fellas, grab your girl because this is the song for it. Here we go!"

The first bubbly chords pierced through the casual murmur of the crowd. The lead singer, a chubby fellow with white hair wearing a red-and-white Hawaiian shirt, stepped back to the mic and sang.

I've got sunshine, on a cloudy day.
When it's cold outside, I've got the month
of May.

"Perfect timing," Nick muttered to himself. Lana and Richie danced as Lana and Nick did, gently swaying back and forth. Nick could see Richie whisper something into Lana's ear and saw her smile. Richie did too.

Lana closed her eyes and rested her cheek on Richie's chest. Nick could see Richie's lips mumble along to the lyrics in Lana's ear.

Other couples started to make their way to the make-do dance space. Out of the corner of his eye, Nick saw one of the boys approach the clique of girls from before. He looked like he was asking her to dance, and Nick cringed, worried he was about to see a public rejection firsthand. Like a car crash, he couldn't look away.

Miraculously, she seemed to say yes, and the boy led the girl to the dance area. It made Nick feel good for the first time in what felt like a long time—to think he had a little part in giving a boy a reason to dance with a pretty girl.

Nick was alone on that itchy wool blanket. The feeling hit him suddenly and powerfully. He stared straight ahead, a blank expression on his face. He thought about the upcoming night. He thought about Richie and Lana and Kimi. He thought about their lives in his hands.

He felt lonely and cold.

His mind drifted to Cassie. He wondered where she was right now, who she was with, and what she was doing. He thought about when she made him promise her to take her to his home at some point. She wanted to meet his dad and his brother. She wanted to see where he grew up. Nick agreed but avoided ever committing to it. Now, it probably wouldn't ever happen. That gave him a pang in his chest.

After a minute, Lana opened her eyes and connected with Nick from across the grass. She waved. He looked away, suddenly feeling uncomfortable watching Richie and his wife share a tender moment.

After another minute, the band finished the last notes of the song. The couples disengaged from their embraces and applauded. The band's singer thanked everyone and then announced the fireworks would start in a few minutes.

Nick watched Richie and Lana walk back to him, Richie's arm slung around her shoulders and her arm wrapped behind his back. Their youth struck Nick at that moment. They could be mistaken for high school kids in love, even though they'd been married for years.

As they rejoined Nick, Richie went to the cooler and grabbed a beer for him and Lana, Nick applauded the two.

"All right, Lana," Richie said. "Now that you've danced with both, you can decide which Morgan brother is better on his feet." Lana shook her head and sat down on the blanket. "I don't want to sway your opinion but don't forget about that ring on your finger."

Lana rolled her eyes. "You were both good."

"That means me," Richie said. "You're lucky I'm so nice. Most guys would kick their brother's ass for dancing with their wife."

"It was her idea," Nick said. His brother was in a good mood, Nick could see. He talked and joked more than usual, and Nick wondered how he could be so easy, so carefree with tomorrow night hanging over his head.

Because he trusts me, Nick thought. It made him sick.

Nick dropped his head down and rubbed his forehead. The night was coming on. Families gathered excitedly in their chairs and blankets, looking up to the sky.

"I'm gonna run to the bathroom," Nick said, suddenly standing up.

Richie and Lana paid little attention to him. Richie lay down on his back, and Lana lay down next to him, using his chest as a pillow.

Nick made his way through the crowd. When he saw he was out of sight of Richie and Lana, he turned toward the trees. He walked through them until he was properly secluded. He bent behind a trunk and vomited. He lurched out the contents of his stomach, his throat and eyes burning. He sat down against the tree and caught his breath. He took a minute to gather himself and then headed toward the resort.

He walked through the large dining room of the resort until he found the bathroom on the other side. He washed his face and gargled water. He looked at himself in the mirror. His eyes red, his cheeks pale. He looked away.

He exited the bathroom and went to the nearby bar. When he entered, it was empty, save for a few patrons exiting to catch the fireworks.

The bartender, a young, skinny kid with a buzz cut in a maroon vest and black shirt, stood alone behind the bar, wiping a glass with a rag. Nick sat down on a black stool.

"Think the fireworks are about to start," the kid bartender said. Nick ignored him and rubbed his hands through his hair, curling it behind his ears.

"Beer and a shot of whiskey," Nick said curtly.

"Okay. What kind of beer and whiskey?"

"I don't give a shit."

The bartender went over to the tap and began to pour a light beer, while Nick stared ahead with a blank expression. He plopped the beer and a shot glass in front of Nick. He grabbed a bottom-shelf whiskey and poured it into the shot glass. Nick grunted when he finished, and the bartender grabbed the twenty-dollar bill from him.

Nick heard the first fireworks go off. He threw back the shot of brown liquor. He didn't react to the bang or crackle of the fireworks; he sipped his beer and stared straight ahead at the display of liquor bottles behind the bar.

The bartender returned with his change. He put the bills down in front of him with a couple of quarters resting on top. He looked out the window behind the bar, trying to find an angle where he could see the fireworks.

"You good here? You mind if I catch some of the show?" the bartender said, pointing his thumb at the back door behind the bar that led to the porch situated outside.

Nick waved his hand without looking at him.

"Just yell if you need anything, or someone else comes in," the bartender said and started toward the swinging back door behind the bar. Before he stepped through, Nick shouted.

"Hey! You got a pay phone around here somewhere?"

"In the lobby, right through that door."

Nick thanked him and waved him away. Nick drank alone. The bar was dimly lit, with only a few lights on the walls. He sat there as the sounds of crackling explosions filled the humid summer air outside. Nick looked around at the empty bar.

What kind of fucking idiot leaves the bar and register like that? Nick thought. He reached over and tapped the sale button on the old register. The bell dinged, and the drawer opened. Nick hovered his hand over.

"Ah," he groaned and closed the register without taking a cent.

He lit a cigarette as green, red, purple, and gold light penetrated through the windows and glowed over his face. Bright light, a crackle or boom, the oohs and aahs of the crowd, a second of pause, and then another light. Again and again.

Nick took a long drag and stared at the money the bartender had placed in front of him. He looked at the quarters. He grabbed them and headed toward the lobby.

He entered through the double doors into the lobby, spotting the pay phone against the back wall, next to the large windows overlooking the harbor. He could see the fireworks exploding over the water through the huge windows. He approached the pay phone.

She probably wouldn't even answer, he thought, quarters in hand. *She's probably busy, away from her phone.* A purple light glowed in the sky.

He grabbed the phone and put in the quarters. He stared at the keypad. He dialed her number. He took a deep breath and dialed the last digit. He closed his eyes and held it up to his ear.

One ring. Two rings. Three rings. Four rings. Five rings. Six rings. Seven rings.

Answering machine.

He almost hung up. He took it away from his ear, but then he heard her voice come on, asking the caller to leave a message. The machine beeped. He put the phone back to his ear.

"Hey, it's me," he said with a slight stammer. "I just wanted to—" He rubbed his eyes. "I don't know, see how you're doing. I'm sure you're with your family right now. I am too, if you can believe that." He cleared his throat. "My dad died. So I decided to come home." Fireworks *whizzbanged* in the background. "It's been pretty good, so far."

He cleared his throat. "I just wanted to"—he looked out at the fireworks over the water—"see how's it going being a lawyer. Who knows, I might need one pretty soon," he said with a flat laugh. He pulled away from the phone and smacked himself in the forehead.

"Jesus, I don't know what I'm saying. I—" He looked around behind him at the empty lobby. "It wasn't all bad, right? There were some good—we were—"

He took a deep breath. "I miss you." He scratched his forehead. He searched for more words. After what felt like an hour, he hung up.

He returned to the bar and his beer. Thirty minutes of whistles and bangs went by with green, red, blue, gold, and white light shining through the windows of the bar as Nick sat alone, drinking and smoking. Nick could hear the clustered, frenetic whistles and furious explosions that indicated the finale.

He grabbed the napkin the bartender had laid out with his beer. He reached over by the register and grabbed a pen. He scribbled a few words on the napkin. When he was done, he crumpled it up and dropped it on the bar. He put out the cigarette in an ashtray and began to walk back. As he left the bar, the young bartender returned. He saw the empty bottle and shot glass. He tossed the empty bottle in the trash and put the shot glass away. He grabbed the napkin and was about to toss it too when he noticed some writing. He carefully unfolded it and spread it out on the bar.

Don't trust Nick Morgan.

He frowned and tossed it in the trash.

Nick made his way through the restaurant and back outside. He walked through the crowd as everyone began to gather their things—rolling up blankets and folding chairs. Nick eventually returned to their spot as Richie and Lana finished bundling everything up.

"Where'd you go? You missed the whole show," Richie said.

"Nah, I just stopped at the deck on the way back from the can and watched it there," Nick lied.

Richie accepted the explanation and rolled up the last blanket. Lana didn't. She squinted at Nick while holding the rolled-up blanket in front of her.

"You call her?" she asked in a low whisper.

Nick looked away.

"You talk to her?"

Nick shook his head. Lana sighed and tapped his cheek.

"Grab the cooler."

Nick grabbed the cooler, and they made their way back to the truck.

16

The Day Of

Lana sat alone in her kitchen, drinking coffee and reading a book in her robe. The early sun cracked through the window into the kitchen, and the morning birds chirped outside. Her eyes darted up when she heard the sound of a bedroom door opening. Nick stepped out in a T-shirt and boxers.

He glanced at Lana ambling over to the coffeemaker.

"How'd you sleep?" Lana said without looking up from her book.

"I didn't," Nick said, pouring coffee.

"Me neither."

Nick sat down at the table, coffee in hand. Lana continued reading.

"You ready?" she said.

"Absolutely," Nick said, his voice low. "Are you?"

"Ready as I'll ever be, I guess."

"And Richie? How do you think he is?"

"Good," she said, sipping her coffee. She looked up from her book. "He trusts you."

Nick stood up and headed back to the bedroom.

"Try to get some sleep," Lana said as he left. Nick waved without looking back.

He stepped into the bedroom and closed the door, locking it behind him. He put his coffee down on the end table and sat on the edge of his bed. He buried his face in his hands. He smoothed his hair back a few times and stared at the wall. He closed his eyes and drew his breath in.

He opened his eyes. He looked at his bag. He went over to it and opened the side pocket on the inside. He pulled out the guns—two pistols. He checked the magazines. Loaded. He put it back and sat on the edge of the bed again. He bowed his head and rubbed his forehead with his knuckles.

He stared at the ceiling and thought—about Lana, Richie, Kimi, and the lie he told them. He thought of what might happen tonight.

Then, he thought of her.

17

Four Years, One Month, and Nineteen Days from the Night

The thin mountain air felt good on Nick's face as he turned his motorcycle onto King Street. He liked the little Sportster, even if it had more rusty parts than not. It'd somehow made the thousand-mile trip from LA to Boulder, Colorado, in one piece.

It was half past midnight when Nick pulled up to the curb in front of the frat house. He could never remember the names, but he could remember which ones his clients lived in by the colors. Jason lived in a red house with black Greek letters.

Nick checked his watch as he turned off the bike. He rarely made deliveries this late at night, but Jason had promised an extra fifteen percent for his troubles. Nick wasn't sleeping anyway. He rarely did.

He double-checked the product was in his jacket and stepped off his bike. Loud music boomed from the house. He skipped the front door and walked around to the backyard, where the party was.

The transaction lasted only two minutes. Nick never idled with chitchat. With the money in his pocket, Nick stepped through the back door into the frat house stuffed with college kids.

He had to piss. Really badly.

He walked down a narrow hallway, brushing past students at every step. He found a bathroom. He tried the knob. Locked. He knocked on the door and an agitated voice shouted, "Occupied!" He continued searching. He went upstairs and tried a handful of doors, all locked. He saw a glass door leading to a balcony.

Close enough, he thought.

He slid open the door and stepped out onto the small, dark balcony overlooking the side of the house. Below, bushes and shrubs grew. *Perfect*, he thought. He maneuvered to the side, unzipped his fly, and began relieving himself.

After a few seconds, he heard the door slide open again. He looked over his shoulder to see a girl step out. She noticed him and looked him over, hearing the last of his stream come to an end.

"Oh," she said. "Sorry."

"It's okay," Nick said, zipping up his fly. "I'm done."

She looked away. She had a pack of cigarettes and lighter in one hand and a red solo cup in the other. She took out a cigarette and lit up. Nick finished gathering himself.

"Mind if I bum one?" he asked. She looked at him sideways.

"Sure. I'm trying to quit anyway."

She handed him the cigarette and was about to hand him her lighter when she pulled back. "Actually, allow me. I know where those hands have been." She lit the cigarette for him.

"Thanks."

They stood and smoked in silence for a few drags. In the background, the loud music and college debauchery ensued. He carefully glanced at her, sizing her up. She wasn't short, but she wasn't tall either. Her brown hair cascaded down past her shoulders. She wore tight, stone-washed jeans and a black turtleneck sweater.

She caught him looking at her. He averted his gaze. She smirked. She turned her head and fully looked him up and down.

"You go here?"

"No," Nick said. "I'm a friend of Jason's."

"I didn't think so."

"Why not?"

She sipped her drink. "I don't know."

Nick ashed his cigarette. "So you know why I'm up here. Why aren't you down at the party?"

"I came for a smoke."

"You can't do that down there?"

She looked at him sideways. "To be honest, I'm hiding from a guy."

"Ah," Nick said. "Boyfriend?"

"No. Just an annoying dude."

"Have you tried asking nicely?"

She rolled her eyes. "I wanna leave."

"Then why don't you?"

"My friend gave me a ride. She doesn't want to leave yet. I think she's in one of those bedrooms back there."

"Call a cab."

"Thank you, Mr. Pisser, I didn't think of that. I don't have any cash."

Nick laughed. "Well, I'm about to leave. I was gonna stop for a slice of pizza on the way. We could grab a bite if you want. Then, I'll drop you off wherever."

She sipped from her cup, leaning forward on the railing. "Nice try."

"I know a great pizza place nearby."

"You mean Bart's?"

"Yeah, you like it?"

"It's my favorite," she said longingly, thinking about her empty stomach and greasy pizza.

Nick held out his hand flat. "I haven't had a drop tonight. Steady as a rock."

She looked at his hand and then Nick. She looked ahead. Nick could see her picturing the melted cheese on a fresh slice. She was almost drooling.

"I make it a point not to get into strange men's cars," she said.

"That's perfect. I have a bike."

She laughed. "Oh god. Yeah, I should've guessed that."

Nick flicked his cigarette. He reached over with his hand. "I'm Nick. Now I'm not a strange man."

She looked at it. "We've been over this. I'm not touching that hand."

Nick drew back. "Right. Sorry."

She smiled. "I'm Cassie."

"Whaddya say, Cassie? I'm offering a ride and pizza."

She finished her drink and dropped her cigarette in it. She tossed the cup down and faced Nick. She crossed her arms and studied him.

"You got an extra helmet?"

"You can have mine."

"Pizza, nothing else."

"Nothing else."

"And then you take me home. No bullshit."

"And then I take you home. No bullshit."

"Because I've got pepper spray in my purse."

"I believe you."

She looked him in the eye. She ran her tongue against her cheek. She stuck a finger in his chest. "Don't make me regret this, Mr. Pisser."

"Yes, ma'am."

*****

Slices of greasy pizza in hand, Nick and Cassie sat down at one of Bart's signature red-and-white tables—Nick with his pepperoni and Cassie with her Hawaiian style. Her cheeks were still red from the cool wind on the bike.

Cassie blew on her pizza. When she bit into it, she quickly breathed with her mouth open to keep from burning herself and drank her soda. She laughed at herself, wiping her mouth with a napkin.

"So," she said when she recovered, "you don't go to school here. You from here?"

"No." Nick sipped his water. "I moved here from LA about two months ago."

Cassie blew on her pizza some more. "Really? California?"

"I was there for a couple of years. I'm originally from Wisconsin."

"Ah, that makes more sense. You sound Midwestern," she said, biting into her pizza. "Where in Wisconsin?"

"Door County."

"Door County," she repeated. "I've never heard of it."

Nick propped his hand on the table, palm facing her and fingers together with his thumb sticking out. "This is Wisconsin." He pointed at his thumb. "This is Door County, a peninsula that separates Green Bay and Lake Michigan."

"Hmm. Sounds nice, surrounded by water."

"It's pretty in the summer. Miserable in the winter."

"Why's it called Door County? Doorway to the Midwest or something?"

"The strait between the peninsula and this island off the end of it, Washington Island, was called Death's Door."

"Ooh, spooky."

"Traders and sailors called it that because ships kept wrecking on its shores. Legend has it, though, that the natives called it the Doorway to Death way before Europeans got there. Apparently, there was a big Indian battle there, a massacre."

"Wow," Cassie said with a mouthful of pizza. "Well, I'm from St. Louis. There's no interesting or ominous story behind that name."

"Are you an undergrad here?"

"Mm-hmm."

"You're not like eighteen, are you?"

She laughed. "I graduate next year."

"What do you study?"

"Political science. But really I'm pre-law." Cassie took another bite of pizza. A stray slice of pineapple dropped onto her plate.

"Ah, good, we don't have enough of those."

She furrowed her brow. "Well, fuck you too."

"Sorry, I'm sure you'll be a good one," Nick chuckled.

She went back to eating. A handful of seconds passed with only chewing. Cassie squinted at Nick's forearm.

"Resist Much, Obey Little." She read the cursive letters that began below the bottom of his wrist and ended at the crick of his elbow.

Nick glanced at the ink on his arm. "Uh-huh."

"That's pretty corny, man."

"It's a Walt Whitman quote. The poet."

"Ah," she said, not impressed.

"I got it after my mom died. He was her favorite."

The blood in Cassie's face drained. She cast her eyes down. "Oh, sorry."

"Now I get to say fuck you too."

"I guess we're even."

Nick went back to eating. He looked around Bart's. The sound system played an Eminem song. Nick noticed an intoxicated white guy in a beanie rapping along to every word for his friends.

"So what'd you do in LA?" Cassie asked, covering her mouth as she talked with her mouth full.

"I didn't *do* anything. I was in prison for two years, spent another year on parole."

Nick enjoyed this part, watching the expression on people's faces when he told them he'd been in prison. It was fascinating to watch people digest the information. Cassie's face, however, revealed next to nothing. Her face was blank as if he'd told her he pumped gas.

"I see," she said as she grabbed her soda. For a moment, Nick saw the slightest concern flash over her eyes.

"I bet you're rethinking this date now," Nick said.

"First of all, this is not a date, big guy. Second of all, I'm gonna be a lawyer, a defense lawyer, so I got no problem talking to criminals."

"How good of you."

"What'd you do?"

"Well, the big one was assaulting a police officer."

"Hmm."

"You want to know why?"

"Do I?"

"Not really."

"Ah, dangerous *and* mysterious. Aren't you interesting," she said sarcastically. She bit into her pizza again.

Nick popped a piece of pepperoni into his mouth. "So why a lawyer? Besides the money, of course."

Cassie wiped her hands. "To help people. Those who don't have the means to defend themselves."

Nick curled his hair behind his hair. "Even the guilty ones?"

"Especially the guilty ones."

"Why?"

"Everyone deserves due process. Most deserve to make a mistake without it ruining their lives."

"What about me? I did it, I admit that. Do I deserve a second chance?"

"Sure. You didn't kill anyone, right?"

"No."

"Well, there you go. Looks like you're getting a second chance."

"Even if I don't feel bad about it?"

"Would you do it again?"

"You mean if the situation happened again, would I do it?"

"Yeah."

"Definitely."

"Why'd you do it?"

"To help my friends. They were going to get caught."

"So to protect your accomplices?"

"Yeah."

"What were you doing?"

"Robbing a house."

Cassie thought for a moment. "This is a very weird date."

"So it is a date now?"

"You did pay."

Cassie finished the last of her soda. She leaned forward. "You have no regrets about it?"

Nick leaned back. "I regret getting caught."

"So no remorse for the victims?"

"It was some rich guy's mansion. We took a little cash, some jewelry. He wasn't even there."

"So because you stole from a rich guy, it doesn't matter?"

"You should've seen this place. A real old money kind of mansion. His granddaddy was probably an oil baron or some shit."

"You sound rehabilitated."

"I got caught, and I did my time. I paid my debt. It doesn't mean I have to beg forgiveness from him or anyone."

Cassie leaned back. "I see."

"You don't like that answer."

"I've heard it before," Cassie said. "The people who say it usually wind up back there."

Nick shook his head. "Nah, not me. I'm straight as an arrow now. I'm just sick of people fishing for an apology, a monologue of remorse from me as if I personally wronged them."

"Well, you *did* break the laws of society. Those of us that live in society might feel you did personally wrong us."

"Does that make me a bad person?"

She squinted. "That one thing? No, I don't think so."

"I don't either." Nick reached over to her paper plate and picked up a scattered slice of pineapple. "However, there's no defense for putting pineapple on pizza. That does make you a bad person."

Although she didn't want to, Cassie laughed.

*****

Nine months later, Cassie opened the door to her apartment and was greeted with a symphony of scents and sounds: garlic, lemon, fish sizzling in a skillet, asparagus in the oven, Soundgarden on the stereo, and burning marijuana.

She breathed it all in. The warm apartment was a welcome reprieve from another brutally cold day of a frigid Colorado winter so far. She stomped her boots and hung up her jacket.

At the stove with a joint between his lips, Nick heard her come in.

"Hey," he said over his shoulder as he poked the fish. "Dinner will be ready in a few minutes. I just threw these trout fillets on."

Cassie dropped her book bag on the ground. She came over to Nick and rested her head against his shoulder. "Smells good in here, in many ways," she said. Nick handed her the joint. She took it and inhaled sharply, holding it in her lungs.

"How was class?" Nick asked, adjusting the heat on the stove. Cassie exhaled and coughed.

"I'm so fucking ready to graduate," she said, sounding exhausted. She handed the joint back to Nick. She reached up and kissed him. She loved how she had to stand on her tiptoes to reach his lips.

"Only a few months now. But you're going to law school anyway. That's another three years of classes. At least."

"I know," Cassie said. "But that's what I *want* to do. I'm sick of all these bullshit political science courses." She went over to her book bag and pulled out a textbook as thick as a pan of lasagna.

"Why'd you choose it as your major then?" Nick asked, turning around and puffing on the joint.

"I don't know. I think I heard somewhere it was a good major for pre-law undergraduates."

She picked up her book bag and carried it into their bedroom. Nick took one last puff of the joint and tossed it in the sink. Nick watched as she dropped the book bag on their bed and traded her jeans for sweatpants. Nick checked on the asparagus in the oven.

Cassie returned to the kitchen in purple sweats and a black Buffaloes hoodie, her hair pulled back into a ponytail.

"Got a lot of homework?" Nick asked, flipping the fillets in the skillet.

"A lot of reading, but I need to get started on this paper for my European history course. We got any beer left?" Cassie made her way to the fridge.

"Should be a couple in there. What's it on?"

Cassie pulled out a bottle. "Something about the Holy Roman Empire. You're going to help me, right?"

"I don't know shit about the Holy Roman Empire, but, sure, I can give you a hand."

"I hate writing. I mean, I know how to write about facts and make arguments and research and all that, but if it's something I don't care about, like an empire from a thousand years ago, it's like pulling teeth."

Nick removed the skillet from heat and put a lid on it, where it'd sit for the next five to ten minutes. "I work Saturday night, so I can help Friday or Sunday night."

Nick leaned down and opened the oven. The asparagus was done. He took out the tray with oven mitts and put it on the counter. He began slicing a lemon on the cutting board. Cassie came up behind him and hugged him as he squeezed lemon juice over the greens.

"I'm jealous of you sometimes," she said, her cheeks pressed against his back.

"A lawyer envious of a high school dropout bartender," Nick said.

"At least you're working and earning. I'm just blowing through money and racking up debt. It'll be years before I can even start my career."

Nick pulled apart Cassie's hands and turned around so they were face-to-face. Due to the height difference, it was more chin-to-forehead.

"Yeah, but when you do start making money, you'll going to be killing it. You'll be the hot shit lawyer driving around a Mercedes, talking on your Bluetooth all day."

"Yeah, because that sounds like me." She stepped away and grabbed her beer and sat down at the kitchen table. "Even when I start working, the first couple years I'll barely be making more than you. Plus, I don't get to go home with tips."

Nick checked on the fillets tenderizing under the clear lid cover. "I think you're exaggerating a bit. Maybe you can start a tip jar for lawyers. Walk around the court with a jar full of cash and quarters."

Cassie laughed. "Still probably wouldn't beat you, coming home with a bunch of twenties and fifties every night, it seems. You must be doing something special to get tips like that."

"Well, you know me and my passion for quality service."

"Makes me think you're doing more than just pouring drinks."

"Well, some nights I like to go to the strip club and dance the night away. I didn't want you to be jealous, but I'm glad I can be honest now."

"As long as there aren't any private dances in the champagne room."

"Well, that's only for the diamond-club members, very exclusive." He went into the fridge and pulled out a beer for himself. "You hungry?"

"Starving."

Nick twisted off the cap to the bottle and tossed it in the trash. He sipped it as Cassie stared at him.

"What?" Nick asked.

"What?" Cassie parroted.

"You've got a look on your face."

"Do I? What kind of look?"

"Like you're thinking about something."

"Am I not allowed to look at you and think?"

"Come on, let me have it."

Cassie picked at the label on her beer bottle, something Nick had noticed she did when she was nervous. Her voice was low, barely able for Nick to hear over the music and commotion of the kitchen.

"I was thinking—"

Nick's cell phone rang. He looked at the caller ID. "Fuck, this is work. I gotta take this. Sorry, two minutes, all right?"

Cassie nodded, disappointed but relieved. Nick flipped open his cell phone and walked into their bedroom, closing the door, but leaving it ajar. Cassie got up from the table to check on the food. From the kitchen, she could see and almost hear Nick talking in their bedroom. His back was to her, but she could hear murmuring and intense whispers.

She couldn't help eavesdropping. Nick hunched over like he was whisper-shouting into the phone. She made out some profanities as the stereo hit a lull between songs.

She saw him close his phone in anger. She quickly turned back to the food. She heard his footsteps come to the kitchen.

"Sorry about that. How's the fish look?" he said, peering over her shoulder.

"Good, I think. You always do that."

"Do what?"

Cassie looked up at him. "You know, go into the other room when you get a call."

Nick reached past her for the spatula and skillet. "I like my conversations to be private." He removed the lid and began to transfer the fillets to a plate, peeling off the skin and putting it back into the pan.

"Who was it?"

"Just Mark, asking if I could come in early on Saturday," Nick said, not taking his eyes off the fish.

"You talk to your boss like that?"

"Like what?"

"It sounded pretty intense from out here," she said. Nick finished peeling the skin and put the pan back on the stove, bringing it to low heat. He added diced garlic and white wine for the butter herb sauce that would go over the fillets.

"Were you eavesdropping?"

"I didn't mean to, but it was hard not to."

"That's just Mark. He talks like that to everyone, and everyone talks to him like that. Everything's a crisis, you know?"

"Ah," Cassie said. She wasn't convinced, but she didn't feel like pushing it.

"Go sit down. It's almost ready. I'll bring it to you," Nick said. She took her seat at the table with her beer.

Nick stirred the sauce, waiting for the garlic to soften to add the parsley and butter. "Oh, what were you going to say before?"

Cassie picked at the label again. "I've been thinking about graduation. And what happens after."

Nick glanced at Cassie before going into the fridge and grabbing the butter. "I thought we already figured that out. You'll go home to St. Louis to attend the *very prestigious* Washington University School of Law."

"I know. But what about you?"

Nick cut two tablespoons of butter off the stick. "What about me? We talked about this. Long-distance is almost impossible."

"I know we said that."

"We've got until May," he said, spooning the sauce onto the plates with the trout fillets. "I wish we had more time, but I can't make you go to a closer school for me."

He added the asparagus and brought the two plates over to the table. "Dinner is served," he said with a smile. Nick grabbed his fork and began to dig in. "Not bad, right?" he said with a mouthful of fish.

Cassie was more deliberate, slowly breaking off a piece of fillet and eating it. She looked down at her plate as she poked her asparagus with a fork.

"What's wrong?"

Cassie kept her eyes down. "Nothing."

"Come on, Cass."

"It's not fair," she said.

Nick sipped his beer. He ran his fingers through his hair. "No, it's not. I finally meet someone like you and you've gotta go away. That's life, I guess."

Cassie took a bite of her asparagus. She swallowed. "I think you should come with me," she said without looking up from her food.

Nick put down his fork and leaned back in his chair. "What?"

Cassie looked up now. "I think you should come with me to St. Louis."

Nick looked into her eyes, but they were without a doubt. "You're serious?"

"I am. I know that's not what we decided, but that was months ago. I think this is something, and I don't want to give up on it because I was too afraid of asking you to come with me. If we bail, we're going to be thinking about what could have been. At least, I know I will."

Nick licked his lips and stared at his plate. "Wow."

"Nothing is keeping you here. You don't go to school. You're not from here. I mean, shit, St. Louis is a helluva lot closer to your home than here is. The lease for this place ends in May. You're going to be moving anyway. Why not move with me?"

She gave him a sweet smile. Nick had yet to say no to that look when she asked—when she *really* wanted what she was asking for.

"I have my job."

"Babe, don't take this the wrong way, but you're a bartender. There are plenty of bars in St. Louis."

"I know," Nick said. "But with my record, it can be hard to find work."

"I get that," Cassie said. "But honestly, this could be great for you too. It'd be a fresh start in a new city. You could even go back to

216

school, get your GED. Hell, you could go to community college or something. You can still do whatever you want. It'll be tough the first couple of years, but we can support each other."

Nick bit his lip and scratched his beard. "Sounds like you've thought about this."

"I know this is asking a lot," Cassie said. "And you don't have to answer right now or anything, but I just wanted to put it out there."

Nick drew in a deep breath. He scratched his beard more and stared at her, scanning over her eyes, her eyelashes, her nose, her lips, her chin, her neck, her hair.

"I've thought about it too," he said.

"Yeah?"

"Of course. I couldn't ask to go with you though."

"Now you don't. I'm asking you."

Nick smiled. "Okay."

Cassie's eyes widened. "Okay?"

"Yeah. Let's do it."

She rose from her chair, and Nick did the same. She threw her arms around his neck, stood on her tiptoes, and kissed him.

When they came apart, they rested their foreheads against one another's.

"I love you," she whispered. Nick kissed her again.

"I love you too. Now, come on, let's eat before it gets cold."

*****

When Cassie entered her St. Louis apartment three years later, there was no smell of cooking food or music. There was only the faint stench of sweat and marijuana. Nick sat on the living room couch, where she'd left him that morning.

When she entered, Nick abruptly stood up and rearranged the filthy coffee table. He stood up, his hands behind his back. "Hey," he said.

"Hey," Cassie said. She dropped her book bag and slowly moved toward the living room. "What's up?"

"Nothing, nothing's up. Just cleaning up a little bit. You're home early. How was class?"

Cassie looked around at the mess. She glanced at Nick before turning back to the kitchen to grab a bottle of water. "Fine," she said, taking a sip of water. She stepped back to the living room. "I called you earlier."

"Shit, did you? I'm sorry. Damn phone must be dead."

Cassie looked around the apartment. It wasn't ever particularly nice, but recently it had fallen to near disgusting.

"Have you gone outside today?"

Nick fiddled with his hands. "Well, I haven't yet. I've just been—"

"Been what?"

"You know, just kind of—" Nick looked around but could find nothing. He searched through his drug-addled mind. Nothing.

"Jesus, look at you. You can't even come up with a lie! You can't come up with a single excuse for what you've been doing all day besides getting high and watching TV."

Nick ran his hands through his hair. "Can we not do this?"

"Do what?"

"Fight. Can we not?"

"I didn't know we were fighting. I thought I was asking you what you did all day while I was in class."

Nick dropped to the couch. He rubbed his eyes. He stared at the floor and massaged the back of his neck. Cassie sat down on the love seat next to the couch.

"Nick, what the fuck? You've been like this for weeks. You hardly ever leave the apartment. You barely talk to me—you barely talk at all! What's going on?"

"Nothing, okay? This is my stuff. You don't need to know about it." Nick stood up and went toward the fridge. He pulled out a beer.

"I don't need to know about it?" Cassie said, standing up from the couch. "Nick, we've been together for almost four years. Why can't you tell me what's going on? Did something happen?"

"The less you know, the better," Nick said, drinking his beer.

"What the fuck does that mean?"

"Just stop, Cass! All right? It's none of your business!"

Cassie froze, startled by his outburst. Her voice caught on her throat. "I'm worried, Nick."

"Worried about what?"

"About you! You don't sleep or go outside. You've completely shut me off, and I can't remember the last time you weren't high off weed or God knows what else!"

Nick scoffed. "You're being ridiculous. You're exaggerating like you always do."

"Are you high right now?"

Nick looked away.

"You are! You can't even look me in the eye."

"So what? Is that the end of the world?"

"Jesus Christ."

"I can't talk to you when you're like this."

Cassie couldn't help but laugh. "*You* can't talk to *me* like this?"

"Yeah, when you get like this. Everything is a big deal and you blow everything out of proportion." Nick stepped past her and back to the living room. He sat down in the middle of the couch, staring straight ahead at the wall.

"Nick," Cassie said, moving toward the living room. "Are you in trouble or something?"

"In trouble with what?"

Cassie stared at him. Nick continued to look at the wall. "Fine," she said and stomped into their bedroom. Nick leaned back into the couch. He grabbed his cigarettes off the table and lit up.

Cassie appeared back in the living room with a box. "In trouble with this!" She slammed the box on the floor. Its lid exploded and out came cash wrapped in rubber bands along with necklaces, watches, and rings.

"Are you fucking crazy?" He kneeled and gathered the things and put them back in the box.

"You're stealing again, aren't you? You've been robbing places, haven't you?"

"What I do for money is none of your business," he grumbled as he continued to gather the things.

"Bullshit! You lied to me! You said you were done with this shit!"

Nick stood up with the box. "Don't give me the holier-than-thou act, Cass. Just don't." He walked past her and back into their bedroom. She followed him.

"I can't believe you would lie to me like this! How long have you been stealing again?"

"I never stopped!" he shouted.

"Are you serious? All this time you've been lying to me?"

"I did it for you! For us! How did you think I could afford to pay the rent for this place? To help pay for your school?"

Cassie said nothing. She wiped a tear off her cheek.

Nick sat down on the bed. "I did what I had to do. For us. Because I love you."

"If you loved me, you wouldn't *dare* try to explain yourself after this, after making me an accessory to your shit, after putting everything I've ever worked for in jeopardy because of you."

Nick rubbed his eyes. "I'm not going to apologize for trying to help."

"Fuck you."

"This is who I am, Cassie. The first night I met you, I told you who I was. It's not my fault you pretended I was someone else."

She laughed. A desperate, exasperated laugh.

"You won't have to worry about helping me ever again."

Nick looked at her. Her eyes bore down on him with animus.

"I'll send someone for my stuff. Don't call me."

She turned and left the bedroom. Nick heard her pick up her bag and slam the door behind her.

Nick fell back on the bed. He stared at the white ceiling for a while until the sunlight faded away. Then it was only him and the darkness.

*****

DETECTIVE VOGEL. Did he ever mention an errand or any business he had to take care of?

RICHIE. Not to me.

LANA. Me neither.

DETECTIVE VOGEL. Did he ever mention a George Collins?

RICHIE. No.

LANA. No.

DETECTIVE VOGEL. Are you sure? Look at his picture. Have you ever seen this man with Nick at any point? Maybe down at the Walleye or something?

RICHIE. No, I've never seen him before.

LANA. Me neither.

DETECTIVE VOGEL. Did he ever mention any other friend of his? Anyone he was meeting?

RICHIE. I already told you no!

DETECTIVE VOGEL. I see. I'd like now to talk about that night. The Fourth of July.

RICHIE. Okay.

DETECTIVE VOGEL. You two, along with Nick and this friend of yours, Kimi Roberts, went to a gala fundraiser at the Egg Harbor Country Club, correct?

RICHIE. Yes.

DETECTIVE VOGEL. Why? Do you go to many fundraisers?

RICHIE. Nick got us invitations.

DETECTIVE VOGEL. Where did Nick get the invitations?

RICHIE. I don't know.

DETECTIVE VOGEL. You didn't ask?

RICHIE. He said he got them from someone he knew at the club.

DETECTIVE VOGEL. But you said he didn't have any friends.

RICHIE. He didn't say it was a friend; he said it was somebody he knew. We didn't care, to be honest.

DETECTIVE VOGEL. Did Nick give any reason for wanting to go to this party with you all?

RICHIE. Open bar. Free drinks.

DETECTIVE VOGEL. Walk me through what happened at the party.

RICHIE. Nothing happened. We arrived, had a few drinks, and danced a little. Then, Nick left.

DETECTIVE VOGEL. Why did Nick leave?

RICHIE. He didn't say why. He said he'd see us later and took off.

DETECTIVE VOGEL. Did you find that strange?

RICHIE. Yeah, the whole thing was his idea to go to the party. But that's Nick, you never know what he was going to do on any given night. Plus, he left our friend Kimi without a date.

DETECTIVE VOGEL. How did he leave? You said you all went to the party together?

RICHIE. He said he'd call a cab, right?

LANA. Yeah, he said that.

RICHIE. Right.

DETECTIVE VOGEL. I see. What'd you do when Nick left?

RICHIE. Nothing much. Drank some more. Watched the fireworks. Went home.

DETECTIVE VOGEL. What time would you say you left?

RICHIE. It was after the fireworks. The fireworks started at ten. I don't know, ten-thirty? I didn't check my watch.

DETECTIVE VOGEL. Is that what you would say, Lana?

LANA. Yes.

DETECTIVE VOGEL. What happened when you got home?

RICHIE. Nothing. We went to bed.

DETECTIVE VOGEL. And Nick wasn't home?

RICHIE. No.

DETECTIVE VOGEL. Did you find that strange that your brother left the party early but didn't go home?

RICHIE. Figured he went to the Walleye or something.

DETECTIVE VOGEL. Did you try to call him?

RICHIE. He called me.

DETECTIVE VOGEL. He did?

RICHIE. I think he butt-dialed me. I answered. He wasn't there.

DETECTIVE VOGEL. I see. At what point did you think something was wrong?

18

The Night

Richie entered the bedroom in a towel, his cheeks pink from the hot shower and his hair gelled and combed. Lana sat in front of the mirror dresser in her robe, applying makeup. She glanced at her husband through the reflection in the mirror.

"You smell nice," she said.

Richie took off his towel and threw on some underwear. He inspected his shirt and tuxedo laid out on the bed. "I hate wearing a bowtie."

"What? You look cute in one."

"I look like a clown."

"Stop it." She glanced at him in the mirror as he dressed. "You're not going to wear an undershirt?"

"It's too hot."

"You'll sweat through your dress shirt, then."

"Not if I have fewer layers on. As soon as we get there, I'm taking off my jacket and rolling up my sleeves."

"Whatever," she said dismissively. "Do you think everything's all right with Nick?" Lana asked.

"What do you mean?"

"He's quiet lately. And there was that whole thing with the fireworks last night. I think I smelled liquor on his breath after."

Richie fiddled with his tie. "What else is new?"

"You don't think he's been a little weird lately?"

"Yeah, a little quieter. Probably just nerves."

"You sure?"

"No, but what else could it be?"

"I don't know."

Richie undid his tie and started again. Lana rolled her eyes and stood up. "Let me." She grabbed the tie from him and began to wrap it around his neck.

"How do you know how to do that?" he said as she focused on his tie.

"I learned it once, and it stuck. It's like riding a bike." She finished and primped it. "There you go." She stepped back and looked him up and down. "Put on your jacket. I wanna see."

Richie grabbed the jacket from the bed and threw it on. Lana ran her hands up and down his torso, smoothing the fabric and buttoning the jacket.

"Not so bad."

They stood like that, not wanting to break themselves from the moment. Richie took a deep breath. "No matter what happens tonight—"

"I know." She gave him a quick kiss and wiped her thumb over his lips.

"I'll be out in a minute," she said. Richie left her as she resumed her meeting with the mirror.

The wind blew Nick's cigarette smoke away, carrying it through the backyard and toward the trees. He sat at the patio table alone while he waited for the others. He checked his watch. Kimi would be there any minute.

He heard the back door slide open and Richie appeared. He wore a simple but handsome black tux, his jacket slung over his shoulder. His face was cleanly shaven, and he smelled of cologne. He sat down at the table.

"Looking sharp," Nick said.

"Thanks." He exhaled as he sat down and looked around.

"Lana ready?"

"In a minute."

The two sat silently together as Nick finished his cigarette. He flicked the remaining butt off the deck. Richie frowned at him.

"You put the bag in my truck, right?" Richie said.

"Yup. Change of clothes and everything else in there."

"Good."

Nick eyed his brother. "You're sweating."

"I can't help it; it's eighty degrees, and I'm wearing a tux. Not to mention—"

Nick pulled out a handkerchief. "Here." He tossed it at Richie. He took it and dabbed his forehead and neck. "Can't have you sweating like a maniac all night."

"I'll be fine." He offered the handkerchief back to Nick. He told him to keep it. Richie rubbed his hands. "So we're doing this. We're not just talking about it. It's happening."

Nick bit his lip. "You can back out any time you want. No shame in that."

Richie rubbed his chin. "Do you want to back out?"

Nick shook his head. "No. I can't now. I'm in all the way."

He took a deep breath. "Then we're doing it."

Nick looked at the trees.

They heard a car pull in. They knew it was Kimi. They sat and listened as they heard her car shut off and the front door open.

"Back here," Richie shouted.

Kimi opened the screen door and appeared. She wore a slim gray dress with a generous neckline and a glittering silver necklace. Her black hair was done up, and her lips looked even fuller than usual with a maroon lipstick.

"Howdy," she said, stepping out into the deck.

"Well, well, look at you," Richie said. "You look nice."

"Thank you, darling," she said, leaning down and touching her cheek to Richie's. "You don't clean up so bad yourself," she said, patting his shoulder. She turned to Nick. She spun in place. "Well? What's my date say?"

"Much too good for me."

She ran her hand over his shoulders and sleeves. "I like the white dinner jacket. Old-fashioned but sophisticated."

"I think he looks like a waiter," Richie said.

Kimi put two fingers to her lips, asking for a smoke. Nick took out his cigarettes and gave her one, lighting it for her.

"Lana will be done in a second," Richie said. They sat silently for a minute, listening to the wind. Nick watched Kimi smoke. She looked like she belonged in an old black-and-white movie with her maroon lips wrapped around a cigarette.

She glanced at Nick. "Richie, could you do me a favor and get me some ice water? I'm sweating like crazy already."

"Yeah, sure," he said, getting up from his chair. "You need anything, Nick?" He shook his head. Richie went inside. Kimi leaned toward Nick and lowered her voice.

"Hey, you got any?" She tapped her nose.

"I thought you were done with that?"

"I know, I know, but with everything, tonight my nerves are kind of fried, and I could use a little straightener. Just to get my head level."

Nick stared into her brown eyes. He did have some. He'd done a line only minutes ago. The little bag of coke rested in his jacket pocket.

"No, sorry," he said.

She groaned. "Damn. What about bud?"

"Kimi, I don't think it's a good idea for us to go up there smelling like a bong. Plus, you know how you get when you smoke—you're gonna be all paranoid, and you don't need that tonight, right?"

She smoked her cigarette. "Yeah, you're probably right."

Nick reached out and took her hand. "Hey, you'll do great tonight, all right? Just relax, it'll all work out fine."

He held her hand, grazing her knuckles with his thumb. He dropped it when he heard the screen door open.

"Look who I found," Richie said, stepping aside and showcasing Lana through the door.

"Oh my god," Kimi said, handing her cigarette to Nick. "You look amazing!"

She was right. Lana looked incredible in her slim black dress. She was even taller in her heels, putting her at eye level with Richie, and seemed tanner than ever.

Nick discarded Kimi's cigarette and stood up to join the others by the door. Richie stood off to the side of the women, holding a glass of water for Kimi.

"Oh, thanks, Richie," Kimi said, taking the glass. She gulped down the water, leaving a lipstick imprint on the glass. "Well, look at us. I feel like I'm back at prom about to take some pictures."

"No pictures tonight," Nick said. He checked his watch. "Come on, it's time to go. I'll drive Richie's truck. You all follow behind in Kimi's car."

They headed through the back door and the living room to the front door.

Nick was the last one through the door. He took one last look at the house before he left. He closed the door behind him.

*****

Nick switched off Richie's truck and pocketed the keys. It was parked on a side road across a fairway from the venue where the party was. He opened the door and stopped. He reached over and opened the glove box. The pistols lay where he put them. He stared at them. He closed the compartment and exited the truck.

When they pulled into the Egg Harbor Country Club Clubhouse, there was a line of cars for the valet. Of the dozen or so cars in line, Kimi's car was the most out of place. Among the Cadillacs, Mercedes, Range Rovers, and Audis, Kimi's cheap compact was the sore thumb that stuck out as it approached the front entrance.

When they arrived at the valet, there was a noticeable curiosity in the young boy's eye. Nick and Richie opened the doors for Kimi and Lana, approaching the clubhouse with their dates on their arm. The kid in a red vest, white shirt, and blue tie stood by the door with a clipboard.

"Invitations and names?" he said, staring at his clipboard.

Richie and Lana exchanged a nervous glance. Nick reached into his jacket and drew out the four invitations. He laid them down on the kid's clipboard with a hundred-dollar bill sitting on top of them.

"Put us down as the Smith party," Nick said. The kid looked up from his clipboard at Nick, who held his gaze. He glanced at Kimi, then Richie and Lana behind them. He took the invitations and placed them in a pile with the others, stuffing the bill in his vest.

"Enjoy the party, Mr. Smith," he said. "Fireworks are at ten. Happy Fourth."

"Thank you, you too." The kid smiled at Richie and Lana as they passed by, and the group entered the impressively large building. A venue reserved for formal parties and weddings of members of the club.

After entering through the arched doorway, the immaculate hardwood floors opened into stairs leading down into the great hall, a cavernous space filled by even bigger windows that faced the cliff the venue looked out on, toward the bay. The sun was approaching its set, sending orange and red glares through the window into the hall that reflected off the framed paintings and art that hung on the wooden walls. Maroon and black bars catered to guests on both sides of the hall under the paintings. A big band orchestra belted out numbers in the corner of the hall, sending brass and string notes throughout the space. Bookending the huge windows were double doors that lead outside to the balcony, where it seemed most guests mingled at the moment, drinks in hand. Servers clad in the same uniform as the door attendant circulated with drinks and hors d'oeuvres.

"Well, this is quite the soiree," Lana said at the top of the steps.

"Keep an eye out for Collins," Nick said. "You all remember what he looks like?" The group did, and they began to descend the stairs. Nick heard Kimi take a deep breath. "You okay?"

"Fine," she said. "Sort of rethinking this dress."

"Why?"

"Looking at some of the other guests, it's a little revealing."

Nick patted her hand. "We want people looking at you, so it seems it's the perfect dress for tonight." They descended the last step. "Let's start with a drink first."

They headed over to the bar. They ordered drinks as Nick scanned the crowd. No sign of Collins yet. Nick grabbed his cocktail and sipped it.

"What did you order me?" he asked Kimi.

"I don't know. It was tonight's special. Supposed to be pretty strong."

He sipped the cocktail and grimaced. "Fucking awful."

"I kind of like it."

"Take it easy tonight. Keep a level head."

"I'll be fine."

Nick leaned toward Richie and Lana. "Kimi and I will go outside to look for Collins. You two stay here and keep an eye out. If you see him, come find me." Nick grabbed Kimi's hand and led her outside.

They stepped out onto the spacious balcony that stretched from the hall and over the cliff. The tops of trees peeked over the railing, and the sun began to dip behind the waters of the bay. They meandered toward the railing, Nick's eyes scanning through the dozens of people mingling about.

"I don't see him," Nick muttered as they leaned on the railing.

"Neither do I," Kimi said, sipping her drink.

"We should go back inside."

"No, we should at least stay out here for a couple of minutes. People will notice if we keep running inside and out."

"We want to draw attention."

"That's suspicious attention, right?"

"Yeah, you're right." He sipped his cocktail and cringed. He dumped it out over the railing and put the glass on a passing server's tray. "Now's a good time to do some alibi work." He looked over Kimi's shoulder to an older couple leaning and talking on the railing. Nick stepped past Kimi toward the bald man who looked remarkably similar to a turtle with eyeglasses.

"Excuse me, sir," Nick said. "So sorry to interrupt you, but you wouldn't happen to have a smoke, would you?"

"No, sorry," he said. He squinted at Nick. "Are you new to the club?"

"That obvious, eh?" Nick said. "Yes, Nick Morgan. How do you do?" He shook the turtle man's hand.

"Tim Vincent," he said. "A pleasure. This is my wife, Anna."

"Anna, very nice to meet you," he said, shaking her hand. "This is Kimi Roberts."

"Miss Roberts," Tim said with wandering eyes over Kimi. He turned back to Nick. "I thought I knew everyone at this club. Anna and I have been members for almost thirty years."

"Wow, thirty years! Well, I've only been in the area a few months and just joined the club."

"Oh, what do you do, Mr. Morgan?"

Nick blinked. "Venture capitalist."

"Ah, that's wonderful. What kind of companies have you invested in?"

"I love that dress," Anna said to Kimi off to the side.

"Oh, thank you," Kimi said. "I've never been to one of these parties, and I was starting to think it's a little too revealing."

"Nonsense," Anna said. "You look gorgeous."

"Oh, thank you so much. I love your dress too."

Nick continued to talk to Tim. "Oh, nothing that important people like yourselves have heard of, I'm sure. Our latest project was this small company that specializes in technology advancements for farming."

"Really? Farming technology?"

"Yes, new tractors and other equipment for crops. We've even tinkered with using drones that can spray chemicals on crops as well as take aerial photos of the land to give farmers a better view of their output and growth. That's what's brought me up here—what with all the farms in the state."

"Are you two engaged?" Anna asked Kimi.

"Oh, no," Kimi said a bit forcefully, causing Anna to raise an eyebrow. "I mean we're not even dating. We're just old friends here with some other friends."

"Oh, I see. Well, you two make a handsome couple."

"Thank you. He wishes, right?"

Anna laughed.

"Fascinating," Tim said to Nick. "Amazing what they come up with these days."

"Right. Say, Tim, I'm still getting to know everyone. You know much about our host tonight? This Collins guy?"

"George? Oh, he's a good man. A real, old-fashioned gentleman. He's been a member for something like six or seven years now. Been doing this holiday fundraiser for five years, I think."

"What business is he in?"

Tim rubbed his chin. "I believe he said something like imports and exports. I think he talked about foreign trade. I'm not exactly sure. Whatever he did, he was very successful at it, as anyone can see."

"Where are you from, Kimi?" Anna asked.

"I'm from here, Door County, born and raised."

"Oh, of course. Where are your parents from?"

"Excuse me?"

Nick cleared his throat. "I apologize for my manners, but I need to get Miss Roberts here another drink if I have any hope of seeing fireworks tonight." He winked and patted Tim on the shoulder. "Pleasure meeting you, Mr. Vincent. I'll see you around the club. Mrs. Vincent, enjoy your night."

With a bow, Nick and Kimi exited the conversation and turned back toward the hall. Mr. and Mrs. Vincent looked at each other.

"Interesting young couple," Anna said.

"Bit of a strange fellow. Could use a haircut and a shave."

Anna sipped her martini. "And to wear a dress like that to an event like this? I thought Asians were supposed to be more conservative when it came to that sort of thing."

Nick pushed open and held the door for Kimi. "I think that went well."

"Did you hear what that woman asked me?"

"Yeah."

"God, why do white people always ask that?"

"I don't know. At least they won't forget you. The whole time Tim was talking to me his eyes were wandering over you and your neckline."

Kimi shuddered as they approached the bar where Richie and Lana still stood. Lana subtly gestured with her head toward the other end of the room.

"What?" Nick asked.

"He's here," Lana said, her voice lowered. "By the band."

Nick and Kimi's eyes darted to the opposite corner where they saw him. He was chatting amicably with a violinist while the band took a break. He looked like a star in his crisp black tux and gleaming silver hair and goatee.

"Yeah, that's him," Nick said. The group nervously eyed him. "Can we all not stare at him?" They averted their gazes.

"So is it time, then?" Lana asked. Nick took a deep breath. He looked around the hall and back at Collins, who had moved on to talking with another guest.

Nick searched for Richie's eyes and met them. "Are you ready?"

Richie didn't say anything, but his eyes told Nick he was.

"All right. It's time to go."

Lana put her hand over Richie's on the bar. She looked up at him. "Be careful." Richie kissed her cheek. As they turned to leave, Lana grabbed Nick and pulled him close. "Don't make me regret this," she whispered with steely sharpness.

Nick nodded and turned to join his brother walking out the side exit near the kitchen.

The brothers walked side by side down the hallway, brushing past waiters and servers. They stepped through the glass door into the humid night. They stepped into the night and toward Richie's truck.

*****

Inside the truck, Nick opened the glove box as Richie started the engine. Two guns spilled out. Nick pulled them out and checked them, putting one in his jacket and putting the other in his lap.

"What's that for?" Richie said.

"Drive, Richie, there's been a change of plans."

"What?"

"Drive."

"No! What are you talking about? Why do we need guns all of a sudden?"

"There's been a change of plans."

"What, are we killing him now?"

"We're not. But someone is."

The words hung in the air. Richie scoffed.

"What? Who? Why?"

"Richie, I'll explain everything once you start driving. Go to the boat launch by Cave Point. We need to go now if we don't want to be late. If you want out now then get out and I'll drive myself."

"What's happening?"

"Richie, get out or start driving!"

Richie stared straight ahead through the windshield. He sighed and put the truck into gear and drove.

Once onto the main road, Richie spoke evenly, looking only at the dark road ahead. "What are we doing, Nick?"

Nick shifted in his seat. "I ran into a problem. My fence, when he was trying to line up some buyers for the car, apparently let the word get out to the original owner of the car."

"And?"

"Long story short is that George Collins isn't really George Collins. His name is Cook. He worked in Miami for this gangster, a real big dick. He double-crossed and killed him and stole his car. His brother—Little Henry is what they call him—took over. He put a bounty on his head worth two million dollars. When he found out the car was on the market, he knew Cook—Collins—wouldn't be far behind. So he got in touch with me."

"Jesus Christ! What the hell have you got us into?"

"It's fine! He doesn't care about the car. He only wants Collins. He sent two guys here. All we have to do is tell him where Collins is and they'll take care of the rest. We do that and we're two million richer."

"That's your new plan? To trust gangsters? Fucking murderers?"

"It's the only plan we have left! I couldn't say no to him, Richie! We're lucky he doesn't send guys to beat the information out of us! He fucking hates Collins so much he's paying two million dollars for an address! All things considered, this is as good as it gets."

"What if he doesn't? What if he decides to kill us once we tell them what they need?"

"That's what the guns are for."

"Fucking hell," Richie said exasperated. "I can't believe I went along with this. I knew it—I fucking knew this would blow up because everything with you does! Now you've got us mixed up with—what?—fucking Miami gangsters?"

"You listen to what I say, you do what I do, and we'll be fine. I know these guys, Richie. I know how they think. They don't want a ton of heat coming down. They'll make it look like an accident, or a bungled robbery or something."

"What about us? What will they make our murders look like?"

"That won't happen."

"How the fuck do you know?"

"If you don't want to do it then stop the car and get out!"

Richie slammed on the brakes. He gripped the steering wheel with force, his knuckles turning white and his jaw clenched. Nick took a deep breath.

"I won't force you to do anything," Nick said. "But I have to go to that meetup. He expects me. If I back out now, he will come after us, all of us. I know this is *completely* fucked—but there's still a way for us to all come out of this rich and happy. I'd like you to come with me, to back me up, because if I'm alone, I'll look weak. But I can't force you. I can only ask you."

Richie shook his head and rubbed his eyes. He stared out into the empty road and its surrounding trees. They bent in the wind. Nick held his breath.

He put the truck back into gear and drove on.

*****

When they pulled into the parking lot of the boat launch, a lone dark car sat—waiting.

"Is that them?" Richie asked.

"Flash your brights."

Richie did. The car flashed their brights back. Richie looked at Nick.

"Don't say a fucking word unless spoken to. Even then, say as little as possible. Here, take this," Nick handed Richie the gun. "Put it in your waistband, at the front. Don't show it off, but don't hide it either. The safety's on. It's right here. Hopefully, you won't need to know that."

Richie held the gun in his hands. He looked at his brother.

"You can do this," Nick said. "Five minutes, that's all this will take and we can go home. Okay? Can you do five minutes?"

Richie's breath shuddered, but he nodded. Nick opened the door and the two got out.

The first thing Nick heard when he stepped out of the truck was the waves. The windy night pounded Lake Michigan's waves against the rocky beach nearby, spitting foam into the air. Even in the black night with clouds shrouding the stars and moon, Nick could see the white caps in the distance.

Two men stood in front of the waiting car when Nick and Richie got out. With the headlights of both cars off, they were only silhouette figures fifteen feet from the brothers.

They were both of average height, a few inches shorter than Nick. One seemed to be completely bald while the other had long hair pulled back into a ponytail. The bald man stood with his arms crossed in front of him while his partner kept his hands behind him.

Nick and Richie stood together. Nick put his hands on his hips while Richie let his lie by his side, trying not to think of the loaded gun pressed against his waist.

The bald man seemed to look them over. "Well, look at you two: Rico Suave and his brother. I feel underdressed, don't you?" He said to the man next to him. Nick thought he picked up a Latino accent in his voice.

"Tell your man to get his hands out from behind him. He's making me nervous," Nick said coolly. Richie side-eyed his brother. The bald man chuckled and looked at his partner, who clasped his empty hands in front of him.

"Well, what do you have for us, kid?" the bald man said. "What do you have for us?"

The bald man chuckled again. He looked to his partner who went to the car and opened the back door. In the brief light from the interior of the car, Nick could see he did have a ponytail and looked to be white. He grabbed a duffel bag from the car and closed the door. He returned to the bald man's side and tossed the bag a few feet in front of him. It landed with a thud. The bald man kneeled and unzipped the bag. He pulled out a flashlight the size of a pen and clicked it on, illuminating the stacks of bundled cash inside.

"Well?" the bald man said.

Nick began to reach into his jacket pocket. He saw the ponytail tense up and move his hand toward his hip; Richie did the same. Nick held out his hand calmly. He pulled out a piece of paper.

"What's that?" the bald man said.

"The home address of George Collins Aka Bill Cook. I even got his alarm code as a little bonus."

The bald man looked at his partner who shrugged. He stepped forward to Nick and Richie. Richie's hand began to wander toward his gun again.

"Easy," Nick whispered as the bald man approached. As he got closer, Nick could see he had a goatee. He wore a tight black shirt over a sculpted torso, and a gold cross dangled from his neck. He walked with an air of loose confidence.

Nick held out the piece of paper, and the bald man grabbed it. He opened it. He clicked on his flashlight again and looked over it.

"He's at a party right now," Nick said as the bald man studied the paper. "Big Fourth of July thing, he'll probably get home late tonight, drunk and who knows what else. Easy work."

The man glanced at Nick and back at the paper. He tapped it with the pen.

"See, the problem is we have no way of knowing if this information is good or not until we, you know, show up at this address," he said.

"I sent those pictures of Collins to your boss. He confirmed it was him."

"I know, I know, I saw the pictures." He sighed. "But for all we know, this is an address to a fucking Dairy Queen, you know?" He chuckled. "Maybe you send us to this address, and while we're waiting all night for him, you take off with our two million. Hell, maybe you're working for Collins himself and setting an ambush for us. You see what I'm getting at?"

"The information's good," Nick said.

The bald man turned on his heel and stepped in the direction of his partner. He turned on his heel again halfway between them.

"But you see our problem, don't you? We just want to make sure we get our money's worth. You understand that, right? I mean, we're talking about two million dollars for an address. It better be the right address. Am I right?"

His partner nodded.

The bald man looked at Nick.

"What do you want as assurance?" Nick said.

"Well, here's what I'm thinking," the bald man said, now circling around the duffel bag on the ground. "You finely dressed gentlemen take a ride with us to this address. We hang out awhile, wait for Cook—Collins, whatever—to show up, and when he does, you guys can walk away with your money, and we'll all be happy knowing we got a good deal."

Nick scratched his beard and looked at the waves. He turned back to the bald man.

"Not both of us. I'll go with you to the house. But the money stays here with him," Nick said, pointing to Richie. "I leave with you, he leaves with the money, to keep us all honest."

"Nick!" Richie hissed under his breath. Nick put up his hand to quiet him.

The bald man tilted his head as he considered the offer. He looked over his shoulder at his partner who seemed to nod.

"All right, you got yourself a deal, *Nick*." He turned and walked toward his car and opened the back door.

Nick stepped over to his brother.

"Nick! Are you fucking insane? You can't go with these guys," Richie said in a hushed voice.

The bald man shouted from behind them, "Oh, and Nick, we'll have to ask you to leave any *toys* behind. For safety."

Nick pulled out the gun and held it toward Richie.

"Take this, take the money, and wait here. It's going to be fine, all right?"

"Five minutes. You said this was going to take five minutes!"

"I know. I know I did. I'm sorry. Richie, please, just stay here with the money. It'll be fine. They won't try anything as long as you got the money. I'll call you when it's done and when we're on our way back. If any other car or person comes here before you hear from me, go. Get Lana and Kimi, go home, pack your things, and leave. I'm serious about this."

Richie sighed. He looked around, exasperated.

"You coming, Nick? We don't want to waste any more time," the bald man shouted.

Nick turned halfway toward him and put up his hand. He looked back at Richie.

"It'll all be okay, I promise. Stay here. I'll call you." He patted his brother on the shoulder and left him. Richie watched as the two men searched his brother. He watched as Nick got in the back seat of the car and watched it drive off.

When he was gone, he looked back at the bag on the ground. While waves split against the rocky shore nearby and the wind howled in his ear, Richie was left along with a duffel bag of money.

*****

Nick sat in the back of the car by himself while ponytail drove and the bald man sat in the passenger seat.

"Nick, buddy, do me a favor and sit on the other side so I can see you," the bald man said. Nick slid over. "Don't forget to buckle your seat belt. You never know."

The bald man turned up the radio playing classic pop hits.

"You know my name," Nick said, looking out the window. "What do I call you two?"

The bald man smiled at his partner and turned to Nick, flashing a gold tooth. "You can call me Hall, and you can call him Oates."

"Of course."

Hall turned back to the road. "All right, Nick, tell us the way. We can barely see ten feet in front of us. These roads are so fucking dark. I don't know how any of you can drive at night."

"You get used to it."

*****

"What's he doing now?" Kimi asked from behind her drink. Lana looked over Kimi's shoulder to the corner of the bar, where Collins leaned against the bar with an arm around a woman.

"He's ordering a drink," Lana said. "He's with that girl, still."

"The young one?"

"Yeah."

"Gross. What're they talking about?"

"I don't have a microphone, Kimi." She sipped her drink. "It looks like they're flirting."

"*Ugh*," Kimi grunted. "He has to be at least thirty years older than her."

"Probably. Still, he's not *awful* looking."

"Lana."

"He's got a few wrinkles, but he's a handsome guy. Plus, he's rich."

"If things go wrong tonight, maybe I'll just marry him, get his money that way."

"He's talking to that guy again. They seem pretty close, like old friends."

"Maybe another possible rich husband for me."

Lana smiled. She put her drink down. "I gotta pee so bad I'm about to burst. I'll be right back, keep an eye on him."

Kimi watched her go and turned to steal a glance at Collins. He was still talking to the pretty young brunette and the other man. The other man was slightly younger but still about Collins's age. He had an erect posture and a serious face with dark eyes. They seemed to scan the room at all times.

Kimi beckoned over the baby-faced bartender.

"Another drink, miss?" he said.

Kimi squinted at his nametag. "No, thanks, Josh." She lowered her voice. "Hey, that gentleman on the end there talking to the brunette. That's the host, right?"

Josh glanced over. "Yeah, that's Mr. Collins. He hosts a Fourth of July fundraiser every year. Well, every year since I've been here."

"Do you know him at all?"

Josh shrugged. "He's around the club a lot. I've only worked summers here the past couple of years, but he's a regular. Nice guy."

"That girl he's with is pretty young."

Josh smirked. "Yeah, that's Mr. Collins. He's got a few girlfriends he brings around. Seems like he's got a new girl every couple of weeks. They're always, you know, around that age."

"Good for him, I guess."

"You want me to introduce you two?"

"No, no, that's all right. What about the guy with him?"

Josh narrowed his eyes toward Collins and the other man.

"Him, I'm not so sure. I don't think I've ever seen him before."

"Okay, thanks anyway, Josh." Kimi dropped a ten-dollar-bill in the tip jar next to her. Josh thanked her and left.

Alone, Kimi sipped her drink and stared straight ahead, keeping Collins in her peripheral. He was still talking to the gentleman with the serious face. Then, Collins's phone rang. Kimi acted as if she was admiring the ceiling as she glanced in his direction as he answered the phone.

His body language changed. He stiffened and turned away from the others so only his back showed to Kimi. She craned her neck to see around other guests. He hung up forcefully and pulled aside the other man. They talked, and after thirty seconds, they parted. George headed to the steps and out the front entrance and the other man toward the side exit—the same one Nick and Richie had used.

"Shit! Shit, shit, fuck!" Kimi cursed to herself as the two men dispersed and left. Lana returned from the bathroom. Kimi grabbed her hand. "Something's wrong," she said out of the corner of her mouth.

"What? Where's Collins?"

"He left," Kimi mumbled.

"He left?"

"He got a phone call. He talked for a minute, then talked to that one guy for a minute and then they both left. Collins went out the front door, and the other guy went out the side exit."

"Shit! I'm calling Richie."

Josh returned and looked at Lana. "Can I get you a refill, miss?"

"Not now, Josh!" Kimi seethed. Josh retreated.

*****

Richie sat alone in the truck with the windows down, listening to the wind. The bag of money was in the back of the truck when his phone started vibrating. He checked the caller ID. Lana. He took a deep breath, unsure of what he'd say to her, and answered.

"Hey," he said.

"There's a problem," Lana said. "Collins is gone. He left the party."

"Already?"

"He got a phone call, that's what Kimi said. He got a call and then he left with this other guy."

"Shit."

"What are you guys doing? Are you still at his house? Did you get the car yet?"

Richie rubbed his lips. "We're almost done. We'll be fine, all right? I'll call you when I'm on my way back."

"What? Richie—"

Richie hung up. He dialed Nick's number. It rang twice before going to voicemail. "Shit!" Richie yelled and slammed his palm into the steering wheel. He tossed aside his phone. It began to ring again. He checked the caller ID. Lana again. He let it ring until it stopped.

19

The Night

Nick stared at his phone until it stopped buzzing. He sat in a love seat in the living room of Collins's mansion. The large windows and French doors facing Lake Michigan were hidden behind curtains, making the cavernous, wooden room so dark Nick could barely see his own hand in front of him. After twenty minutes or so of sitting in the darkness, his eyes began to adjust, and he could see the silhouettes of furniture and windows around him.

Hall returned. Nick heard the squeak of his shoes on the hardwood.

"Where is he?"

"He should be here any minute."

"You sure?"

"You heard me call him. Didn't he sound scared to you? He loves that car. He wouldn't let anyone take it."

"You sure he'll be alone?"

"No. I can't guarantee anything, but I've never seen him hang out with anyone besides a girlfriend."

Hall clicked his tongue. "Hate to see a civilian get caught in the crossfire but—"

"Yeah."

"What's he usually carrying for protection?"

"Just a .22 around his ankle. He brings it everywhere though. And I think he keeps another piece in his car."

Hall sighed. "Shouldn't matter much. Oates is a dead-eye shot. As soon as he pokes his head out of his car, he'll be done."

"Good."

Hall came around and sat at the love seat opposite of Nick.

"You don't seem to be very remorseful about all of this."

"As long as we get paid."

"You already were. When this is over, we'll drop you back off, and you can go on with your life two million dollars richer. That's a lot of money."

Nick scratched his beard and said nothing.

Hall propped his elbow on his knee and rested his chin on his knuckles, staring at Nick. "Not my style."

"What?"

"Handing over two million dollars just for an address. If it were up to me, I'd just kill you and that other guy after we were done Collins."

Nick's neck stiffened. His eyes glanced at the gun in Hall's hand, hanging casually below his knees. Nick thought how quickly he could lunge at him, maybe wrestle it away from him if he tried to pull it on him. Not quick enough.

Hall smiled. "But that's not what the skip wants. No, he was very serious about this. 'No funny business,' he said. 'Pay the money, do the job, and come home.'"

Nick wanted to breathe a sigh of relief but worried it might jinx it. He held his breath in.

"And he said there'd be a sizable bonus for us if the job's done nice and clean, so what the fuck do I care, right?"

Nick gulped.

"I gotta admit, you got some skill, kid. You were right about the alarm and the cameras too. We found the security system room and disabled them—destroyed the tapes too. You've done this before, haven't you?"

"Never this."

"But something like this, right?"

Nick tightly gripped his wrist, rubbing it. "I've pulled some jobs on places like this."

Hall nodded and looked around, impressed. "I bet you could pull some nice swag from a house like this." He leaned back on the couch and stared at the ceiling. "Yeah, this is a real nice fucking place. I've always been more a beach house guy myself, but I gotta admit, there's something cozy about this log cabin shit."

He took a deep breath and stood up. "You want some water or anything? I think I saw some water bottles in the fridge."

Nick shook his head.

Oates called from the kitchen near the front door. "He's here."

Hall smiled and cocked his gun. "Showtime, kid." He reached behind him and pulled out another gun. He flipped it in his hand and held the butt of it toward Nick. "Stay here, watch the back door, and don't do anything stupid." He disappeared out of the room toward the front door.

Nick could see lights from a car flood through the windows and illuminate against the wall and back windows. He stood up and crouched against the corner leading down the hallway to where Hall and Oates waited. They were crouched next to the front door and window looking outside. Nick looked at the gun in his hand. He clicked off the safety. He closed his eyes and took a deep breath.

He could make out faint whispers from Hall and Oates but no words. He closed his eyes and leaned his head against the wall. He worried his heartbeat was so loud that it'd echo in the empty room. His eyes crept around the corner again. His breathing sounded like a jet engine to his ears.

He turned back and stared straight ahead at the wall and tried to control his breathing. He wiped his brow and pushed a wayward strand of hair out of his eyes. He looked ahead at the windows and focused on his breathing. He didn't hear anything from Hall or Oates. He began to wonder what they were waiting for. Collins had to be in sight now, out of his car. They had to have a shot by now. *Why don't they do it already?*

His eyes darted right. Even behind the curtains on a moonless night, Nick thought he saw a shadow scamper past the window. His throat seized up. He gripped the gun in his hands until he felt like he would snap the butt of the pistol right off.

The back door broke open. A flashlight beamed. A gun fired.

*****

Richie bit at his nails. Every two seconds he looked at his watch. Every time a thought grew louder in his head.

This is taking too long.

He looked at the gun on the seat next to him—Nick's gun that he handed to him before getting in their car. He bit his lip and looked straight ahead at the swaying trees and listened to the whistle of the wind through their branches.

A ringing pierced through the night and made Richie jump. He grabbed his cell phone and opened it quickly.

"Nick?" he said hurriedly.

There was no response.

Richie thought he heard breathing, but he couldn't be sure.

"Nick? Is that you? You okay?"

Still nothing. Then he heard some movement, a slight moan, and what sounded like the phone dropping to the ground.

"Nick! Are you there? Where are you?"

Total silence now.

"Fuck!" Richie thought about hanging up and calling the police, but that thought quickly faded. He smacked the steering wheel with his palm. He looked at the gun next to him. He started the truck and went in the direction of Collins's mansion.

When he got close, Richie pulled off the side of the road and into a nearby driveway. In the original plan, they were to use this driveway to hide their cars while they stole the Talbot-Lago. Nick said the house was for sale and unoccupied.

The car. Richie remembered what this was all about again: a car. *A stupid fucking car.*

He parked and stepped out of the truck with his gun. He crouched behind the truck and looked around. He listened. Only the trees.

He crouched down the driveway and down the ditch of the side of the road toward Collins's place. He peeked down the long driveway. There was Collins's car, the driver-side door open. As he got closer, he could hear the interior door beep. There was an unsettling stillness to everything. He reached Collins's car and looked inside. Empty.

He looked ahead and saw the front door open. He looked around and crept closer. As he approached, he noticed bullet holes in the front door and one of the windows. When he reached the door, he noticed a smell. Iron.

He took a deep breath and carefully stepped inside, holding the gun out in front of him.

Next to the door was a body. Its bald head was face down on the floor with a hole in its skull. Richie suppressed the urge to gag. He closed his eyes and moved on. He froze as his shoe crushed a piece of glass underneath it.

He gingerly picked his foot up and stepped through the hall. He came upon the kitchen to his right. There was debris everywhere with broken glass, plates, glasses, and wood from the shelves destroyed. He peered over the kitchen island and another body lay behind it. Richie looked away immediately. He squeezed his eyes shut and breathed heavily. He opened them again.

It wasn't Nick. It was Collins, still in his tuxedo. His eyes open and staring at the ceiling. Empty.

Richie moved on through the hallway into the living room. He jumped as he came around the corner to see another body slumped against the wall. The urge to vomit was almost unstoppable, but he kept breathing. He opened one eye to look at the body.

He didn't recognize him. It wasn't Nick or one of the two gangsters from Miami. He was middle-aged, around the age of Collins. He was in a tuxedo too. A knife protruded from his chest. His head was slumped over, and blood trickled from the corner of his mouth. Richie tapped his leg, and his whole body collapsed onto the ground.

There was a trail of blood from the body. Richie followed it to find another body on the floor in the living room. It looked like the other gangster from Miami, the one with the ponytail. He was slumped behind a love seat, a chunk of his shoulder missing and blood forming underneath him.

As he looked at the dead gangster on the ground, Richie heard a gurgling.

He snapped around, his gun pointed. He saw Nick sitting down, his back resting against a chair.

"Nick!" Richie shouted and rushed to him.

His white jacket and shirt was mostly red now, prominently around his stomach and chest. When he kneeled beside him, Nick's head lolled over to see Richie. His jaw was slung open, but the corners of his mouth curled into a weak smile.

"Ri—," he tried to say before coughing blood.

"Nick! Jesus Christ! Oh, fuck!" He grabbed his brother's hand. He reached into his pocket with the other and pulled out his phone.

Nick's free arm swung up and landed on Richie's with the phone. Richie looked at him, and Nick shook his head. He coughed.

"You came," he said softly.

"What happened? Are you—I'm calling an ambulance!"

"No," Nick said hoarsely.

"Nick, you're going to die!"

Nick reached out and grabbed his brother's hand.

"It's okay. I'm okay."

"No, you're not okay!"

Nick coughed more blood. "I know." He took as deep a breath as he could, labored and raspy. "But you're okay."

"I'm going to call for help, okay? It's going to be all right. You're going to be fine!"

Nick reached out again and grabbed his brother's hand. Richie clasped both of his hands around Nick's bloody palm.

"I just—" He drew in a scratchy, agonizing breath.

"What? What, Nick?"

"I wanted to say sorry." He stretched his jaw. "For leaving you again."

"You're not leaving again! You're not going anywhere! I got you! You'll be fine!"

Richie opened his phone again. As he began to dial, he looked at his brother again. His jaw hung down and his eyes fell to the floor.

He gave a weak smile.

"You're good."

He was still.

"No, no, no!" Richie pulled his brother close. "Please no, please no, please no," he whispered in his brother's ear.

He pleaded to Nick and anyone else who would listen. He squeezed him tight, as if it could stop his little brother from going. He asked and begged and promised and prayed.

There was no answer.

*****

RICHIE. When he wasn't home the next morning, we thought maybe something was wrong because we knew he wasn't with Kimi and he wasn't with us.

DETECTIVE VOGEL. What'd you do, then?

RICHIE. We started going to his usual bars and hangouts, seeing if anybody had seen him. No luck. Then, around noon, I got a call from the police. To come down and identify a body.

DETECTIVE VOGEL. This all happened yesterday, on the fifth?

RICHIE. Yes.

DETECTIVE VOGEL. Richie, why do you think your brother went to George Collins's house that night?

RICHIE. I don't know.

DETECTIVE VOGEL. I'd like to show you some more pictures. Do you recognize any of the men here?

RICHIE. No.

DETECTIVE VOGEL. I'll ask you to be as sure as possible. Lana?

LANA. No, never seen them before.

RICHIE. Who are they?

DETECTIVE VOGEL. They are the four other men found dead along with Nick and George Collins.

RICHIE. Who are they?

DETECTIVE VOGEL. These are Alberto Flores and Seth Schroeder. Their ID says they're from Miami, Florida.

LANA. Miami?

DETECTIVE VOGEL. Correct. This last man is Stephen Thompson. He's from Alaska.

RICHIE. Who are they? Why were they there?

DETECTIVE VOGEL. We don't know, but we're still finding out about them. We believe Flores and Schroeder are both linked to drug trafficking in Miami. We're coordinating with the Miami PD and DEA for more information. So far, there's nothing suspicious about Thompson, but we have a feeling there's more to him too.

RICHIE. Jesus. Do you at least know what happened? Why?
DETECTIVE VOGEL. No, that's why we're asking you, Richie. We're at
a loss.

20

Two Days after the Night

Richie stared at the photographs of Flores, Schroeder, and Thompson. He thought about Flores's skull with a hole in the back of it, bleeding next to the front door, and the knife in Thompson's chest—the way his body slumped over when he touched it.

Vogel sighed and rubbed his forehead.

"Richie, Lana, I hope you're being as honest with me as possible."

Lana looked up accusingly. "Of course we are. Why wouldn't we?"

"I don't know," Vogel said, sounding tired. "Five people are dead, including your brother. Two are drug movers from Miami and a mystery man from Alaska. There were no drugs or money found in the house. Nothing seems to be missing. There's no obvious motive we can see. We're looking for something—anything that could point us in the right direction."

Richie rubbed his knuckles. "I don't know what to tell you, Detective. All I know is my brother's dead."

Vogel nodded. He collected the photographs and passed them to Kucharski. "Well, thank you for your time, both of you. If there's anything else you think of, anything at all, please contact me." He stood up and adjusted his suit. Richie and Lana remained seated. Richie stared at the floor while Lana rubbed her face.

"My condolences," Vogel said. He turned on his heel and exited the Morgan home, the two sheriffs in tow. Neither Richie nor Lana bothered to say anything as they left.

They were alone. The air felt heavy and thick, suffocating Richie, keeping him from leaving the couch. Lana wrapped her arms around his neck and pulled him close. Her eyes began to glisten.

They stayed like that for a while. It could have been seconds, minutes, or even an hour as far as Richie knew. Time felt different now. Sometimes it inched along, while other times it felt like it moved on without him. He stared at their front door and thought of who he would never see walk through it again.

Lana cleared her throat, and Richie blinked, snapping him out of his trance.

"Did you talk to him at all?" Lana whispered. "Before…"

Richie sighed. "Yeah a little. Before…"

"What'd he say?"

Richie stared blankly ahead. "He said he was sorry," he said flatly. "He said, 'You're good.' And then he was gone."

Lana sighed and rubbed the back of his neck. She wrapped herself around Richie and rested her head against his chest.

"You are good," she said.

Richie stared ahead and wiped his cheek. He sniffled.

"You should get to work. You're going to be late."

"I love you," Lana said, still pressed against him.

"I love you too." He cleared his throat. "Go on, go to work. I'll be fine."

"No."

"No?"

"I'm not leaving you alone. I'll take a personal day."

"I don't want you to get in trouble."

"Fuck 'em."

Richie laughed, softly at first, but then growing as Lana joined him. When it subsided, Lana grabbed her husband's hands, holding them between her own.

"Let's just go," she said. "I'll give my notice. We can sell the house and the bait shop. Take that money and go somewhere else. It's what he wanted us to do. He wanted to give us a fresh start. Now we can."

Richie looked at his wife and her hands wrapped around his. Lana released one hand and brought it to the back of Richie's neck, her fingers turning his face to hers. She kissed him on the cheek. Richie rested his head on her shoulders. Lana's nails caressed his scalp.

"I already miss him."

"Me too."

"I don't see him for nine years, he's back for a couple of months, and now he's gone two days and I already miss him."

"I know."

Richie yawned.

"When was the last time you slept?"

"Well? I can't remember."

"Me neither. You should sleep," Lana whispered in his ear.

He did need sleep. He couldn't rest last night. Or the night before. When he closed his eyes, he saw him. Nick lying there—bloody and limp. Richie could still smell him. The mix of sweat and blood coming off his brother.

"I see him," Richie said. "Every time I close my eyes, I see him."

"Then look at me."

She slid down the couch and patted her lap. Richie stretched out onto his back, his head in her lap. He looked up at her as she ran her fingers through his hair. He felt safe there. He closed his eyes and rested.

21

Three Years, Six Months, and Two Days after the Night

The cold St. Louis wind followed Cassie. It whistled past the heavy green door as it closed behind her and settled inside Monty's. Her chin was tucked into her brown scarf, and her eyes watered from the whipping wind.

Monty's was as it always was. Julie manned the bar. Louie sat at the end, closest to the TV. Jerry ate his Thursday night cheeseburger alone in his booth. Allen smoked at the other end of the bar.

One thing was different: a man sat in the middle, drinking a can of beer.

"There she is!" called Julie when Cassie stepped inside and revealed her tired face beneath her scarf. At her cry, Cassie grinned. Julie emerged from behind the bar, her arms out wide.

"The future Mrs. Grigson!" she squealed as she embraced Cassie. "Congratulations, sweetie!"

"Aw, thanks, Julie," Cassie said with a hearty laugh as Julie rocked her back and forth in her arms.

"You deserve it, honey," Julie said with a tap on Cassie's cold nose that made her giggle. "Come on, we gotta do a celebratory shot!" she said as she galloped back behind the bar.

"Ah, I don't know," Cassie demurred as she set her bag down in her usual spot, the middle of the bar. Five seats away, the unknown man glanced at her. Cassie removed her jacket and dropped it on the stool next to her. "I just came in for one drink. I gotta work tomorrow."

Julie popped up from underneath the bar with two shot glasses. "Oh, stop it," she demanded. She grabbed a bottle of whiskey and pointed it at Cassie. "You only get engaged once. Well, not in my case, but you only get engaged for the *first* time, once."

Cassie smirked. Julie was about a decade older and had finalized her second divorce only a few months ago. Julie poured whiskey into the two glasses.

"A toast of top-shelf stuff, on the house."

"Thanks, Jules."

Julie raised her glass, and Cassie did the same. "To the future Mrs. Jacob Grigson," she said. "And a lifetime of happiness." They knocked glasses and threw back the whiskey, slamming their glasses upside down after.

Cassie cringed. She hated doing shots. Julie furiously rubbed her hands together. "All right, time for that one drink. The usual?"

"You know how I like them."

"While I make it, you're going to tell me how he proposed. I saw some of the photos on Facebook. It looked amazing!"

"Yeah, it was nice," Cassie said. She took a deep breath and rubbed her eyes.

Julie frowned. "What's the matter, sweetie?" she asked as she muddled. "Most—hell, *every*—girl I know who could get a guy like Jacob to get down on one knee wouldn't shut up about it until the wedding. Then they wouldn't shut up about that until they had kids."

Cassie laughed flatly. "It's nothing. I really am excited and everything. It's just been one of those days, you know?"

Julie added rye whiskey to the glass and stirred. "Work?"

"Yeah."

"I'm sorry, honey. Seems like every time you come in here you've had a shit day."

"Because even shitty days get better when I come in here and see your gorgeous face," Cassie said. Julie blew her a kiss as she added ice to the cocktail and stirred. She added a slice of orange, and lastly, like Cassie liked it, she spritzed ginger ale soda on top. She laid the concoction in front of Cassie.

"All right, come on. Tell me about it," Julie said. "I'm your therapist. Session has started."

Cassie took a deep breath and wrapped her ink-stained fingers around the cocktail. "One of those days where I wouldn't mind switching careers with you."

Julie wiped her hands with a rag. "A big-time lawyer like you wanting to trade places with a bartender at this shit heap? First time for everything."

"Seems like you never have a bad day."

"Well, not when you come in," Julie said with a wink. She started wiping down the counter of the bar. "Come on, lay it on me. What happened today?"

Cassie took a sip of her drink. *God, that's good*, she thought.

"Ah, don't worry about it. It's just another one of my pro bono clients."

"You're a good person doing that—helping people who need it. Helps me sleep at night knowing you're out there."

Cassie shook her head. "Opposite for me. Some of the shit my clients go through…"

"Keeps you up at night?"

"Makes me restless."

"Well, what's this latest one keeping you up?"

"He's only a kid, barely nineteen. He's actually smart and all, but he can't stay out of trouble."

"Sounds like most men I know."

"I've helped him get out of doing serious time before. But he can't stay out of trouble—or doesn't want to. This time, he's looking at years because he was with friends who decided to hold up a liquor store. One of them shot the clerk. He's all right, but now the kid is an accomplice to armed robbery and attempted murder."

"Jesus. Some never learn, huh?"

"He said he thought they were only going to get some beer."

"Do you believe him?"

"I want to. He seems like a good kid, but I don't know. It seems like he never really had a chance."

"What'll happen to him?"

"Maybe I can knock down the time a little, but not that much. Maybe help him get into one of the softer places, but I doubt it. That kid won't survive prison. If he does, he's not going to be the same when he comes out."

Julie sighed. "I'm sorry, baby."

"Sometimes I don't feel like I make any difference."

"Nonsense, of course you do."

Cassie smirked and sipped her drink. "I shouldn't even really be telling you this. It's privileged information."

"Don't worry. Bartender-client confidentiality."

Julie threw down her rag and looked around the bar. "I'm gonna grab a smoke. You want to join me?"

Cassie shook her head. "Nah, I quit."

"Watch the place for me. Keep these fellas in line."

"No problem."

Cassie sipped her drink as Julie grabbed her coat and escaped out the back door. Cassie stared at her drink and listened to the corner TV blast football highlights.

There were a few seconds of silence before a voice approached from her right.

"Congratulations," the man said.

Cassie looked at the man five seats down, drinking his beer. He looked to be in his early thirties. He was tall with broad shoulders that stretched the gray crewneck he wore.

"I'm sorry?" Cassie said.

He pointed at her left hand, gripped around her glass, and tapped his ring finger. "I didn't mean to eavesdrop, but it was hard not to with how loud she talks," he said.

Cassie looked at the diamond on her finger. "Oh, right. Yes, thank you."

"When's the wedding?" the man asked, scooting one seat closer.

"Uh, we don't know yet. He proposed on New Year's Eve, so it's barely been a week.

"That sounds romantic," the man said. "Judging by that rock, it's going to be a hell of a wedding."

Cassie wasn't sure if she was flattered or offended. She looked at her ring. *It is a helluva rock.*

"Thank you. Are you married?"

The man flashed his left hand and his gold band around his ring finger. "It'll be ten years this summer."

"Wow, congratulations. I hope I'm that lucky."

"Thank you. I'm sure you will be."

Cassie sipped her drink. "Any advice for someone getting started?"

The man rubbed his chin, which had a thin layer of fuzz on it. She could hear his nails scratching the short fibers.

"There's nothing you can really do to prepare for it," he finally said with a shrug. "It won't be easy, that's for sure. Even if you're madly in love. If you're not, it'll only be harder. Impossible, even."

"Ah. How comforting."

He rubbed his chin again, thinking. "But even happy stories can have sad endings."

Cassie furrowed her brow. "Huh."

The man chuckled. "My brother once told me that. I don't know if I even believe it, but it sounds pretty good, right?"

Cassie smiled.

Julie reappeared behind the bar. She came over to the man. "Another beer?"

"Yes, please," he said, handing over the empty can and dropping cash on the bar. Julie grabbed another can and cracked it open for him. He thanked her and took a long sip, savoring it.

Julie asked Cassie if she was ready for another, but she declined, citing her need to drive home soon. Cassie downed the last of her old-fashioned and put the empty glass down. She stood up to leave.

"He used to work here."

Cassie stopped. She squinted at him. Julie, on the other side of the bar, glanced over her shoulder.

"I'm sorry?"

"My brother. He used to work here."

"Oh," Cassie said. "Well, I've been coming here for years. Maybe I knew him."

The man drank again and wiped his lips. "You did."

"Excuse me?"

The man reached across their divide with his hand.

"My name is Richie. Morgan."

Cassie slowly reached out her hand and took it. Richie watched the understanding crawl over her face.

"Morgan?"

The corner of Richie's mouth twisted into a grin. "Yes. Do you mind if we talk, Cassie?"

*****

Cassie ran her fingers over the condensation of the fresh old-fashioned in front of her. She wiped it on the stained table of the corner booth. Richie sat across from her, leaning his elbows on the table and his hands clasped around his can. He kept his eyes down until Cassie finally spoke.

"I don't—," Cassie started. "I don't really know what to say."

"That makes two of us," Richie said with a nervous laugh. "You know, I thought about what I might say, how this might go a thousand times in my head. Now, for the life of me, I can't remember a single thing."

Cassie slowly nodded.

"I thought about calling. So many times, I had my phone in one hand and your number in the other and even dialed it out, but I never could."

Cassie bit her lip. "I think I know what you're here to tell me."

Richie took a deep breath, slowly exhaling.

"Yeah. Nick's—"

Richie didn't have to finish. Cassie stared at the table for a few moments. Richie waited. She sniffled and reached to her side to grab a tissue from her purse. "Goddammit," she muttered to herself. "I'm sorry," she said, pulling out a tissue and dabbing her eyes.

"Nothing to be sorry for."

"I'd like to say I'm surprised. But the way he was…"

Richie sipped his beer.

"When did he…?"

Nick thought for a moment. "About three and a half years ago."

Cassie's eyes widened.

"I wanted to tell you sooner—when it happened, but I was sort of busy with family stuff. And it was hard to track you down. Nick never told me much about you. Only a name and a city."

Cassie dabbed her eyes again. "That sounds like Nick. He would never tell me much about you or his family either. He told me his brother's name was Dick."

"I figured as much," Richie chuckled. "I go by Richie now."

Cassie smirked. She wanted to say something, but her chest ached, and she didn't feel like talking. She let a silence fall between them. She sipped her old-fashioned. She put it back down but kept her eyes on it.

"Should I even ask how?"

Richie grimaced. "It's a long, hard story to tell."

Cassie frowned.

"He was—he was shot."

"Jesus Christ. Why?"

Richie exhaled a deep sigh.

"I was selfish," Richie said suddenly. "I was in trouble and needed some help, and Nick tried to help me. But in the wrong way. I was an idiot and let him. But I don't blame him. I should have known better. I let it go too far, and Nick paid for that mistake with his life."

Cassie was stunned silent.

"I'm sorry. I know this is a lot to throw at you all at once."

"No, it's fine," Cassie said. She frowned, staring at the table, deep in thought. "You said three and a half years ago?"

"Yeah."

"So that would be like the summer of 2008, right?"

"July 4, 2008."

Cassie leaned forward and rubbed her forehead. She scoffed. She laughed lightly to herself.

"I'm sorry. It's—," she said, shaking her head. "I think he called me around then. Yeah, the night before the fourth."

Richie straightened in his seat.

"I remember because I was at my parents' cottage and that was the first time he even tried to talk to me since we broke up. I didn't recognize the number, so I didn't answer, but he left a voice mail."

"What'd he say?"

"He said he was checking in on me. But he was talking strangely. I think he said something about maybe needing a lawyer soon, as a joke. I didn't listen to it until the next day, and when I called the number, it was a phone at some resort hotel."

Richie said nothing. Cassie reached into her purse and pulled out an old pack of cigarettes. They looked like they'd been in the bag for months. She lit up.

"I was worried. But I was still so angry with him." She exhaled smoke, coughing slightly. "I've thought about what would've happened if I'd answered that call."

She sipped the last of her drink. She lightly laughed.

"You know, I really thought we'd get married. That sounds so crazy and stupid looking back."

"Doesn't sound that crazy."

"Come on, you knew Nick. Could you ever see him getting married?"

Richie grinned softly. "No, probably not."

"I can't believe I thought I could change him."

"I think you did."

"Clearly not enough." Cassie cringed at her harsh words. "Sorry, I didn't mean to—"

"It's okay." Richie sipped his beer. "I still think you did though."

Cassie blew smoke.

"I knew Nick. And, yeah, for the most part, he was the same Nick from before he left. But I'll say this: the old Nick never would have done what he did for me and my family."

Cassie gulped.

"Maybe you don't think so. But the Nick I knew before he left wouldn't have tried to help me. I think that's because of you."

Cassie dropped her cigarette into her drink. She stared at the wooden table. She fiddled with her hands. Richie reached into his pocket and pulled out his wallet.

"I want you to have something," he said. He pulled out a paper, one that looked like it'd been in his wallet for years. He pushed it across the table to her. "I hope the next time you feel like you don't make a difference, you look at that."

He stood up and put on his jacket. Cassie slowly reached out and pulled the paper toward her. It was a photograph. She unfolded it.

"Is this your family?" she said, looking up at Richie. He smiled.

Cassie looked at the family in the photograph. They were on a beach. Richie was in the middle with a wide smile. A woman with golden hair that cascaded down her shoulders was kissing his cheek.

On Richie's shoulder sat a toddler. Richie's large hands wrapped around his chubby legs. The little boy was laughing. His tiny hands held onto his father's forehead.

"You have a beautiful family."

"That's my son. We adopted him a couple of years ago. Nicky."

Cassie looked at Richie and the picture again. She squinted, studying it. Her eyes began to glisten.

"If it wasn't for Nicky's uncle, we never would have had a chance for a fresh start. To start a family. It only seemed right as a name."

Cassie laughed. She looked back at Richie.

"It was nice to meet you, Cassie," Richie said.

"Thank you."

Richie turned and left. Cassie felt the rush of cool wind when he opened the door, heading back out into the cold.

Cassie stayed in the booth, staring at the picture.

She smiled and wiped her eyes.

About the Author

Robert Cowles grew up in Wisconsin where he spent much of his childhood in the setting of this story, Door County. After graduating with a journalism degree from Marquette University, Cowles worked in copywriting and digital marketing before pursuing his goal of becoming an author.